A RECKLESS IMPULSE

The low light made the tears in her eyes glisten. She rushed to wipe them.

He took her hands in his so she would not work so hard at being brave. "Weep if you need to. No one will think the less of you."

She let him support her while she gave in and the tears flowed.

It was sympathy that led him to press a soft kiss to her crown, but more than that stirred in him when he did it. She did not seem to notice.

The tears tapered off but she remained against him, sighing out their remnants. He should release her now, set her away. He didn't, but instead submitted to the reckless impulse to hold her longer.

She stirred, as if wakening from a dream or a daze. She looked up at him. Her eyes still glistened and her face appeared luminous in the dusk. Not thinking or caring about consequences, he did what he should not do. He kissed her.

Praise for *A Devil of a Duke*

"Rich with scandal and sensuality, Hunter's second Decadent Dukes Society Regency (after *The Most Dangerous Duke in London*) features a fabulous heroine, a secretary with a criminal secret who falls for a man far above her station . . . Scintillating love scenes are plentiful in this page-turning tale, which is enhanced by a cast of memorable characters and smart, witty protagonists."
—*Publishers Weekly*, STARRED REVIEW

"Readers who crave historical romances served up with a surfeit of searing sensuality and plenty of sharply nuanced characters will snap up this sterling addition to Hunter's Decadent Dukes Society series."—*Booklist*

"With a delectable blend of clever ripostes, scorching sensuality, and masterly plotting, Hunter's latest sees the most infamous of the Decadent Dukes fall head over heels."—*Library Journal*

"Another passionate, adventurous, captivating romance from a grand mistress of the genre. Hunter combines a heated love story with a feminist vibe with a dangerous mission led by unconventional characters. Thanks to the snappy dialogue, readers will find the pace never slows as they try and keep up with a bold thief and a devilish duke engaged in a subtle game of seduction. Readers will adore the smart characters who actually talk to one another as they set aside foolish misunderstandings in favor of communication."—*RT Book Reviews*, Top Pick

Praise for *The Most Dangerous Duke in London*

"The writing is lively and the characters fun, and the duke's cronies promise to make good heroes in future books. A thoroughly enjoyable read."—*Kirkus Reviews*

"Hunter has created an intelligent, fast-paced romance, chock-full of sensuality and spiced with mystery."
—*Publishers Weekly*

Books by Madeline Hunter

The Most Dangerous Duke in London

A Devil of a Duke

Never Deny a Duke

Never Deny A DUKE

MADELINE HUNTER

ZEBRA BOOKS
KENSINGTON PUBLISHING CORP.
www.kensingtonbooks.com

ZEBRA BOOKS are published by

Kensington Publishing Corp.
119 West 40th Street
New York, NY 10018

All Kensington titles, imprints, and distributed lines are available at special quantity discounts for bulk purchases for sales promotion, premiums, fund-raising, educational, or institutional use.

Special book excerpts or customized printings can also be created to fit specific needs. For details, write or phone the office of the Kensington Sales Manager: Attn.: Sales Department. Kensington Publishing Corp., 119 West 40th Street, New York, NY 10018. Phone: 1-800-221-2647.

Zebra and the Z logo Reg. U.S. Pat. & TM Off.

First Printing: May 2019
ISBN-13: 978-1-4201-4394-2
ISBN-10: 1-4201-4394-8

ISBN-13: 978-1-4201-4395-9 (eBook)
ISBN-10: 1-4201-4395-6 (eBook)

10 9 8 7 6 5 4 3 2 1

Printed in the United States of America

This book is dedicated to the loving memory of
Warren Archer (1946–2018),
my husband,
my best friend,
and my hero

Chapter One

Davina touched the crown of her bonnet to make sure it was still angled correctly. She smoothed the leather of her gloves. The anteroom in which she sat held two other people, both gentlemen from their bearings and garments. She assumed she would have to wait for them to be seen first.

The summons had arrived three days ago, impressive in its cream laid paper, exquisite penmanship and crested wax seal. It instructed her to arrive at St. James's Palace at one o'clock today, and to give the summons to a page at the door of the Tapestry room. That young man had brought her to this chamber to wait.

What a commotion that letter had caused. Mr. Hume, her employer, had insisted on reading it, then demanded her attention for almost an hour while he instructed her on how to behave, what to say, what not to say, and how to subtly make threats without doing so outright. She hoped she would be spared the last. On her lap she had the letter her grandfather had received from Court. Surely once it was seen all would be rectified.

She fingered the other paper she carried, the one in her

father's hand where he explained all he knew about the legacy. He had given it to her when he became ill with the malady that would kill him. *I am entrusting all this to you, for what good it will do. Still, you've a right to know.* She wished she had him beside her now. His quiet, steady manner had always given her confidence.

A different page appeared in the chamber. He approached her. The two gentlemen did not take that well. Their glares followed her while the page escorted her out.

She was almost never nervous, but her stomach churned now. Still, she needed to keep her wits about her if she were going to speak to the king.

The page brought her to an office not far from the anteroom. A man greeted her and bade her sit on the blue-silk upholstered chair near the large window. He then sat nearby in a wooden chair that kept his posture very straight.

"I am pleased to meet you, Miss MacCallum. I am Jonathan Haversham. I am of the Household."

He meant the king's household, of course. Perhaps he was an important functionary in it. Maybe not. For all she knew Mr. Haversham was nothing more than a very old page. He certainly wasn't a young one. He looked to be about fifty, his gray hair had turned sparse on the sides and absent on the top. Lean and angular, his heavy-lidded dark eyes and wide, flaccid mouth gave the impression he resented having to deal with her.

"Your petition for an audience was received," he said.

"I have sent others."

"I am aware of that. I am sure you can imagine how busy His Majesty is. He is not indifferent to the concerns of his subjects, however, so he has asked me to speak with you."

So she would not see the king. At least she was being

seen by someone, however. "As I explained in each of my letters, I have evidence that my great-grandfather's estate was taken by the Crown after he died. I know that in many such cases the property was later returned to the family. I have a letter from the king's father that he would do the same for us." She handed over an old folded parchment. "The king himself told me when he was in Edinburgh that he would address the matter."

Mr. Haversham perused the letter. "What makes you think your grandfather was the heir to these properties?"

"He told my father that he was, before he died."

Mr. Haversham smiled slightly. "There have been errors on such matters."

"The last king did not think so." She gestured to the letter he still held.

"The last king was at times confused." He looked down at the letter. She wondered if he wanted to claim it was a forgery. That would be hard to do, because it bore a seal. "Do you have whatever proof was sent to the palace, to convince the last king of your grandfather's claim?"

"I assume it was kept by the king."

"We have found no evidence of it."

Her heart sank. She could not guarantee there ever had been evidence, so she could hardly now demand they find it.

"The king, *this* king, the living one, told me personally that he would look into this and deal with it. He was in Edinburgh and I had an audience. You were not there, but I am sure he remembers and, if not, there were others like you present who certainly do. The man who obtained the audience for me does." *I have proof of this at least, so don't try to put me off.*

His lips thinned and folded like a frog's. "No one

questions that meeting, Miss MacCallum. We will indeed look into it. We have already begun. Hence my comment about the proof. It will be needed. Kings do not hand over land to claimants merely on their say-so. As for this," he waved the letter that he still held. "It will figure in the final determination of what to do once that proof is found."

She took the opportunity on one wave to snatch it away. "I will hold it, if you do not mind. I would not want it to be lost and I am sure you have thousands of letters here."

"Of course. As you wish." He glanced at the letter greedily.

"I will also endeavor to provide yet more proof, to support that which was sent all those years ago," she said. "I am determined to settle this."

"As are we, I assure you." He stood and offered his hand to help her up. "You will give His Majesty's regards to the duchess, I hope. He was delighted to receive her letter."

Davina doubted that. However, that letter was probably why she had been received by anyone at all. If not for the Duchess of Stratton, this entire journey to London would have been a waste of time.

Again a page escorted her through corridors and chambers until he deposited her in the drawing room.

No one took note of her. A few glances came her way but immediately moved on. Too unfashionable to be important, those fluttering lids said. She didn't care. She had not come here to impress anyone with her style and wit. She had come for justice, for herself, her father, and the grandfather she had never met.

Her mind returned to her meeting. She picked through the memory, seeking evidence it had gone better than her dampened mood believed. As she did so, the door to which she walked opened and a man entered.

She halted in her tracks. Considering what had just transpired with Mr. Haversham, this man's presence only increased her consternation.

He entered like he had been here a hundred times before, which he probably had. No need for him to gawk at the large chamber's appointments the way she did.

He made his presence known through no effort or intention. Everyone noticed him arrive. Some ladies repositioned themselves so they might catch his eye.

He stood taller than anyone else and his bearing insinuated a man who did not bend easily. His vague smile implied tolerance more than friendliness. His handsome, chiseled face, with its straight nose and square jaw, reflected the Germanic blood brought into the family line by a great-grandmother. His eyes, more a dark gray than blue, created a steely gaze that shot through all that it saw.

Eric Marshall, the Duke of Brentworth. The most ducal duke, he was called.

Davina had been introduced to him several days ago, at a party to celebrate the Duchess of Stratton finally taking credit as the patroness of *Parnassus*, a woman's journal of increasing renown. Davina had been invited because she contributed essays to the journal. That was the only reason she knew the duchess, or any of the other ladies present. Almost everyone in attendance far surpassed her in social standing.

The duke had condescended to have some conversation with her at that party. She had held her own, using the opportunity to take his measure. One should do that with a person who might be an enemy. Of course, she had known when they met that she would have this meeting today, and had anticipated a much more favorable outcome then. A summons from the king gave one a lot of confidence when meeting a duke.

She had no interest in conversing with the duke today. She averted her gaze, and aimed through the chamber, turning her thoughts again to the potentially insurmountable problem of finding more evidence to support her petition about her legacy.

It was rare for Brentworth to receive a summons to Court. Granted, it had not been a true summons. More of an invitation, to the extent that kings ever invite instead of summon. *His Majesty would be happy to receive you tomorrow at two o'clock.*

He entered St. James's Palace at fifteen minutes to two, wondering why the king would want to see him at all. He and the king did not rub well together. The king was a fool and Brentworth was not, so they had little in common.

He considered that it might have to do with the meeting he had attended earlier in the day. The king may have learned about the renewed efforts to again pick up the question of abolishing slavery in the colonies. He might want to voice his views on the matter and think an informal conversation with a duke would be the best way to do that.

Brentworth had no idea what that view would be. This king was not known for engagement in political questions, or in much, really, except his pleasure. He probably did have opinions, however. Most men did, no matter how ill-informed those men might be.

It was not a drawing room day, so few people were about. There was no crush in the anteroom of those hoping to obtain vouchers to watch the nobility on parade. He strode through that chamber and the next and entered the drawing room. At most twenty people moved through it, chatting.

He did not announce himself to any of the pages. They knew him, and upon his arrival one hurried across the chamber and disappeared through the door that led to some offices.

He idled in the drawing room, awaiting either the king himself or an escort to wherever the king lounged. While he did he saw a young woman in serviceable blue garments and bonnet stride across the chamber. He recognized her as Miss MacCallum. He had been introduced to her at a party earlier in the week. She was a writer with an unusual interest in medicine.

She had impressed him with her ability to hold her own in a chamber full of nobles and members of the ton. He could not ignore that during their brief conversation she had been sincerely unimpressed with his title or status. That almost never happened, especially with women. Most peers would be annoyed. He had been intrigued.

Her bonnet obscured most of her blond hair, hiding its short length. That cropping had been apparent at that party despite a heroic attempt to disguise it. He had concluded that her interest in medicine derived from a serious illness of her own, a recent one in which her hair had been cut off to help with the fever.

Right now she appeared both out of place and distraught. He intercepted her before she could leave.

"Miss MacCallum, what a pleasant surprise."

She halted abruptly and blinked away whatever had been distracting her. She executed a neat curtsy. "Your Grace."

"Are you unwell? You appear haunted."

She glanced back at the door that led to the long wing

with offices. "Not haunted so much as distressed that my business here is being treated lightly."

"You have business at court?"

"I do. I think it unlikely it will ever be addressed as it should be, however. I learned that much today." Her features, too bold to be fashionable, moved easily to express her thoughts and moods. Right now she appeared to be fighting both despair and fury.

"It is nothing serious, I hope."

The anger won. "Do I appear to be a woman who would waste a monarch's time with frivolous matters?"

"Of course not," he soothed, drawing her aside. "If you were in some way insulted you must let me know. I will make sure it does not happen again."

"Not insulted as such. Just dismissed as unworthy of fairness." She looked down on herself, on the neat but simple blue muslin dress and deep blue spencer. "Perhaps if I had dressed like . . ." She gestured to the ladies chatting nearby. "Like them, it would have helped."

Probably so. "Not at all. You look fine." *Solid and honest and with a character not dependent on garments and fashion.* A self-possession that he had noticed when they met at the Duchess of Stratton's party still ruled her, but her distress softened her enough that his protective nature emerged. "Can I help in some way?"

His offer startled her. She regarded him, cocking her head, as if she considered ways in which he could indeed help before thinking better of it. "It is a private matter, thank you. Only the king can help me, and I fear he will not. I must decide whether to accept that or battle on."

"If you are in the right, do not lay down your arms now. The Household strives to protect him and remove problems before they even know if a problem truly exists. If you persevere you may yet succeed." Oh, how smoothly it all came out. He did not really believe a word of it. Those men back there would bury whatever she claimed needed fixing forever if they thought it best for their master.

She nodded firmly. "You are correct. Your reminder is well taken. I can still muster the evidence I need to get his attention."

The door across the chamber opened and a balding crown emerged. Miss MacCallum noticed. "I must go now, Your Grace. I do not want to see that man again until I am ready for him."

She dipped a fast curtsy then disappeared while the bald head worked its way across the large chamber. It finally stopped right in front of Brentworth.

"Your Grace, thank you for coming."

He knew Haversham. The man had been in the king's tow for decades. He could not see him without thinking of Shakespeare's Julius Caesar. *Cassius has a lean and hungry look. Let me have men about me that are fat*.

"My liege summoned me. Or so I thought."

Haversham flushed. "I wrote at his instruction, but today he asked me to speak for him."

"I am not accustomed to having anyone, even a king, foist me off on a clerk."

"Foisted? Good heavens no. Not at all. It will save you much time if I do the preliminaries, so to speak. Explain a few things. Then should you meet with His Majesty you will not have to wait on his explanation, which might be less direct." He coughed into his fist. "If you understand me."

He understood. It could take the king an hour to say whatever Haversham would complete in ten minutes. "At least you were not so stupid as to have me delivered to you by a page."

"Of course not! Truly, it is best if we speak privately

before—that is, the matter is of some embarrassment to His Majesty and he would prefer if I— If you could sit with me over here, I will try to explain."

Here were two chairs tucked behind a statue in an attempt to create a bit of privacy. Brentworth threw himself into one of them and waited for Haversham to get on with it.

"As you know, after the Jacobite rebellion, a number of Scottish titles were attainted. In the case of some commoners, lands were taken," Haversham began. "In a few cases, the lands of deceased feudal barons reverted to the Crown due to there being no heirs or descendants. In such cases, official attainder was not pursued."

"All of that was settled a generation ago."

"True, but—on occasion, we will still receive a petition to reopen the matter regarding this estate or that. Someone will claim to be the descendant of one of those men, and want the land back. Charlatans normally. Adventurers." Haversham dismissed the frauds with a sneer. "It happens more often than you would guess. Some petition the Crown after the College of Arms rejects the claim. We have a letter we send to all of them, warning them off under penalty of imprisonment. That normally does it."

"And when it doesn't?"

"I deal with them. It is lengthier, but eventually they go away."

"Good. Why did this bring me here today?"

Haversham appeared surprised. "Oh! I thought you knew. Well, this *is* embarrassing." He leaned in. "Recently, such a descendant came forth. Only this one has a letter from the last king that all but acknowledges the claim."

"How awkward for you."

"Most awkward. It is not a forgery. It is a signed and

sealed letter all but admitting that the descendant is indeed a descendant and all but promising the estate will be returned. Well, of course the king was mad at the time. Who knows what he would write? Yet, there it is."

"Do you want my advice? Is that why I was summoned here? I think you should—"

"With respect, Your Grace, that is not why you were invited. When I came out and saw you I assumed you knew. You were speaking with Davina MacCallum. She is the claimant in question. She is insisting on another audience with the king to discuss the matter. I have been charged with seeing that never happens."

"*Another* audience?"

"I regret to say they met in Edinburgh."

"If a five-minute audience will placate her, I don't see why—"

"In addition to the letter from the last king, I regret to say she has a promise from this one, obtained in Edinburgh. The entire matter promises to be a potential embarrassment to His Majesty. A very big one. It is vital that the whole story does not be bandied about."

Eric wanted to laugh. Davina MacCallum had the King of Great Britain all but hiding in the cupboard to avoid her. His estimation of her rose immediately.

"Haversham, all of this is interesting, even entertaining. I regret that I do not know the lady well enough to influence her, however." He stood. "My advice is that the king just give her the land. I suspect he is no match for her."

Haversham bolted to his feet. "My reasoning exactly. Not the part about whether he is a match—I would never be so disloyal as to agree to that—but about returning the land. Much cleaner. No embarrassments. There is only one problem. Someone else now holds that estate. He is not likely to think our solution is so clever."

Finally they were down to it. "I will speak with him on the king's behalf, if that is what is wanted of me. Who is he?"

Haversham licked his lips. He offered a trembling smile. "You."

Chapter Two

In late afternoon Davina entered the house on Bedford Square that served as the home of the Parnassus Club. Established by the Duchess of Stratton a year ago, the club only had female members. Davina had been inducted upon her arrival in London, on the day a month ago that she came to meet Mrs. Galbreath, the editor of the journal who had purchased two of her essays.

As exclusive as any club, this one required a vote for admittance and fees from its members. However, she had been included as a charity case—Mrs. Galbreath did not put it that way, of course—and the membership turned out to be quite democratic. While there were many ladies who stopped by to relax in the salon or gamble in the room set aside for that, some women were not ladies at all.

And a few, like the club's treasurer, were important ladies now, but had not been well born. Davina assumed everyone recognized that latter quality just as she had, but unlike many others it relieved her. As a result, she and the woman born Amanda Waverly and now the Duchess of Langford had formed a fast friendship.

Amanda sat at a writing table in the library when Davina arrived, her dark-haired crown bent over a pen. She wore a simple linen apron atop a luscious dress the color of amaryllis.

"Are you working the accounts?" Davina asked. "Or writing a letter?"

Amanda looked up and greeted her. "The accounts."

"You do not care to use the office?"

"The office normally suits me fine." Amanda glanced aside to where three women sat near the fireplace. "But Mrs. Bacon's gossip suits me better. I can eavesdrop from here."

"Naughty woman. I will not interfere with either activity. However, at the party I overheard something myself. The duchess spoke of visiting today to meet with Mrs. Galbreath. Has she done so?"

"They are in Mrs. Galbreath's chamber."

"Does the duchess normally leave immediately after they chat? Or might she avail herself of the club's amenities?"

Amanda set her pen into its holder. "Why do you ask? Do you want to speak with her?"

"I thought if we greeted each other in passing, perhaps a few more words could be exchanged."

Amanda's smile stretched more with every word she heard. "I have a better idea. When she comes down I will tell her you wish to speak to her."

"I do not want to impose on her." *Again*, she almost added. She had imposed quite a lot when during a casual conversation she had asked for that letter to the king.

"I don't think she will see it that way. I didn't when you addressed me.

That was different. Davina caught the words. This new duchess might be insulted at the implication she was not as ducal as the other duchess.

Humor lit Amanda's eyes. "She is not going to eat you,

Davina. I am sure she will be interested in whatever you want to tell her." She cocked her head and looked at the door. "In fact, I hear them coming now."

Feminine chatter preceded the two women down the stairs and into the library. "After the meeting on Tuesday we will vote," the duchess said to her companion. She then noticed Davina. "I am so glad you are taking advantage of the club, Miss MacCallum. I like to think you have found a sanctuary here."

"I have, Your Grace. It is not far from my residence, so I can avail myself of the peace here any day I want after my duties are completed."

"I have told her she must visit the booksellers and choose a few medical books and tracts for the library," Mrs. Galbreath said. Mrs. Galbreath, a fine boned, elegant blond woman, lived here and served not only as editor of *Parnassus* but manager of the club.

"She came today because she wants to talk to you about something, Clara," Amanda said.

"Do you? Well, let us find a quiet spot so you can." She gazed around the library and pursed her mouth when she saw the three women ensconced near the fireplace. "We will go to the dining room, so no ears overhear by accident."

Amanda flushed at the insinuation there might be eavesdroppers around. She bent over her accounts again. Davina trailed the duchess out of the chamber and across to the dining room.

Calling it that had become a misnomer because it rarely served for dining now. Rather it had been set up for gambling, with small tables and a wager book. Mostly, Davina had seen women playing whist for money, but once a member had served as a dealer for *vingt-et-un*.

The duchess took a seat at the far table near the doors that led to a small garden. She invited Davina to sit with her.

"As I told you last week, I have come to London for a reason," Davina began. "It was not to be a tutor. That was merely a way to get here."

"You want to speak with the king about an important matter to your family on which the king made promises. Has that finally come to pass?"

"I was summoned to the palace today, due to your letter on my behalf. Without your influence I doubt it would ever have happened."

"It was not my influence, but that of my father whose shade stands by my shoulder. The king has no love for *me*. However, it is good to know that I still have some influence, small though it may be. And I am joyed that you had your audience."

"I did, but not with the king. I met with a man named Mr. Haversham."

She received a kind, regretful smile. "It is not easy to see a king, especially this one. You are being rebuffed because he does not want to be reminded of his promise."

"I expect so."

"You said you met him at a dinner during the festivities in Edinburgh. Was he in his cups? Stupid question. Of course he was. And there you were, a pretty young woman and he agreed to help you in order to be gracious and perhaps more. Oh, do not feel you have to tell me. His habits are well known, as is his eye for the ladies." She tapped her fingers against her chin. "May I ask what this is about? You did not offer the information last week, and I did not press you, but—"

"It involves a legacy. One that has been ignored over a long time. His father had also agreed to rectify the situation, you see. Only then he went mad, and . . ."

"So two kings promised to help with this and neither one did? That is not acceptable. This one is afraid you will put it out that he does not keep his word, or even honor that of his father."

That was what her employer Mr. Hume had said. *Your greatest weapon is the gossip that will make him look bad.*

The duchess pondered the matter a few moments. "I think you will hear more of this from the palace. I think they will either settle matters as you want, or try to buy you off in some way. You must decide if you are willing to allow the latter, and if so what this legacy is worth to you."

"Why do you think this will happen?"

"I suppose because it is what I would do if faced with your determination."

Davina hoped that was a compliment. She wondered if Haversham had seen what the duchess seemed to see in her.

"I hope you are right." Davina stood to take her leave. "I thank you for your help in opening the palace door for me. I hope I have not been too bold in requesting your aid."

The duchess laughed. "You have been most bold. As it happens, I admire that in a woman."

"I am glad for that, and very grateful."

The duchess stood too. "Let me know what transpires. Someday perhaps you will tell me all about this legacy. I think there is an interesting story there."

Eric stretched out his legs and gazed at the inky red liquid in the glass he held. His two friends, the Duke of Stratton and the Duke of Langford, had already finished theirs. In ten minutes or so it would be time to join the ladies.

"It was good of you to come," Langford said to no one in particular and everyone in general.

"Of course we would come. A small dinner party is

an excellent way for your wife to test her new wings," Stratton said.

"You can invite a few more to the next one," Eric said. He took a sip of the port. "This went well, and dinner parties are all much the same except for the number of chairs."

It had been the smallest of dinner parties, with only three couples present. A first stab at entertaining for the former Amanda Waverly, it had indeed gone well enough. She could use a bit of help with the menu, but the cook should get her in hand. Or else one of the ladies would. Stratton's wife Clara would not hesitate to instruct the new duchess if she decided it were necessary.

"I told her it was too few, but she was so nervous . . . Well, she was not born to this, of course." Langford ran his fingers through his dark curls the way he always did when worried. Eric knew his friend did not care if the dinner went well or not. His wife did, however, and the concern was all for her contentment.

"Perhaps her next attempt should be an afternoon gathering. A salon," Brentworth said. "Another one for that journal, for example." Thus did his mouth speak his mind, which had been occupied for the last days with a certain essayist for that journal. Davina MacCallum thought to connive her way to taking one of his estates, did she? She was in for a sad reckoning on that scheme.

"It was good of you to come to that too," Stratton said with a meaningful glance at him.

Not good. Necessary. Duchess or not, that journal was controversial and Clara claiming ownership was sure to bring down criticism on her head. Not that either she or Stratton cared. Both were accustomed to controversy, even scandal. It was a friend's role to ease that if he could, however, and Brentworth knew his presence would silence at least some of the wags.

"I enjoyed it," he said, although that was an exaggeration. "I even took one of the journals home and read it. Lady Farnsworth does not hold her fire in her essays, but then I would never expect her to. The historical essay was well done, although I have never heard of the author. And Miss MacCallum's contribution was . . . interesting." Quite interesting. He grudgingly admitted she had a talent for engaging prose.

"Amanda says the woman is interesting, so her writing would be too, I expect," Langford said.

"Do you know her yourself?" Eric asked.

Langford shook his head while he poured more port and passed the bottle to Stratton. "I spoke with her briefly at the party. A few words. Amanda has formed a friendship with her, however. I thought it odd that she hails from Edinburgh but does not sound especially Scottish. Amanda said she lived in Northumberland in her childhood."

"Her essay combined the description of a traveler with the advice of a physician. Except, of course, she is not a physician."

"Her father was one, Amanda told me. She would travel with him in the summer, to care for people in rural parts."

"An apprentice, then," Stratton said, in a casual tone that belied how extraordinary the observation was.

"It sounds like it," Langford said. "I think she may continue his work now that he is gone."

"Except *she is not a physician*," Brentworth said again.

"Better someone who knows something about medicine than no one who does, is how it is probably seen by those she tends," Stratton said.

"Nor can she continue his work. I am told she is a governess," Brentworth added, mentioning a point given to him by Haversham.

"She began in that situation very recently, right before

coming to Town. She signed on with Hume a month or so ago."

"Hume? That radical?"

"The same. In his mind he hired a tutor for his daughter, not a governess," Langford continued. "Miss MacCallum is responsible for teaching a whole range of academic subjects to his daughter. That was how she occupied herself in Edinburgh. Not as a governess."

Brentworth thought about the essay in the journal. "I think Davina MacCallum may be a radical too." It would explain a lot if she had politics as a motivation, not greed. For one thing, she had not struck him as the sort to cheat to enrich herself. But to bring Scottish lands back under Scottish ownership— He could see that being a goal that allowed a twisted rationalization that cast cheating as not cheating.

"Why would you say that? My tutor did not adopt my father's politics, so why would she adopt Hume's?"

"I don't think she adopted anything. I think she knows him because they already held sympathy for the same cause."

"Cause? Singular?" Stratton said. "I assume you mean the Scottish cause. I think it is safe to say that after the executions in '20, the remnants of that cause have finally been put to rest forever."

"Amanda reported no political views at all of her new friend, least of all that one," Langford said.

"Her essay described travel east of Glasgow where that trouble was centered. Her patient was the wife of a weaver. She made reference to his unfortunate absence from the home the last few years and the trials that created. He was probably one of those transported."

"Does it matter? I doubt she has come to London to assassinate anyone," Stratton said.

Brentworth let that pass. *No, she came to London to steal hundreds of acres from my legacy.*

Langford peered at Brentworth hard. Brentworth suffered it. With most men he would be confident that absolutely nothing would be discerned, but this was Langford who knew him too well and who possessed an annoying ability to bore beneath the armor.

Langford smiled like a devil and mischievous lights entered his blue eyes. "You don't really give a damn about her politics. You are just looking for an excuse to be interested in her for any reason, and that one will serve your purpose."

Stratton's eyebrows shot up. He scrutinized Brentworth too.

"Nonsense," Brentworth said. "You have no idea how very wrong you are. Your ongoing infatuation with your wife has you assuming all men are idiots like you, Langford. I have no interest in overly self-possessed Scottish women of peculiar education and manner. Now, isn't it time we join the ladies? You two are boring me."

"*Overly self-possessed*, was she? You have already spent more time considering her character than you do most women." With a cocky smile of victory, Langford rose to lead the men out.

Indeed he had, but not for the reasons Langford assumed.

Chapter Three

The house on Saint Anne's Lane in Cheapside did not appear large, but London houses could surprise you. Some of them, though narrow, rambled back almost an entire block. Eric assumed this one did not. It had been let by an M.P. after all, and not a wealthy one at that.

It probably proved convenient enough to Angus Hume's attendance at sessions, however. Also to those meetings of radicals that he no doubt attended too. Hopefully that was where Hume was right now. Eric mounted the few steps to find out.

He presented his card to the servant who opened the door. "I am calling on Miss MacCallum."

She paused over the card. Her freckled face flushed beneath the brim of her white cap. Flustered, she invited him to sit in a little room beside the entry before she hurried away.

The chamber served as a small library. Nice windows looked out on the street and good furniture offered comfort. He perused the books, wondering if they belonged to Hume or had come with the house.

"Your Grace, we are honored."

Not a woman's voice. Damnation.

He turned to see Hume right inside the doorway. The man affected an artistic look in his shoulder-length hair and mustache, made more dramatic by its deep copper color. On the other hand he favored fashionable clothes, so Eric at least did not find himself treated to some exotic turban and robe.

He did not like Hume, and not because the man was a Jacobite who flirted with sedition in condemning the Union of Scotland and England. There were radicals, and then there were radicals. This radical was of the type that wanted to turn everything upside down tomorrow. He had once suggested that the only way to have the necessary change was to exile all the nobles. Privately he was known to have spoken fondly of how the guillotine handled the problem in France.

"Hume. Good to see you. You appear hale and fit." And happy. Smugly happy. Like most wiry men, Hume always gave the impression that he held in a burgeoning energy. Right now he looked fit to burst with it.

He knew. The damned Jacobite was aware of Miss MacCallum's claim. Haversham would have apoplexy if he found out.

"I am healthy as an ox, I am glad to say. The house-keeper said you want to see Davin—Miss MacCallum."

The familiarity was not truly a slip. It had been a deliberate declaration of—what?

"That is correct. Is she at home?"

"She is in the schoolroom with my daughter. She normally holds lessons until two o'clock."

"It is one thirty. Perhaps this once you will allow her to end them early. Although if you require it, I will wait."

"No, no, we can't have that. When a duke condescends to call, he must be accommodated. I have already told the housekeeper to inform Miss MacCallum of your arrival."

"How good of you."

Hume strolled around aimlessly, looking at the furnishings as if he were the guest. "Can I ask why you called?"

As if you don't know, you annoying rogue. "No."

"I am of course responsible for Miss MacCallum. May I at least ask if this is a social call?"

"It is a private matter."

"Ah."

Ah, indeed.

"You met her, I think," Hume said. "No doubt your perception of her matches my own. She is a most determined woman. Strong-willed too. She is not cowed easily."

"How unfortunate for you to have a servant with those qualities."

"Oh, she is more than a servant. We have taken her into our family. She is one of us." He sent a direct gaze with that, to be sure that last sentence carried all kinds of meaning, which left Eric to wonder which one applied in reality.

"I am sure she appreciates her good fortune."

"Well, there is good fortune, and then there is truly good fortune, isn't there?"

Eric hoped Miss MacCallum arrived before he had to listen to Hume explain how her future good fortune would come at the Duke of Brentworth's expense. The man was itching to do just that.

"I have been negligent," Hume said. "Allow me to have Mrs. Moffet bring you some refreshment." He aimed toward the door to call for the housekeeper. "I will call my mother as well, so she can greet you."

Eric did not want refreshment. He did not even want to

stay in this house, where he was sure ears would be listening. "Please do not. This is a business call, and I would not want to disturb the household. I will wait in the garden, however. The day is fair."

"Certainly. I will show you the way."

Davina stared in the looking glass, then groaned. Hopeless.

She had hurriedly changed into a decent dress, though hardly one suited to receiving a duke. That did not bother her as much as her hair. It hung in loose waves on either side of her face, skimming her jaw. It almost looked fashionable. Unfortunately, it hung the same way all around her head. Long locks had not been gathered into a knot on her crown the way anyone would expect.

She scowled at her reflection, but not in distaste at her appearance. Rather, she fumed over the idiocy of cutting her hair. Had Sir Cornelius gotten to her in time, the quack her landlady in Edinburgh called in would not have had the chance. Sir Cornelius was a scientist and knew the ancient practice of cutting off hair during bad fevers did nothing a cool compress would not achieve.

You are alive, aren't you? that quack had snapped when she complained after the fever passed. Yes, alive, but that illness had taken a toll in her face, her weight, her hair, even her outlook. She had gone into that fever a girl and emerged a woman.

That was what she saw in the looking glass. A woman with features too bold and hair too short and goals too ambitious. A woman with something she had to do that had now been delayed too long.

She stood and smoothed the pale ocher muslin of her

skirt, and left her chamber to go down to the library. She did not expect it to be a pleasant meeting. There was only one reason the Duke of Brentworth would have come here today.

She found Mr. Hume loitering outside the library door. "He has gone to the garden," he said, falling into step and guiding her toward the back of the house. "I had intended to have my mother sit with you as a chaperone, but in the garden there is no point because he will only request you walk with him."

"I do not need a chaperone, least of all with this man. Nor did you think so. You just wanted your mother to listen."

"That is not true. You are as yet unmarried. You should not—"

"Mr. Hume, we both know why he has called. I am in much more danger of being browbeaten than importuned." She paused at the door in the morning room, which led out to the garden. "I appreciate your concern and your interest in my welfare, but, please, allow me a moment to collect myself. A dragon waits out there, and my sword is very small."

He patted her shoulder in reassurance. "Find me in the library when he leaves." He went away.

Davina faced the door, closed her eyes, found the core of her strength, then walked outside.

The duke stood twenty feet away. He did not stroll amid the plantings or even look at them. Rather he stood tall and erect, his profile carving the landscape, his brow slightly furrowed.

He appeared crisp and precise and sternly, impressively handsome. And displeased.

He must have heard the door, because he turned his head to watch her approach. Oh yes. Very, *very* displeased.

Amanda had said that mothers with eligible daughters did not even try to lure him because they found him too formidable. Davina understood that now. Here he was in all his privilege, his lean strong form containing an energy that contradicted his casual stance.

She made her curtsy and he his bow. "How generous of you to call," she said. "I fear the household will not be the same for days."

"I will not stay long. I apologize for taking you away from your duties."

"Nora, my charge, is delighted, and I don't mind having an excuse to partake of the garden in midday."

He looked toward the house. "Would you walk with me? I need to discuss something with you in privacy."

"Of course."

He set his hat and crop on a nearby bench. They began to stroll through the garden. She ignored how his close proximity made him very large and a bit overwhelming. She would not allow him to bully her. Not that he had done anything to imply he sought to do that. Then again, she wondered if it was the goal of how he presented himself to the world.

"I have been to the palace," he said. "I was informed why you were there when I saw you. I know about your claim, and your petition."

She turned her head to look up at him just as he turned his head to look down. "You could have told me," he said. "If not at the salon when we were introduced, then at St. James's when we met there."

"I thought it better not to until I heard back from the king."

"More likely you were hoping I would not learn about this nonsense until you wreaked all the trouble you could."

"Did you come here to insult me? We do not know each other well, and this is not looking like a promising friendship."

His jaw flexed. "The king is no more pleased by your persistence than I am."

"Then he should not have promised me to take up the matter."

"How did that happen? What exactly did he say to you?"

"He was in Edinburgh for the Scottish festivities. My father was associated with the university and had many friends there who helped me after he passed. One is Sir Cornelius Ingram. He was knighted for his scientific work."

"I know of him."

"He agreed to try to arrange for me to see the king. He had me attend a banquet as his companion, and introduced me after the meal."

"A meal at which His Majesty drank freely, no doubt."

"I could not say. I did not count the glasses of wine he consumed."

"Trust me, he was well into his cups by then."

"He was not foxed, if you are trying to suggest that he did not have his wits about him."

He stopped and faced her. "Such wits as he possesses are easily lost to drink. So, the meal was done, Sir Cornelius pushed you forward and made an introduction, and there was no cut from the king." He narrowed his eyes on her face. "Your hair was longer then. It was cropped more recently. The king saw before him a pretty young woman with a winning smile and he behaved as all men do."

"Not all men. You, for example, are behaving boorishly whether I am pretty or not. As for the king, he was polite and gracious, which is what I would expect a king to be." She tipped up her chin and looked him in the eye. "We spoke a few minutes, then I explained my situation. He was sympathetic."

"I'm sure he was."

"He said that when he returned to London he would direct his men to look into the matter and see what could be learned, and that he would support a bill in Parliament to rectify any oversight and to clarify matters, lest someone claim there should have been an attainder even if there was not."

He appeared surprised to hear that last part. She suspected his mind had gone in that direction. *Your great grandfather died at Culloden fighting against Great Britain, and if there had been an heir there would have been an attainder due to his criminal act.*

"He probably did look into the matter and learned you have no claim and there was no oversight. Hence his avoiding you."

"If he had looked into it, he would have learned I am completely at rights."

He inhaled tightly. He appeared like a man reining in his temper. Only she had not seen anything to indicate he had become angry.

"Perhaps you would be good enough to explain your situation, as you call it." He gestured to a stone bench, inviting her to sit.

She perched herself on the bench. He did not. He loomed in front of her. Huge now. A tower of black garments and chiseled visage watching her.

"Before my father died, he shared a family secret with me," she began. "He also entrusted a letter into my care. One from the last king. It all pertained to my family's history and my grandfather's identity as the rightful heir of the Baron of Teyhill."

"The baron perished at Culloden. He had no heirs. His only child, a son, died around the same time."

"So it was believed. That son, however, did not die. He was spirited off to Northumberland and given into the care of a farming family there."

"Why?"

"For his safety. The baron's people did not trust the British army. They believed that after the defeat and his father's death he would be harmed."

"Our armies do not kill innocent children."

"What nonsense. Of course they do. Of course *they did*." She glared at him, daring him to disagree.

He did not make the claim again.

"And so he was raised there," she continued. "My grandfather became a clerk, and married, and my father was born. He in turn eventually returned to Scotland and studied to become a physician in Edinburgh. Before my grandfather died, however, he revealed his true identity to him."

"It would ring truer if he had revealed it to the Lord Lyon much earlier."

He referred to the authority in Scotland that served much like the College of Arms in England, as arbiter of titles and heraldry. "He was not sure of it earlier. Nor did he hold the land as is required of those feudal baronies. He sought proof, so the lands would be returned to him, and then the title. Sought evidence."

"Which he did not find before he died, correct? If he had, this claim would not have been delayed by over a generation."

"In his own mind he was sure enough that he wrote to the king and presented himself as the son of MacCallum of Teyhill. Whatever that letter said, it resulted in the king responding with great encouragement. Had my grandfather lived longer, it would all have been settled then.

Only he didn't live longer. Before he died, however, he gave my father that letter and told him about the history."

He paced away slowly, thinking. "You have no proof of this except a family story from the sound of it."

"My grandfather had more, I am sure. It was in the letter to the last king. Only now I am told that letter is lost. Or so Mr. Haversham claims."

"He has no reason to lie."

She stood. "Doesn't he? How awkward it must have been when the king's men realized who now held that land. Not some other Scot, or even an English lord from the border lands. Not some viscount or baron of recent patent. No, it was a duke. Not any duke. Brentworth. A powerful duke who makes lesser men tremble. The king must have thought it was the worst luck for it to be *you*."

"If you are accusing the king of lying to you in order to avoid an argument with me, you overestimate my influence. He and I have argued plenty in the past over more important matters, but as the king he wins. That is how it works, Miss MacCallum. He and I are not friends and he does not care if I am the object of a claim from a Scottish woman with nonexistent proof."

"If you and he were not friends, he would enjoy giving me the lands. Instead they are claiming all the proof is gone."

"That is because it is *in fact gone* if it ever existed. You should give this up. It will come to nothing."

"I cannot do that."

He sighed with deep exasperation. "You have no proof other than a surname that is so common as to be meaningless to your claim."

"I will find more."

"How? It all happened almost a hundred years ago."

"I will find it. My grandfather was not a fool or dishonest. If he wrote to the king, he knew he was the heir. I will find whatever he found that convinced him of that." She sat again, firmly. "You are the one who should give it up."

He paced forward and glared down at her. "There is no way that will happen. I am Brentworth. We do not hand over parts of our estate easily, least of all to women with dubious stories about unfounded inheritances." He made the vaguest bow. "I will take my leave now, lest we have a row. Good day to you."

"I thought a row was what we were having already."

With a quelling glance in her direction, he began walking up the garden path.

"Don't you fear being known as a cheat?" she called after him.

He paused long enough to face her. "Don't you fear being known as a fraud?"

Chapter Four

The woman was impossible. Irritating as hell.

Eric fumed about the conversation with Davina MacCallum while he rode back to Mayfair. She had been damned sure of her story, considering she had no proof at all. Anyone else would have at least hesitated before all but declaring war. But not Miss MacCallum.

Was she a fraud? Eric had met a few in his day, and they usually showed the same confidence. They had to. Enough questions would be raised that it hardly helped to raise them first.

The notion that she might be perpetuating a bold, audacious swindle had provoked an odd reaction while he was in the garden. Anger, mostly, and—disappointment. The combination resulted in a sensation that discomfited him. What did he care if she was shown to be dishonest? Yet something in him rebelled at the idea.

He never became angry. Well, rarely. Yet here he was riding through London with a jaw so tight his teeth were grinding. He kept seeing her sitting there, the dappled sunlight making patterns on her short locks, calmly explaining how her family should receive those lands.

The English army did not kill children. But he could not

say that with confidence, and she knew it. He had not been there, and who knew what happened in every case of heirs of rebels. And whether it ever happened or not, what mattered was what others believed might have happened.

Northumberland back then had been full of Jacobites who supported the Scottish revolt. Catholics mostly. It had been a center of significant rebellion on its own in those years, and many of its own sons had fallen at Culloden. If one wanted to send a child to sanctuary, that would be one place to choose.

Damnation, her story at least held a certain logical consistency. But it was only that, a story. A story and a letter from a king half mad and on his way to delirium.

He cursed under his breath. She was going to be trouble, maybe for years. Just looking at her he could tell she would never give this up. Why would she? *She* had nothing to lose, and much to gain.

It would have to be *those* lands, too. He never thought about that Scottish estate if he could avoid it. Even now, while he paced his horse through town, memories wanted to take over his mind and throw him back in time to wallow again in guilt and remorse.

He escaped that dark cloud by chewing over what he knew and what she did not know but claimed to know. He ruminated over that conversation with Haversham. By the time he reached Mayfair he concluded that the real danger did not come from Miss MacCallum but from the king who would be anxious to protect his name and honor. That caused him to ride to a house other than his own.

The butler took his card even though they knew each other well. "His Grace is not at home, Your Grace."

"I am calling on the duchess, not Stratton."

"I will see if Her Grace is at home then."

He waited in the drawing room. He assumed Clara would decide she was at home, out of curiosity if nothing else.

By anyone's calculations, Clara was the last woman Stratton would have married. Their families were old enemies, and it turned out Stratton could lay the blame for unforgivable sins at their doorstep. Yet he and Clara had fallen in love, against all odds.

Their union represented the triumph of optimism and pleasure over the obligations of blood and duty. Being a realist Eric had not held much hope for the longevity of their great love, but here they were today, still smitten like new lovers. Which was probably why Stratton allowed his wife a level of independence unusual even for duchesses. Not that Clara would have it any other way.

She indeed was curious enough to receive him, although he had to wait almost half an hour for her to enter the drawing room.

"You caught me unawares, Brentworth, and it is not a day on which I receive. I had to rush to dress for you, and it took forever to get my hair to look right."

Her chestnut hair had been twisted and curled expertly. "Perhaps you should cut it. I expect short locks are fairly easy to dress."

"Excuse me?" She gave him a suspicious look, as if he toyed with her.

"Never mind. You could have come down in whatever you wore. I am a friend and we do not have to stand on ceremony."

Another suspicious look, one that caused her eyes to appear hooded. "How generous of you. As if you would receive me in a banyan."

He had to smile at that, along with her.

She strolled to a divan and invited him to sit. "I doubt

this is the typical social call, so forgive me if I ask what it is you want."

"I am wounded. Why would you think I want something?"

"Because you have never paid a call on me alone in all the time we have known each other. If my husband is not here, neither are you."

He wished he had been more careful about that. It had been a stupid negligence.

"Goodness, Brentworth, you almost appear uncomfortable. Your need must be great indeed. Out with it, and I will count in your favor that you asked me directly, instead of having my husband do it for you."

"I will be frank. I have reason to think you wrote to the king regarding Miss MacCallum."

"How do you know?"

"Haversham."

Her eyebrows rose. "Just as well it was handed off to him. He owed my father for interceding in a matter when he was a young man, so he will do right if he can."

"Right by whom?"

"Why, by Miss MacCallum, of course."

"So you know about her claim?"

"Not the particulars. I only know she was promised attention to a problem with a legacy and that promise had not been kept. That is disgraceful. Kings can't lie about such things."

She did not know the facts of the matter. He debated what to tell her.

Clara, unfortunately, was very sharp and her mind was right with his on that point. "How did Haversham come to tell you about any of this?"

"He sought my advice on a part of it." Not a lie.

"At least they are finally doing as was promised and

investigating her claim. I hope you can help. She is alone in the world now, since her father died. She keeps body and soul together by being a tutor for girls, but who knows how long she will find such situations? Eventually she will have to take service as a governess, I suspect, and that would be a waste." She ended her diversion into Miss MacCallum with a smile that then firmed. "And how can I help you help Haversham?"

"I have a favor to ask."

"You almost choked on that. I expect it is rare for you to ask a favor of anyone. Well, let's hear it."

"It would be best for Miss MacCallum if her matter was handled discreetly."

"Best for the king, you mean."

"Nothing good will come from this turning into drawing room gossip."

"Brentworth, did you come here to ask, *as a favor*, that I keep silent about this?"

"I would never insult you by implying you gossip. I am more concerned with that journal of yours."

To say she sat up and took notice would be an understatement. "The journal? We do not write about squabbles over inheritances. Unless—*ohhhhhh*. There is a story here, you mean. A scandal or something that could feed the gossips for a year."

"Hardly that interesting. However, I am asking you *as a favor* to desist in any inclinations that you may develop regarding the entire affair."

Her excitement dissolved into a pout. "It is cruel of you to dangle this then snatch it away. I expect if I do not agree to this favor you will then ask my husband for the favor, and I will in turn have to hear his petition."

"I would rather not."

"Which means you still might." Her eyes narrowed.

"Why do I think you are not doing this to help Haversham and the king but yourself in some way?"

He gazed back passively. Innocently.

"You have your favor. With one condition. Should at some point this be ripe for publication, *Parnassus* gets to do the story first. There are times when nothing else but all the facts will clear the air and silence the lies."

"Condition accepted." He stood. "Thank you."

She rose too and walked with him to the door. "It was an easy favor to grant. Now, of course, you owe me one. That should be fun."

Davina did not join Mr. Hume in the library after Brentworth left. Instead she took a long walk and released her anger in long, purposeful strides. Her path took her far afield, and as a result when she returned to the house on Saint Anne's Lane, the family had already sat to dinner. She entered the chamber as quietly as she could and slid into her chair.

During her entire walk she had thought about her meeting with the duke. She had to admit that while he did not frighten her, she understood why some women found his attention discomforting. His presence and attention carried no real danger but rather a compelling but subtle vitality that was hard to name. Perhaps it was called power. She could see some people becoming tongue-tied when that gaze leveled at them.

Mrs. Hume sipped her soup and Nora only glanced in her direction before reaching for a roll from the breadbasket. It was Mr. Hume who made a display of noticing her arrival. He paused midsentence of his description of a political meeting. His thick eyebrows, copper-colored like his hair, rose a fraction over his blue eyes. The mustache he wore like a badge of his radical ideas moved above the small pucker of his lips.

He waited for the housekeeper to bring her some soup before speaking again.

"You were gone a long while, Miss MacCallum." He removed his pocket watch to look at the time, as if he did not know it already. "A good three hours."

"I took a long turn through town. I felt the need for exercise."

"Not fitting," Mrs. Hume muttered. The old woman did not like Davina and made no pretense on the matter. She did not approve the unusual terms Davina had demanded before taking this position. As a result she often scolded when Davina displayed the independence that had been at the top of her list of necessary accommodations.

"How did you spend your afternoon, Nora? Miss MacCallum's absence left you on your own."

"I visited my friend Anna," Nora said. "She has a new doll she carries everywhere. If I were younger I might be envious, because it is French. But I think it silly to carry around a doll when one is thirteen."

"Better a doll than a book too complex for your young head," Mrs. Hume said.

"Mrs. Hume, I was brought into the household to encourage the complexity you decry."

Mrs. Hume's snowy face turned pink. "That I should have to suffer such impertinence from a governess . . ."

"She was hired to be a tutor, Mother. Not a governess. She is not being impertinent in explaining the truth."

Davina gave Mr. Hume a look of gratitude. It could not be easy for him to disagree with his mother, especially about how and why the tutor did not behave like a normal servant.

Face red now, Mrs. Hume excused herself. Her exit

would have been dramatic except that her departure could not be abrupt. Afflicted with bad bones like many elderly women, she required aid in standing and a cane to walk, both of which Davina jumped up to supply.

"May I leave too?" Nora asked.

"You may," Mr. Hume said.

"You can study your Latin verbs," Davina added. "We will drill tomorrow."

Nora neither groaned nor objected. A biddable girl, she seemed to enjoy her studies. Davina wondered how long that would last. Soon fashion and young men would turn her head, and common notions of what a girl should know and need not know would influence her.

Davina ate the cook's stewed fowl. Mr. Hume drank his wine. His long fingers gently held the stem of the goblet as if it was made of crystal instead of pewter. Davina waited for Mr. Hume to broach the topic begging to be addressed.

"Did Brentworth indeed come about the legacy?" he finally asked.

"Yes." She sometimes regretted informing Mr. Hume of her reason for accepting his offer to serve as tutor to his daughter. She had debated whether to even take the situation. For one thing, she suspected that Mr. Hume, whom she had met socially in Edinburgh, was a little too interested in her in ways she was not interested in him.

At their meeting where she accepted the charge, she had stated her reason. *I need to go to London to petition the Crown, and that is where you live much of the year.*

Regrettably, Mr. Hume had concluded that the truth might serve other ambitions in addition to any he harbored regarding a romance with her. His interest had expanded to her history, plans and fortune.

"What do you think of him?" he asked.

"Proud. Well aware of his consequence and standing."

She paused. "Intelligent. I was not expecting that. I wrongly assumed he would be lazy, rich, and spoiled, like a character in a satirical print."

"The English aristocracy is not entirely composed of mental laggards given only to self-indulgence. Mostly, but not totally. I did warn you that Brentworth would be formidable."

Mr. Hume liked to think he was her adviser in her quest. He had expectations of political gains that were not part of her own goals, and they kept his nose a little too close to her business. For Davina, this mission was entirely personal. She had plans for that property. She wanted to turn that big house into a place where medical help could be given to the rural people her father had cared for when he could. It would be a way of continuing his work, and his memory, as well as giving her own life a purpose it had lost when he passed away.

"Any duke is formidable, sir. This was a superior formidable, however. He reveals nothing." *He would never narrow his eyes like you do when calculating his next move. He would never show his hand.*

He nodded in acknowledgment of her perceptions. "Does he know what you are up to?"

"Our conversation in the garden proved he knows all of it. He thinks I am a fraud. That I have made it all up. I should have waited until I had more evidence, I suppose. Only I thought the evidence that my grandfather sent would be all that was needed. Instead, it can't even be found."

"Or so they say."

"If they say it, it is as good as true." She considered Mr. Hume, who sat there looking sympathetic. "I don't think I will progress if I wait on Mr. Haversham. I need to present my case to someone else who has the king's ear.

Can you help me obtain an audience with someone close to the king?"

Mr. Hume pondered her request, but she knew his influence probably did not extend that far. Not only was he an MP from Scotland, but also he was known as a radical one who continued to oppose the Union and who spoke out loud and long about the trouble there a few years ago, the so-called Radical War. The court was not likely to do him any favors.

"I can see," he said. "You must know that I will do whatever I can to help you. We will find a way." His blue eyes warmed.

His expression made her uncomfortable. Mr. Hume had done nothing untoward since she took up her situation a month ago, although he had begun addressing her by her given name too soon, and been hurt when she requested he desist on the familiarity.

He was not an unattractive man. His fashionably cropped curls held an unusual dark copper hue rarely seen outside Scotland. His eyes could be appealing when they did not express what they did right now. He was not a big, bulky Scot, but rather slender and wiry, so he cut a figure that current fashions favored.

She liked him as a person. She simply wished he did not think about her the way he was thinking this instant.

She excused herself. Once in her chamber she settled at her writing desk and penned a list of all the kinds of evidence it might be worth looking for.

Chapter Five

Davina bumped her way through the crowded, narrow street. Goods poured out the shop doors and tradesmen could be seen working their crafts behind some of the windows. People stopped to browse or buy, and others hurried along on their way home for dinner.

She kept to the side, watching the signs dangling overhead, looking for one of a cobbler. Mr. Hume had sent her here, to talk to an old man named Mr. Jacobson, who occasionally attended the political meetings he frequented. Mr. Hume thought this man had lived his youthful years in Northumberland in the region where she had been born. Possibly he would know something of use to her.

That Mr. Hume had not accompanied her implied this would probably not be a successful outing. She suspected he had given her this man's name and direction in order to appear helpful.

She spied a sign with a boot up ahead. Perhaps this Mr. Jacobson was not a cobbler but a bootmaker. She squeezed past a cart, suffered its donkey's strong odor, and ducked through the doorway.

Boots in various stages of creation lined one wall, and leather hung from another one. An old man, big and pink-faced and with cropped gray hair, straddled a bench near the window, nailing the bottom of a boot. He squinted as if he could use spectacles. He did not appear to hear her enter.

"Good day, sir. Are you Mr. Jacobson?"

He looked up, still squinting. "I am. I don't do women's boots, though."

"I am not here for boots, although yours appear quite fine. Mr. Hume met you and thought you might be able to help me."

"Hume? That troublemaker? What's he doing, sending a woman to me? All talk, he is, and let someone else take the lead ball, that's all that one is." He returned to his work. "Nearly came to blows over all his talk causing trouble but him never being the one to risk his neck."

"This has nothing to do with politics. I came to ask you if you knew my family in Northumberland. He said you came from there, near Newcastle."

"'Tis a big county, lass."

"Yes, very big. Yet there are long and wide family connections in it, and it is always possible you knew them if you lived near the village of Caxledge. It is near Kenton."

He nodded grudgingly. "Possible, as you say. I didn't live far from that town when I was a lad. What's the name?"

"MacCallum."

"Scot. Well, that narrows it a bit. I knew MacCallums. Went to church school with one. He wasn't Catholic, or a Scot to hear him, but his father wanted him to get some learning, and that was one way to do it."

"That could have been my father. He was educated at the St. Ambrose School in Newcastle but started at a local parish school."

"Could have been him, then. He was younger than me,

and I didn't stay long, what with taking an apprenticeship, so we did not know each other well. I can't tell you much about him."

"It was my grandfather I was hoping to learn about. His father, James."

Mr. Jacobson set down his tool. His brow hooded his squint. "Seems to me my father knew him, at least in passing. Fostered nearby, I think. An old couple. Forget their name."

"Mitchell. Harold and Katherine."

"I wouldn't know. There was some bad feelings when he left the church as a young man. Haven't thought about that in years. Odd how old memories come easier these days than new ones. I only remember because my father thought it wrong for him to then send his son to the school if he left the church. That's probably the only reason I recall your family at all." He paused over his own words, then shrugged. "One reason at least."

"There is another?"

He sat in thought, as if pawing through old parchments in his head, looking for the right document. "A strange thing to say, I thought," he spoke to himself.

"For whom to say?"

His profound distraction lifted. "My father. When MacCallum died, he told my mother. It was odd enough it stuck in my head. MacCallum caught fever and died, he said."

"Not so odd to tell her if they had attended the same church when younger."

"MacCallum caught fever and died, he said. The baron is gone." He grinned. "Carried himself like one, I suppose. Made you take notice, now that I picture him. It was a name they must have given him to goad him about that."

"Probably so." Her astonishment made it hard to get the words out.

"Proud, I suppose. A common enough sin. There are worse. Although he weren't the best family man either, now that I poke my brain about him. Put his son in that school, but he'd leave his family from time to time and wander off for a spell. Kept needing new situations for clerking because of it. Seems to me my mother had something to say about that. She didn't approve, of course." He chuckled. "Never saw my father dare to take a holiday from us or his work, I'll tell you that much. She wouldn't a had it."

"Few women would." *Where did he go when he left for a spell? How long would he be gone?* This man would not know, but she wished he did.

"I went back there, oh, ten years ago. Don't remember word of them. Don't remember you at all."

"My father left when I was thirteen. We moved north after my mother died."

"Ah. That would explain it, then. Not more I can tell you. As I said, I didn't know any of them much."

She wished he could tell her much more, could regale her for hours with stories and memories. She wished he and her father had been good friends, so he might fill the hole inside her with details she could cling to. "I thank you for telling me what you do remember. It was good to hear about my grandfather, and about my father when he was young."

He picked up his cobbler's hammer. "Was an easy service to provide. Tell that fool Hume to come and get some boots. The ones he wears don't fit him proper."

"I will do that." She took her leave and went out to the street, where she released her excitement. Finally, she had something to indicate she was not on a fool's errand. While it was possible her grandfather had been called the baron due to his bearing, it could also have been a reference to his history, known to those alive when he was brought to the region. It wasn't much, but it was more than she had expected this visit to give her.

The little clue distracted her until someone brushed past and jostled her to alertness. She paid better attention to her path then, but walked home with a lighter heart than she had experienced in months.

Stratton hailed Eric and galloped his horse across the park. Eric stopped and waited for him, then noticed that Langford brought up the rear.

"Odd to find you here this early," Stratton said while his horse snorted and whinnied in the crisp autumn air. "I thought you would be sequestered at one of your meetings."

"The day is chilled but fair, and I needed a ride to clear my head." He turned his horse and paced along while Langford bore down on them.

Stratton fell into place on his right. "If we are interfering with deep thought, we will ride on."

"Clearing one's head means you put deep thought aside for a spell." *I am riding in order not to think about a Scottish woman who is trying to steal land from me.*

Langford took up position on his left. The wind proved too strong for hats, so all their hair blew around their heads.

"And here I thought you had such deep thoughts plaguing you that you could not afford to put them aside," Stratton said.

"I am spared thoughts that deep."

"Interesting," Langford murmured.

Eric glanced over at him, then turned his attention to Stratton. Both of them appeared ever so uninterested and casual. Studiously so.

Damned if he was going to offer up thoughts, deep or otherwise. If they waited for something, let them wait.

They all turned toward the reservoir.

"We haven't seen you much the last few days, but Clara said you called on her, so you must not be playing the hermit," Stratton said.

"I never play the hermit." *Hermit* implied total retreat, and also self-denial. He did not engage in either, ever, although there were times when he might not be very social.

"Well, not since that time when we were much younger," Langford said.

Eric did not respond. He could not believe Langford had mentioned that, or even remembered. Memories crowded forward again, about how he had not been a hermit at all then, merely engaged in something no one could know about. *Fire. Madness. Inexplicable loss of control . . .* He closed the door forcefully on the impending reverie.

"It was good of you to call anyway," Stratton said.

"Why was it good of me?"

"There has been some talk about her and that journal since the party, so it was good of you to show again that you hold her in high esteem."

"She told you about my call?"

"Only that you did call."

"And now you wonder why."

"Not at all. If you choose to call on my wife when I am not at home, that is fine with me."

"It isn't as if he thinks you have designs on her,"

Langford said from the other side. "He'd never suspect that, would you, Stratton?"

"Of course not."

"I think she did tell you why I called. What did she say?"

Stratton shrugged. "She only said it had to do with the journal. Hence my thanking you for letting society know your high esteem again."

Eric debated whether to leave it at that. Eventually, the problem with Miss MacCallum was going to get out, however. If the king's Household knew, eventually the world might. Who knew if Hume would be discreet. Probably not, if he saw some profit in talking.

"It did concern the journal. However, it also concerned Miss MacCallum."

"I told you," Langford said triumphantly to Stratton. "As soon as you said the journal, I thought, *and who writes for that journal?* Hmmm? I told you he has a fascination."

Eric chose to ignore Langford. The alternative was to thrash him and, tempting though that might be, they were in the middle of the park and he loathed creating a scene. "There is no fascination. There is no interest. There is only annoyance and a good deal of pique. Not only with her but with your wife, Stratton."

"I trust you did not call on Clara to scold her. I won't have it."

"Hell, no one scolds Clara. Even you don't, nor would any man who wants to live five more minutes. I merely called on her to ask a favor. And she graciously granted it."

That stopped the two of them in their tracks. He rode on. A patter of hooves brought them to his two flanks again.

"What favor?" It was Langford who had the cheek to ask. "You have told us this much, you may as well tell the rest. Clara may never confide in Stratton, but Amanda will surely tell me if I work my wiles on her."

"I have no reason to think Amanda knows about this."

"Of course she does. Or she will. She said all they do at that club is gossip. They are worse than men, according to her."

Knowing how successfully Langford worked his wiles, that meant Amanda would indeed tell him if he was determined to find out.

"Miss MacCallum has come to London to petition to have lands returned to her that she claims were confiscated several generations ago and given to someone else. That is her true reason for being here, not to write for *Parnassus* and not to serve as a tutor."

Langford's brow knit. "So who has the lands now?" He glanced askance at Eric. "Ohhhh."

"She had a meeting at St. James's a few days ago. As did I. The king has been avoiding her, but that became impossible because *someone's wife* interfered and wrote to the king on her behalf." He glared at Stratton.

"Not much interference," Stratton said defensively. "The king does not like Clara."

"He could not ignore a duchess, though, could he? He had Haversham speak with her. And with me."

Stratton reddened. "You had the temerity to meet with Clara and ask her to stop *interfering*?"

"I asked her to allow matters to resolve themselves. I asked her not to publish anything about this in that damned journal of hers. That is why the king agreed to have Miss MacCallum be heard out. He knows about that journal, and your wife's patronage of it, and he probably imagined being shown as a liar in it."

"A liar?" Once more, Langford could not allow anything to pass. How like him.

"There had been a promise a few years ago. I was very thankful Clara indeed said she would not publish anything."

"That is not like her," Stratton said. "She must like you more than I realized. I always thought that she and you—"

"Yes, yes. Well, I sweetened the favor a little. She gets the whole story if there is ever one to tell."

"I trust you included the provision that Lady Farnsworth would not be the one to write that story," Langford said. "Because even if you are in the right, she can make you look like an ass."

"Still bitter about that, are you, Langford? Since the lady all but adopted your wife, you should probably let that water flow under the bridge."

"What are you going to do about this?" Stratton asked. "Can you disprove her claim?"

"I'm the one holding the lands. Let her *prove* her claim, not that there is anything to prove."

"I doubt that is how the king sees it," Langford said. "He probably wants you to fix the problem."

He probably did. Haversham had all but said as much. Damnation.

"Maybe you can just buy her off somehow," Stratton said. "Find a compromise."

"I am not inclined to compromise. Nor would either of you if you were in my position. Are we all to give away parts of our estates to any swindler with a sad story? I intend to prove she is the fraud she is."

"You are sure of that?"

"She has no damned *proof.*"

"I suppose if you need to prove she is a fraud, you will have to get to know her," Langford said. "Spend some time with her to catch her up on her inconsistencies. That sort of thing."

"Probably so, hellish though it will be."

Out of the corner of his eye, he saw Langford grin broadly across at Stratton. Stratton responded with a slow smile of his own.

He turned to give Langford a furious glare, but by then Langford looked as innocent as a babe.

Chapter Six

It was all Davina could do to keep her mind on the lessons. She kept finding ways to avoid having to, by giving Nora mathematical problems to work on her slate, and a Latin passage to translate. All the while, she sat with books open in front of her, pretending to prepare for tomorrow, while in reality her thoughts dwelled on Mr. Jacobson.

It would be helpful to find another Northumberland native who had the same memory, but she doubted that would be likely. It would have to be someone at least Mr. Jacobson's age, and from the area around Caxledge. What were the chances of that? Even Mr. Jacobson would have never been found if he had not gotten into an argument with Mr. Hume at a recent meeting.

She had learned that much at dinner last night, after returning from the boot shop. Mr. Hume had been all curiosity. When she described Mr. Jacobson's dislike of him, he explained about the argument. It had yielded the information about Mr. Jacobson's history, however, so he considered it a row worth having.

Then he had said he would think about her next move and they would discuss it later. She assumed that meant today.

She had already decided her next move. It waited on her

writing table in her chamber. Last night she had composed a letter to Mr. Haversham, explaining she had met a man whose father knew her grandfather as the baron. Perhaps Mr. Haversham would take her a little more seriously when he learned that.

As expected, Mr. Hume wanted to discuss her problem. He waited until his mother and daughter left, but asked her to stay in the dining room. To her discomfort, he then moved to sit closer to her. Not right beside her, but closer than normal. Within arm's reach.

"I have ruminated on your discovery," he said. "I think there are several options for further action."

"I agree. One is to go to Northumberland."

He drew back, horrified. "And what of us—I mean, what of Nora's lessons?"

"I am sure a good finishing governess could take over."

"I don't want her finished. I want her educated."

"Surely there are women who can provide an education besides me. This is London. And I only said it is obvious that is one path, not that I am leaving tomorrow."

"I was thinking more of a newspaper advertisement, seeking others from that area. There must be some in London. Probably many. I would gladly pay the fee."

She had not considered using the newspapers that way. She admitted to herself that Mr. Hume was proving useful. "I would prefer to pay the fee myself. How do I accomplish this? Present myself at the paper and ask to put in a notice?"

"I will help you. We only have to write it out, then I will bring it to them."

They spent some time deciding which papers to use. Fifteen minutes later, they had a plan. Mr. Hume insisted that contact be through a third party, and recommended a stationer nearby.

"I thank you for your advice, sir." She slid off her chair and stood. "I will go and compose the notice and make several copies. I will leave them in the library with some money, because you have offered to bring them around."

"You do not need to hurry off, Miss MacCallum. If we put our minds to it, we can probably think of other things you can do. I already have several in mind myself."

She wondered what those might be. Unfortunately, he was looking at her in that too warm a manner again. "I need to finish this tonight, then get my rest so I am fresh for Nora in the morning. Perhaps tomorrow you can tell me your other ideas."

"As you prefer."

She hurried up the stairs to write her advertisements.

Two days later, two things occurred at breakfast that ensured Eric would not enjoy the day.

The first happened while he perused the *Times*. He normally did not read the advertisements, but because they appeared on the front page, one could hardly avoid them. This day, while he scanned them to see if any of his partnerships were calling for more funds, his gaze landed on a short notice and halted there.

Desire to make contact with anyone who once lived near Caxledge in Northumberland. Replies with directions can be left at Montague Stationers on Norwich Street."

Norwich Street was not far from Hume's home. While any number of persons might want to contact someone who once lived in Northumberland, he suspected he knew who this person might be.

The second thing to happen was far more disagreeable. A hand-delivered message came while he read his mail. It was another invitation to be received by His Majesty, this time at three o'clock.

He had planned to spend the afternoon doing other things, and fought the temptation to respond with his regrets. That would never do, much as he wanted it to do very neatly. And so, at quarter to the hour in question, he entered St. James's.

No Haversham greeted him. Rather, one of the pages immediately showed up to escort him. Across the large chamber they paced, through the door, and through several chambers until they reached a private one used by the king.

His Majesty waited there in all his corpulent excess. He looked displeased, which transformed his mouth into an unpleasant pout. Seeing Eric hardly changed his demeanor. Ever since Eric had voted against his divorce, the king had let his dislike be known.

Haversham stood beside the king. He smiled a greeting, along with a bow.

"Brentworth," the king said. "Good of you to come. We've a situation here and need to plan how to address it."

"His Majesty refers to Miss MacCallum's claim," Haversham said.

"He knows what I refer to," the king snapped. "Don't you, Brentworth?"

"I deduced that much. Two invitations in a week, no less. This matter can't be serious enough for that."

"It's damnable serious."

"I think he was making a joke, Your Majesty," Haversham bent to speak in the king's ear. "He was not making light of your concern."

"I can speak for myself, Haversham. Yes, it is serious.

Whenever someone wants to steal land from my inherited honor, it is most serious."

It was not the answer the king wanted. He frowned furiously. "You only inherited it because my father gave it to a Brentworth before you. It is officially ours to give or take."

"It has been a very long time since a king has taken lands from a duke without that duke being attainted," Eric said. "A very, very long time." He looked the king right in the eye. "The peerage would not take such a thing well at all, as I'm sure your advisers have explained."

That quelled the king. He looked at Haversham desperately before regaining his severity. "See here, it may be serious for you, to your mind, but it is much more serious for us. We'll not have this minor bit of land resulting in our name being bandied about. Or that of our father! She went to Stratton's duchess and told her about this, and who knows where that will lead. That woman owns that damn journal and has no sense of decorum. She savaged her own family in a story, so expecting her to respect the Crown is hopeless. Furthermore—"

"The duchess will not print rumors and innuendo. It is not in her nature, nor would it benefit her journal. If it gives you any reassurance, she has promised me as a favor to desist in any interest in this until the matter is settled."

"The gossips will get hold of it anyway. They always do."

"As you may know, I dislike being the object of it as much as Your Majesty, perhaps even more. Regrettably, I cannot silence every gossip."

"There are some who don't like us," the king muttered petulantly. "They will whisper we can't keep our word. Disparage our honor. Defile our father's name too. This must be . . . must be . . ."

"Nipped in the bud?" Haversham offered.

"Ripped out by its roots would be better," the king snapped. He settled back and focused on Eric. "We've a plan."

Hell. "Do you indeed? I trust that it is not that I just give her the land. Every charlatan in the kingdom will be making up stories and claims against peers' properties, then. Nor would you want me to accommodate a fraud, I am sure."

"And if she isn't a fraud?" Haversham said.

"Do you have reason to think she is not?"

"She is a most unlikely fraud, that is all."

Eric could not believe the utter lack of reasoning at work. "Let us be frank. If this claim came from a man of ambiguous history, based on some story told by his father, no one would give it the slightest credence. But let a handsome woman be the liar, and suddenly she is plausible."

The king's eyes brightened. "So you find her handsome? We did, but not in a typical way."

"Handsome or homely, she still has no proof and should not be encouraged."

"But you referred to her as handsome."

"Yes, fine, I find her handsome. Can we return to the matter at hand?"

The king looked back at Haversham smugly. "He thinks she is handsome. We told you our plan would work."

Eric did not like the king's sudden confidence. "What plan is this?"

The king gave Haversham a direct look. Haversham cleared his throat. "His Majesty thinks there is a way to compromise her claim quickly, at no cost to you."

"What the hell does that mean, *compromise her claim*?"

"Give her half a loaf, so to speak, so she is contented."

"If you mean give her half the land, I refuse. Does no

one else see the dangerous precedent this could create?"
Eric battled to keep his tone even, but as so often happened
with the king, his temper was beginning to rise.

"Not half the land, no," Haversham said. "Not give her
any, in a manner of speaking. The plan is that—"

"Stop talking in circles." The king leaned forward and
balanced his weight on his hands, which he set firmly on
his knees. "Everything will be fixed neatly if you marry
her, Brentworth."

Eric just stared.

"You are past the age. It is time. Why not this handsome
woman?"

Eric kept staring.

"The thinking is that should her claim be proven, it will
not matter if you are married," Haversham said soothingly.
"The lands would have been joined already. And if it turns
out she is a baroness—"

"Madness that they allow women to inherit titles up
there, but we are stuck with it," the king inserted. "But it
won't matter if you are married, will it? Better, actually.
Good blood on both sides, then."

"And if she isn't a baroness but a lying female scoundrel?" Eric said.

Something in his tone had Haversham sweating and the
king shrinking. The king nudged Haversham.

"There is reason to believe she is not," Haversham said.
"That letter from the last king, for example. Her name.
There is a fair chance she is correct in her claim."

It was time to kill this plan. Now, before the king
warmed to it even more. "I do not know anything about
this woman. Nor do I think there is a fair chance she is
correct. In any case, I have no intention of marrying her.
Find another plan."

The king frowned darkly. "Don't know her well? Hell, we didn't know our wife at all when she was chosen. We don't worry about such things. Duty, duty." He made an ugly face. "Nor did you have any sympathy for how that affected us, so don't expect us to be overly concerned with your marital bliss now. We say you will marry her."

"You don't get to say that and you know it. I'll not have my life become a convenient solution to a problem of your own making."

"We are your king, damn it."

"And I am Brentworth."

"As Brentworth, it is your duty to—"

"My duty is to the Crown. Not to your whims." He stood. "I will take my leave now, with your permission. I repeat, find another plan."

"We will no longer receive you if you do not do as we say," the king yelled when he reached the door. "You will be banned from Court, from our presence, and all society will know of our disfavor."

"Do your worst, Your Majesty. Only remember that if society learns of your disfavor, it is apt to also learn the reason for it."

Eric prided himself on clear thinking. Logic and reason marked his consideration of any matter. He therefore found it extremely uncomfortable to find his mind jumping from one indignant curse to another for the next few hours.

The conversation with the king would have been comical if it had not been so outrageous. Where in hell had he decided he had the power to decree that a duke marry? They weren't living in the Middle Ages. No doubt all the toadies around him acquiesced to his slightest desire, and he mistakenly had grown to believe anyone would.

I am Brentworth. Hell yes, he was Brentworth. He would be ostracized from Court? What a welcomed respite that would be.

Marry that fraud? Not likely. Not ever. Yes, he needed to marry, it was past time, etcetera. He had already planned to take care of that next season. He'd pick some dutiful girl and get on with it. But not at the command of someone else. Not at the point of a sword.

Was the king going mad like his father? Or was this just a desperate move by a king foreseeing how his honor might be mocked by the people he sat with at dinner parties?

By evening, he was still pacing his house with his jaw as tight as a screw press. He called a footman and sent him out with a message. A half hour later, Stratton arrived, entering the library like a man in a hurry.

"Are you unwell?"

Eric saw the mask of concern on his friend's face. "Not unless fury's fever counts."

"The note—it was vague—*Come at once if you can*, it said." Stratton took a deep breath. "You have never done that before. I thought perhaps you had been stricken in some way. Hell, I didn't even wait for my horse to be saddled. I came on foot. I *ran*, damn it."

"My apologies. I have been stricken in a way, however. When you hear about it you will understand."

"Will I be taken by fury's fever too?"

"It is my hope that you will bring me to my good senses so maybe I will laugh."

He pointed to the decanters. Stratton poured himself some whiskey. "If you also sent for Langford, do not wait on him. He was going out tonight and will not receive your message until very late."

"I did not send for him. He would enjoy this too much. Then I would have to thrash him and the night would end poorly."

"If he would enjoy it, perhaps I will laugh even if you don't. What has happened?"

"I saw the king today. At his request. Regarding Miss MacCallum's little problem."

Stratton pursed his lips. "Why do I think the conversation did not go well?"

"Because it didn't. The king devised a clever plan, you see. A way to make his obligations go away. His solution was to command me to marry the woman. He was not joking either. He meant it, as did that worthless Haversham."

Stratton's mouth twitched, but he avoided laughing. "What did you say to that?"

"*What did I say?* Damnation, I refused, of course." He repeated the conversation, so Stratton would know all of it.

Stratton got up and poured more whiskey. He sat again. "So you reminded the king that he did not have the power to make such commands, and you all but dared him to do his worst." He paused. "You lost your temper with him."

"Not completely, but, yes, I was a bit sharp." More than a bit, now that he thought about it.

"That is unlike you. Completely so. It is not how I would have expected you to respond. The Brentworth I know would have listened, promised to consider, then gone home and devised his own clever plan that was far cleverer than anything the king and Haversham could ever concoct." He examined Eric thoughtfully. "So why did you do it the wrong way instead?"

It was enough of a scold to cause some chagrin. "I was caught unawares, I suppose."

"That is also unlike you. Do you want my advice? I dare not give it unless you say you do, because you are acting like a madman on this topic."

"I am not acting like a madman."

"You are not acting like the man I have known most of my life, that is certain. It is well you did not call for Langford because he would have theories regarding that point that you would not want to hear." He leaned in. "But you already know that, which is why he was not invited."

"You are here instead because you give better advice, and, yes, I do want to hear it."

"First, you apologize to the king. A nice letter will do. Otherwise—you will have no more consultations by ministers. No more invisible hand in the deepest of state matters. No support from the government for any bills you particularly favor. He is still the king, and even weak and constrained, he can make his power felt if he chooses. He rarely does because he is lazy, but he *can*. But of course you know that too."

He knew it. Damnation. "I trust you do not expect me, in this letter of apology, to capitulate on the notion of marrying that woman."

"If you were acting like the Brentworth I know, I would. You have to marry someone, and why not her if it solves the matter of those lands? You have never expected love in a match, or even wanted it, from what I have seen, so it matters little who you marry."

"I'll be damned before I—"

Stratton held up a hand, stopping him. "I accept that you refuse the idea, so I am not advising that. However, in your letter, you might assure the king that you will find another way to appease her. Then you only have to find a way that does."

Eric paced to a window, drew the drape, and gazed into the dark outside. Appease her? He could probably find ways to do that, much as it would infuriate him to appease a fraud.

While he stood there, a renewed calm descended. It had been good to call for Stratton. He hadn't been himself lately, especially where Miss MacCallum was concerned. He had allowed his annoyance to have its way. This really was a simple matter if one addressed it rationally. He had helped devise the most complicated diplomatic responses in times of crises for the realm. Surely a Miss MacCallum could be dispatched with ease.

"I will say that it is very odd to be the one giving advice," Stratton said from the divan behind him. "Normally, it is the other way around."

"Yet you have been more helpful than you can know." He watched the streetlights, and noticed that one kept changing position. Not a streetlamp, but a lamp on a carriage. From the way it swung, he assumed it was moving fast.

"Of course, Langford would say you are only behaving out of character because you found this woman appealing, and are disappointed to discover she is an adversary."

"Langford is an ass sometimes." The lamp kept coming, growing bigger with each instant.

To his surprise, it stopped in front of his house. A door opened and a man jumped out of the coach.

Two minutes later, the library door opened and Langford barged in without announcement or ceremony. He stopped short on seeing Stratton, but then strode right up to Eric.

"I came as soon as I could in order to tell you."

"Tell me what?"

"It is out. Everywhere, I assume. It was being discussed at the dinner party. I had Amanda feign illness so we could leave. I came here after I brought her home."

"What is out?"

"You. Miss MacCallum. Her claim on that land. It will be everywhere by morning is my guess." Having done his duty, Langford looked around. "What are you doing here, Stratton?"

"Visiting."

Langford took that in the stride he made toward the decanters. "Well, just as well you are here. There is plotting to be done."

"I do not need your help plotting," Eric said.

"Of course you do." Langford came back, glass in hand. He threw himself into a chair. "You will have to find some way to buy her off if you don't want to be the subject of gossip and prying for the next half year."

Gossip. Prying. He could live with the former. He definitely did not want the latter, especially about *those* lands.

"Do you want my advice?" Langford asked.

"No."

"Yes," Stratton said.

Langford stretched out his legs and sipped some whiskey. "The way I see it, you want the lady pliable and open to compromise. As an enemy, she never will be. She will be on her guard, and suspicious that you seek to press an advantage. Which will give her the advantage instead."

"Do you always talk so much when you plot?" Eric asked.

Langford ignored him. "So how to make her a friend instead of an enemy? I ask you, Stratton, how did you do that with Clara?" His blue eyes twinkled as if stars had entered them. "Don't be shy. Tell Brentworth here how it is done."

Stratton looked at Eric. "He has a point."

"When it comes to women, I usually do," Langford said with supreme contentment. "That is what you need to do, Brentworth. Befriend her. Charm her. Kiss her. Hell, seduce her if necessary. Otherwise, the most discreet duke in the world will have everyone nosing into his business until hell freezes."

Chapter Seven

Two days later, his letter to the king composed and sent, Eric presented himself again at Hume's house. No rows, he told himself as he faced the door. Even if the woman irritated him, even if she provoked him, no arguments.

Once more, the housekeeper put him in the little library. Once more, Angus Hume joined him first.

He had sworn no rows with Miss MacCallum. Hume was another matter.

"We are honored again," Hume said.

"I waited until two o'clock so I would not pull her away from her duties this time."

"How gracious of you. Still, I expect there will be some time before she joins us. Women and their vanities and all that."

"She does not strike me as vain. However, your point is well taken." He turned to the bookcase and pretended to browse the bindings. "Can I thank you for letting it about that she has business with me?"

"Rather more significant than business, don't you think?"

"My question stands, no matter what word we use."

Silence behind him. Then a burst of energy came across

the chamber like a wave. "The king was not doing as he promised. Now, with society aware, he will be forced to."

"You have complicated matters more than was wise. For one thing, the king was not the problem. I was. And I made no promises, so I have no obligations."

"He could make you relinquish—"

"I am Brentworth, and he would never dare it." He turned to face Hume. "What is your interest in this?"

"She is in my house and is my responsibility."

How noble he made it sound. The scoundrel saw gain in helping her, of one kind or another. "Does she know what you have done? How you have made her the object of whispers and gossip? That many will call her a fraud and charlatan fit only for prison?"

"That will pass. Then she will regain those lands and everyone will know how it came to be that her family lost them and why," Hume said with a snarl. "Scotland will cheer when she bests you."

"It will be a very small victory."

"Not so small. As the great-granddaughter of a hero of '46, she will be famous. She will marry one of her own kind, and be a baroness."

He did not ask who Hume envisioned as a good Scottish match for Miss MacCallum. Hume probably saw himself at the top of the list.

Anger threatened to get the better of him again. Stratton would be appalled. He glanced toward the door, hoping it would open so he would be spared this scoundrel's presence.

It did open, but not to Miss MacCallum. Rather a bent old woman entered, her cane taps on the floor punctuating the silence while she walked.

"Allow me to introduce you to my mother," Hume said.

Eric wondered if he was expected to chat with Mrs.

Hume, as if he had called on her. Fortunately, after a few words she tapped to a corner and took position on a chair.

"I know you will not mind if she remains in the chamber during your call," Hume said. "It threatens rain outside, so the garden will not do this time. Do not worry that she will overhear. She is all but deaf in one ear."

The mother's presence would ensure no rows, so Eric did not mind at all.

Miss MacCallum finally arrived, her short hair swinging free around her head. She offered half a smile, then gazed pointedly at Mr. Hume until he made his excuses and departed.

She noticed Mrs. Hume in the corner. "My apologies, Your Grace. It could not be avoided." She gestured to chairs set near the opposite corner. "Let us sit here, if that will suit you."

The front windows sent diffused light over her after she took her chair. It turned her hair a silvery gold and her eyes a deep sapphire. She wore the same pale ocher dress as the last time. A limited wardrobe. Small wonder she wanted those lands.

For reasons Davina could not fathom, the duke did not launch into an explanation of his arrival. Rather, he sat there looking at her. Sizing her up, she assumed. Though he'd had enough time for that in the past, so unless he was indeed slow witted, he should not need to do it now.

"I assume you have come about my inheritance," she said, breaking the stretching silence.

"I have mostly come to warn you that any hope of discretion has been lost. Your claim is being discussed in drawing rooms all over town today. It will continue for some time."

She swallowed the curse that almost slipped out. She had wanted to avoid this. It could never help, and might make a resolution harder. In particular, if the king's negligence about his promise was well known, she no longer had the implicit threat of the world finding out as a weapon.

"I told no one."

"I did not think you had. Even the duchess is vague on the particulars. I think this was the work of someone who thought it would put the king's feet to the fire. That was a mistaken belief."

"Indeed it was."

He glanced at Mrs. Hume.

"She appears to be asleep, but she is not," Davina warned quietly. "And while half deaf, the ear facing us is very good."

"I do not care if she hears what I am about to say. Let her, and let her repeat it to her son. It was he who spread the story of your situation. He admitted it before you came in."

She had guessed as much. Who else could it have been? "He thought to help me, I am sure."

"He thought to help himself. He has plans about all of this." His gaze penetrated hers. "But I think you know that."

She felt her face warming. "My own plans are very simple, and that is what matters."

"It is not my place to ask, of course, but—" He appeared unsure of his words. "I hope he has not—He thinks of you as more than a servant or a tutor, I believe. A woman in your situation is vulnerable. I trust he has not—"

He suddenly appeared a man discomfited by an ill-fitting jacket. She was certain that was a rare occurrence. So rare that the discomfort only begat more discomfort.

She let him remain thus for a ten count, wondering if

there were some way to document what she was seeing. No one would believe her just on the telling of it.

"I know of his interest," she finally said. "I do not share it, and he is aware of that. He has in no way insulted me the way I think you fear."

That satisfied him, mostly. "If that ever changes, if he— you are to tell someone. Tell the Duchess of Langford. I am told you are friends with her."

"I will be sure to do that. Did you call in order to warn me about the gossip and my employer's designs? How kind of you."

"I came to warn you, yes. As for your employer, that was an impulse."

"And here I thought you never had any of those."

His smile almost appeared chagrined. "They are not frequent. I did come about him, however. How do you know him?"

"We were introduced at a meeting. An historical one, lest you assume I share his politics."

"I am surprised he attends any other kind."

"This particular society has a special subject. Its mission is to reestablish Scotland's history, lest it be lost in all the romantic notions becoming so popular."

"The public likes those notions. Hence their popularity."

"They can have as much of it as they want, and wear plaid to their hearts' content, so long as the true history is not eclipsed. Truth is always best, don't you think?"

"It is hard to disagree with the rightness of truth, Miss MacCallum. Some history, true though it may be, is best not to dwell on, however."

"I do not dwell. I merely honor it."

He looked as if he wanted to say more but declined to do so. Perhaps he had decided to avoid an argument today.

"I am glad you called, Your Grace. It gives me an opportunity to tell you that I have found more proof."

Any indication that he was experiencing an uncharacteristic lack of confidence disappeared. He did not straighten or puff up. If anything, he relaxed in that chair, his strong hands resting on the arms and his feet placed just so in order for his half-outstretched legs to convey his utter lack of concern. His pose turned that chair into a throne.

"Have you now? Am I to learn what it is?"

"I have met a man who remembers my grandfather, and that he was called the baron by those who knew him since he was a child."

"It may have only been a reference to his manner."

"It may have been a reference to his history."

"Did this man who remembered him say anything about that history, to give you reason to believe that?"

She wanted to lie. Badly. She wanted to smugly announce that he had regaled her for an hour with all the details and produced a letter from his own father that revealed the entire episode. That would set this proud duke back on his heels for at least a moment or two.

"It is enough for me to be even more confident that I am pursuing a just cause," she said instead.

"Finding this man was convenient to that cause."

"Mr. Hume—" She tripped over her words in midthought. *Convenient?*

"I wondered if Mr. Hume had not helped you find him."

"I hope you are not saying that because Mr. Hume was involved, you do not trust this proof as truthful. Mr. Hume is not dishonest, whatever else you may think of him."

"Had the proof been real proof, I would have wondered about the sudden discovery of someone to provide it.

However, because it is not proof at all, I will not insult Hume with that suspicion."

Insult her too, not that he said as much. "I think that short of resurrecting from their graves those who brought my grandfather to Northumberland, and procuring their testimonies, you will not believe any proof I obtain."

"That is not true. However, a passing reference to a man as baron, if indeed that memory is accurate after all these years, does not make him a baron's son. If I call a man an ass due to his behavior and manner, he will not start braying." His gaze caught and held hers. "Is Mr. Hume looking for others who might have proof? There are notices in the papers that I believe indicate he is."

"Those are *my* notices, paid for by *me*."

"I am sure you will receive responses. A lot of them."

"You are?"

"Of course. As I said, the word is out. The notices are clearly yours. There will be those who hope to profit from this, who will tell you whatever you want to hear. When it starts, let me know. I will listen with you, and make sure the liars are revealed for what they are."

"Perhaps some won't be liars."

He smiled vaguely. "Perhaps. In that case, we will hear the proof together."

She did not believe he would *ever* hear *any* proof correctly. However, she would love to see his expression if someone came forward with knowledge of that time that was accurate and true. "Should I receive responses that appear they might be fruitful, I will send word to you of my meetings, so you can be present if you so choose."

"Thank you. Now, I should take my leave before Mrs. Hume falls over. She has been stretching and leaning in our direction so long and so precariously, I doubt she can keep her seat much longer." He stood and bowed. Then he paused and gazed down on her. "Primrose."

"Excuse me?"

"In this light, you should wear a dress the color of primrose, I think."

He left without further ado.

That afternoon, Davina remained in the library, alone now, reading. Not that many pages in her book were turned. Her mind kept going back to the duke's call.

He had almost been friendly at first. Gracious. Charming. He might have been deliberately trying not to frighten her the way Amanda said he did most women. It had been difficult to think of him as an enemy during those first minutes.

And his concern about Mr. Hume—that had not been feigned. It touched her that he had perceived she might be importuned and felt moved to reassure himself that was not happening. Nor had his concern been misplaced. Sir Cornelius had insisted on accompanying her when she let a room with a family in Edinburgh after her father died. Only later did she comprehend that it was not the chamber he wanted to examine.

Of course, the duke's softness could not last. By the time he left, she had almost been as vexed with him as the last time. They did not have a row, but he had still left her fit to scream.

She forced her mind back to her book, only to be interrupted one page later by Mrs. Moffet.

"Something came for you." She handed over the sumptuous letter.

It was from the Duchess of Stratton, inviting her to the theater the night after next. Davina peered at the page in amazement. Of course she would go. She dared not decline. Only what could the duchess want with her?

"There is something else." Mrs. Moffet handed over a card. "He has called. Just now."

He was Mr. Justinian Greenhouse. Davina had been introduced to him at the duchess's salon for *Parnassus*. She remembered him because he knew Mr. Hume for some reason that escaped her now. As did his face. She vaguely recalled a very thin man, early into his middle years, with sparse dark hair. He also walked like a dancing master. That memory came clearly.

"He's still at the door," Mrs. Moffet said.

"Mr. Hume will be angry if you leave one of his friends on the street."

"He's not here for Mr. Hume, is he?" Mrs. Moffet pursed her lips. "He is calling on you."

"I can't imagine why. I barely know him." She sat up and smoothed her skirt. "Well, bring him in, I suppose."

While she waited, Davina realized that just possibly Mr. Greenhouse was responding to her notice in the newspapers. He was from Northumberland, after all. It could be that he realized the notices were hers and had decided to—

"My dear Miss MacCallum." Mr. Greenhouse advanced on her with long strides and a simpering smile.

Davina took one look at his eyes and knew for a fact that this had nothing to do with her notices. This was a social call. A special kind of social call.

How exceedingly odd.

Chapter Eight

Eric attended the theater alone. He wanted nothing to do with society tonight, but he did want to listen to music, and the first part of the program had a pianist playing Beethoven.

He settled on a chair deep in his box and sent the usher away when he tried to light one of the lamps. There, in the darkness, he waited for the music to start.

As had happened too often lately, his thoughts meandered in the direction of Davina MacCallum. He could hardly ignore her intrusion into his life now. Several rude questions had been put to him in his club last night regarding her claim. The whole world seemed to know his business on the matter.

Worse, some fellow from a newspaper had waylaid him when he left his house this afternoon, wanting to ask questions. *You don't have to talk to me, but its best you do,* the brash pup had said while getting in his way. *Otherwise I'll have to make something up*. Oh, how he had chuckled at his own joke. Eric had wanted to use his horse crop on the fool.

He might have forgotten the incident if not for the last

question, thrown after him while he rode away on his horse. *So where is this land?*

Inevitable that people would wonder and ask. It was the heart of the story, wasn't it? Only he did not want anyone—not Davina MacCallum, not Parliament, and certainly not newspaper writers—poking around that property, or asking lots of questions about it.

He forced his thoughts to more productive matters, like the negotiations at work for bringing the bill regarding slavery to the Commons. It had to go there first. Too many lords owned properties in the colonies that made use of slaves. All fine and good for Britain to outlaw its trade, but to do so on those distant estates would be costly in the extreme.

The only solution was to pay them off. Unfortunately, he could not make most of the others agree to that. The notion of compensating slave owners for the loss of their slaves sickened right-thinking men. It sickened him too, but this would never progress, not now and not in fifty years, unless it was done.

While the music started he turned over various strategies in his head. Just when one was forming that held some promise, he was distracted by a broad gesture by a man in a box across from his.

It was Langford, and he was all but hanging over the balustrade, demanding Eric's attention. His wife gestured too, only more discreetly.

Langford realized he had commanded Eric's attention. With a wide sweep of his arm, he pointed to his right. He clearly wanted Eric to look there. To do so would mean getting up and walking to the balustrade and hanging over like Langford. Eric had no intention of doing any of that. He closed his eyes and gave himself over to the music.

Five minutes later, a firm hand jostled him. He opened his eyes to see Langford hovering above, looking exasperated.

"Did you not see my direction?"

"I did. Whatever you thought I needed to see is not of interest. I don't care if some woman arrived half naked, or if some idiot is falling down drunk. I only want peace."

"You want to see this, I promise you."

"No, I do not."

A firm hand grasped his shoulder. "Come with me."

He followed. Langford was easily amused and had probably seen some outrageous gown. He also was a gossip, so it might be unexpected evidence of a liaison that would set tongues wagging. Whatever it was would not be worth the bother.

He trailed Langford to the door to another box. Stratton's box. "Unless Stratton has grown two heads, there is no drama in there."

"You would think not, but wait." Langford opened the door to present the box.

The very crowded box. So crowded that Stratton appeared annoyed. His duchess kept smiling at her visitors, but she also looked dismayed.

Stratton saw them and pushed his way to the back of the box. He shook his shoulders as if he needed to resettle his coat. "Hell of a thing. We were planning a quiet night and this is what happened."

Eric peered through the dim light at the faces. Men, almost all of them. He knew most of their names, but a few he did not recognize. Bright-eyed and gracious, they all kept their attention settled on the front of the box and the duchess.

The duchess turned to speak to her companion. That other woman turned her face. Eric understood why Langford had dragged him here.

Miss MacCallum sat beside the duchess. And Miss MacCallum was the object of all the attention.

"What is she doing here?" he asked Stratton.

"Clara invited her. She doubts the woman enjoys much entertainment and wanted to treat her."

"More likely she has heard the truth about that legacy and wanted the whole story. The gentlemen all know most of it already, that is clear." Langford gestured to the men angling to get an introduction from the duchess to Miss MacCallum. "Nothing like a woman of property to draw the admiration of the younger sons."

"She is not a woman of property," Eric corrected.

"Of course not," Stratton soothed.

"She, however, does have expectations," Langford added. He surveyed the little scene with what looked suspiciously like pleasure.

"Very small expectations," Eric said. "A gnat's worth at most."

"That does not seem to be the general opinion, from the look of it."

No, it didn't. The popinjays were out in force. Miss MacCallum did not even look surprised. With her damnable self-possession, she chatted and smiled as if she had expected this to happen.

Hell if he intended to watch. He decided to leave, only just as he was about to, the duchess saw him. Her gaze locked onto his. Her smile turned brittle. Her eyes narrowed and darkened. She beckoned him with her finger.

"It looks as if Clara wants to talk to you," Stratton said blandly, as if he did not know better than anyone that when Clara had that look in her eyes, even brave men sought shelter.

"I'll be your shield if you want to retreat," Langford said. "Or even when you advance. Yes, I think it would be best if I stand right beside you and try to distract her with flattery and such."

Stifling a heartfelt sigh, Eric made his way to the duchess and Miss MacCallum.

A fan smacked his chest as soon as he stepped close. Langford, good to his role, stepped quickly so no one else saw.

"You deceived me," the duchess said.

"I did not lie to you."

"I did not say lie. I said deceive. Do you think you are too clever for me, Brentworth? You knew the whole story, but you kept the best part from me when you asked for your favor."

"I do not agree my involvement is the best part. Rather it is the worst. However, it was my hope no one else would ever know of it."

Langford edged into their conversation with one shoulder. "You look too ravishing to bear tonight, Duchess." He flashed his seductive smile. His new position meant that Eric could no longer see Miss MacCallum out of the corner of his eye.

Clara speared him one impatient glance. "Go away, Langford."

Yes, go away. At least move. It is Miss MacCallum who looks ravishing tonight and you are now in the way of my seeing her. She wore blue tonight. Pale blue, like an iced pond. Not primrose, but it still flattered her.

The duchess aimed her dark gaze back on Eric. "Imagine my astonishment, Brentworth, when a friend confided to me the very information I had promised you to keep silent about. Only she knew *more* than I."

"I expect that in the competition for gossip, such a development would be disheartening."

"Are you mocking me?"

"Not at all, Clara." Langford finally shifted enough for Eric to see beyond him. A young man who looked fresh out of university had engaged Miss MacCallum in conversation while he expertly blocked the other swains from intruding. *You go away too, boy.* He hoped Hume had apoplexy when he learned how the suitors were lining up. Served him right for feeding the beast of gossip.

Clara was saying something. He saw her mouth move, but he heard nothing other than Miss MacCallum's laughter.

"Duchess, send for me at your pleasure and I promise to come so that you can upbraid me to your heart's content. Langford, do whatever it is you do to make vexed women smile. Now, excuse me, please." He pivoted and walked the few paces that took him to Miss MacCallum. The young man noticed him first. The pup flushed, as if he had been doing something wrong. Which he had. Eric just looked at him until he took his leave.

"That was an interesting display of silent power, Your Grace." Miss MacCallum's lips pursed. "At my age, it is not usual to have men warned off like that."

"He is a fortune hunter. They all are."

She laughed, and her eyes turned to sparkling gemstones. "I have no fortune."

"They hope for the best on the question. Eventually, one will propose and take the big gamble. When disappointment comes, you will pay a bigger price than the fool you married."

"I do not see how. I never had a fortune and will not miss the one I don't have."

"You will be married forever to a man who planned to receive that which he never did. And you will be at his mercy."

"Unpleasant, to be sure. How good of you to look out

for me again." She turned and flashed a few smiles at gentlemen hanging back but looking hopeful. "If I promise not to marry any of them tonight, will you allow them to amuse me?"

No. "Yes, of course."

"Thank you. It is a rare treat to be the object of all this attention." She gazed past him again and flashed another smile. He all but heard her mind think *Go away, Duke.*

He took his leave. Langford intercepted him as he went to the box's door. "That seemed to go well," Langford said, sardonically. "It is understandable that she can't stand the sight of you. I half-expected you to get the cut direct."

"She would never give me the cut direct."

"She wouldn't dare, you mean. A pity, though. If she had tonight, I could have dined on the story for a month."

"Shouldn't you be attending to your wife? You have left her alone for a long time."

"She won't mind, because I'll have stories to tell when I return."

"I am so glad I could be your entertainment tonight." He aimed for his own box, hoping the music would provide the distraction he had sought when he came here tonight. More likely, he would mostly hear the music of a woman's laughter.

Please meet me in Russell Square at three o'clock.

To receive such a note was odd enough. She was not the kind of woman to receive requests for assignations.

The signature made it stranger yet. The letter had come from Mr. Haversham.

Davina did not know what to make of it. Should he want to speak with her, would he not ask her to come to

St. James's? She doubted he only sought to save her the time of traveling across town.

At three o'clock, she entered the square. Rather than search for him, she decided to sit on a bench and let him find her. He did so five minutes later.

"Would you like to take a turn?" he asked after they shared greetings.

She stood and strolled beside him. He appeared even more gaunt in the full light of day. Shadows formed in his hollow cheeks and the light made him squint. His mouth still reminded her of a frog.

"I thought this would be more convenient for you," he said. "Also less formal."

"How thoughtful. And here I assumed the peculiar place you chose meant you are not speaking for the king."

"You are perceptive. And correct. I am not speaking for His Majesty. I am only conveying my own view of how things stand."

"And how is that, sir?"

"Not good. Not good at all. His Majesty is most displeased that the matter is being bandied about. I explained that you had no cause to do that. In fact, you lose a useful weapon in its happening. He insisted on knowing the source, and was even more displeased to discover it was your employer, Angus Hume. Now he thinks the whole thing is a Jacobite plot to discredit him." He laughed lightly. "Nonsense, of course."

"Of course. Utter nonsense."

They paced on.

"And yet," Haversham said. "Once he gets a notion in his head, well . . ."

"If you know of some way I can end the gossip or turn this around, I will endeavor to do so. However, I can hardly silence people if he and the duke cannot. I am the least influential party."

He slid a gaze over at her. "The only way to silence them is for you to withdraw your request. For now, that is. Allow it to die down, and in a year or two—"

"In a year or two, you say. Then in another year or two. It has already been one year or two. A few, in fact. I am determined to settle this now, Mr. Haversham. I would never have come all this way otherwise."

He stopped walking. He covered his mouth with his hands and frowned in thought. "It might help your case if you were allied with someone the king trusted. The involvement of Hume has him agitated, you see. Suspicious."

"Is not the Duchess of Stratton esteemed enough to be someone he trusts?"

"He thinks she will publish a damning article in that journal if given the chance. No, she is not the alliance I meant. I speak of a more permanent one. You are still of marriageable age. If you had a husband, a man the king trusted, it would probably do much to aid your case."

She managed to keep walking, but this suggestion, put out as calmly as a comment on the weather, stunned her. What did the king expect? That she stand on a street corner with a sign around her neck, offering to marry any man acceptable to the king?

"It would be necessary for the man to be English, of course," Haversham added.

"Why is that?"

"So you are not unduly influenced, and instead are correctly influenced."

"I see."

"There are some sons of peers who would most likely

apply for the position. Younger sons, of course. The heirs would need more assurance of a fortune than can be given."

"Of course."

"I could arrange some introductions. It would be subtle."

She pictured all those subtle arrangements and assurances, and the romantic pursuits that were anything but heartfelt, and the proposals. She could see herself getting caught up in it, much as she had at the theater. What woman would not enjoy the flattery and attention, especially after years of having none?

What had the duke said? That if she inherited nothing, she would still be stuck with this man forever. No matter how honest she was, no matter how blunt, he would blame her and feel he had been trapped.

Of course, the duke had not put it that way. He had said *when* she inherited nothing, not *if*.

"I ask that you do not arrange any introductions," she said. "I am not interested in marriage under such conditions."

He accepted it, but his lips thinned. "I understand. It was my duty to try, because it seemed one solution to me. I believe that if you had such a marriage, your claim would be accepted, you see."

"Because such a husband would control me and the land, you mean."

He did not respond, which meant she was right.

"If you reconsider, please let me know. It truly is the fastest way to finish this. You would get what you want and His Majesty would be relieved of this worry he has now."

"It may be the fastest way, but not the only way. I trust you are looking into the claim. You are likely to find something, and that would also finish this."

"Of course. Of course." He gazed up at the sun. "I must go now. Allow me to escort you back to your home."

"I think I will stay here for a while longer, thank you."

He gazed around the square, assessing it. She imagined him thinking, *Not Mayfair, but she should be safe enough in daylight.* After he left her, she walked the short distance to Bedford Square, found a private chair in the club's library, and did some hard thinking.

Chapter Nine

Eric prided himself on equanimity and discretion. He was known for both, and it went far in gaining him access to the confidences of the most senior ministers in government. On many a day he sat with one of them in his study and they pondered the realm's response to a threat or diplomatic problem. Like the Brentworths before him, he never served in a government position, but his influence was not small.

On this particular afternoon, he did not sit with a minister. He did not contemplate a diplomatic problem. Rather, his guests were Stratton and Langford, and he gazed at a gossip sheet that Langford had just placed ceremoniously in front of him.

"I thought you should see it," Stratton said.

"*We* thought you should," Langford said.

Eric picked up the paper and immediately found the reason why. "What in hell is this?"

"It is a very curious writer who has a nose for scandal," Langford said. "I have had a few dealings with him. Or rather, my name has."

Langford was no stranger to scandal. He mostly ignored when his name became fodder for the gossips. There had been a few times when Eric envied his friend his ability to never give a damn. But then, just as Brentworths were discreet, Langfords had, down through the ages, been scandal prone. After a few generations such traditions probably invaded one's blood. After a few generations of numerous inoculations, the blood probably becomes immune.

"Amanda buys a few of those scandal sheets," Langford explained. "She brought this one to my attention today."

"If it were anyone except you, the fellow probably would not poke so hard, but you are a good story due to so rarely being the subject of one," Stratton said.

"Are you suggesting that if I flaunted every mistress and engaged in drunken brawls like Langford here, I would now be spared?"

"I rarely brawl and never when drunk," Langford said. Then he shrugged. "Well, perhaps once or twice I was foxed."

"Yes, I am saying just that," Stratton said.

The article indeed poked. Since its writer had no facts, he resorted to innuendo. Why was a certain peer so obstinate in refusing to hear the claim against some lands he held? It was not as if said peer visited them often or needed the income. Indeed it was said the manor house was a ruin and uninhabitable, so said peer could not even be bothered to maintain the property. Had the means by which his family acquired those lands been in some way irregular? Were there family secrets attached to that spot of Scotland? Etcetera.

"He claims my coachman said he has never taken me there in the seven years he has served me."

"Has he?" Langford asked.

"No, but I am disappointed if Napier spoke to this man. He knows I will not like it."

"Do not do anything rash regarding Napier," Langford

said. "Napier may not even know to whom he spoke. He surely did not understand the importance of it."

Eric threw down the paper. "What importance would that be?"

Langford chose that moment to groom some lint off his coat sleeve. Eric turned to Stratton instead.

"If this writer does not retreat, and truly pokes, is there anything about that land that would be better unknown?" Stratton asked. "All families have their secrets."

"Nothing at all. Let him poke away for all the good it will do him." He stood and looked out the window. "It is too fine a day to spend in here. I think I will ride along the river for a few hours. Join me if you like."

"I have another engagement," Langford said.

"I am free, however," Stratton said.

They thought he had not seen the meaningful look they shared before answering. He led the way out, assuming Stratton would be doing some poking now too.

He could not gallop forever, so he eventually slowed his horse to a walk. On one side, the Thames flowed rapidly. On the other, Stratton fell into place beside him while they passed the string of low buildings that flanked the river outside London.

"Have you decided what to do about Miss MacCallum? You seem to be holding your fire. Langford thinks it is because of the fascination he attributes to you."

"Langford's head might get turned fast by any passing pretty face, but Brentworths are made of sterner stuff."

"Then you find her pretty?"

He shot Stratton a glance in time to see his grin.

"Attractive enough."

Another grin. "If I were Langford, I would ask *enough for what*?"

"Thank God you are not he, then."

They paced on. Stratton surveyed the scenery. Eric watched him do so.

"You may as well say now whatever it is you are going to say eventually, Stratton."

"I thought to let some time pass first, so it does not appear I am—"

"Poking? Well, you are, so get it over with."

"As I said, you seem to be holding your fire. I will leave that observation there, and suggest that if you do not want to engage in battle with the woman, perhaps you should seek a truce."

"A truce requires compromise. Even if I were willing, she is not."

"You do not know that. The thinking is that perhaps half a loaf will satisfy her. Half the lands, for example. Or a settlement for half the value."

"Pay her off, you mean, to be rid of the nuisance. That is the thinking. Can I ask whose thinking?"

"Langford's and mine."

"And?"

"Fine. The ladies have weighed in as well. Do not give me that Teutonic look of yours. Clara thinks as clearly as any man and is excellent at strategy, and Amanda brings special skills to any such discussion."

"They are her friends. Their opinions are not objective."

"And yours are? How big is this property that you are allowing your name to be dragged through the gossip mill and are risking your influence in government? What are the rents? Do you even know? Have you ever been there?"

"It consists of about a thousand hectares. The tenants mostly raise sheep, so the rents vary but are respectable."

Silence greeted that. It stretched. They approached a tavern and Eric considered whether he fancied a pint.

"So you do know something about this land," Stratton said.

"It is my obligation to."

"Is it true the house is a ruin? Have you ever seen it?"

Eric decided a pint would be a good idea. He stopped his horse, swung off, and tied it to a post. He entered the tavern and took a place next to the window that overlooked the river.

Stratton followed a few minutes later. He regarded Eric with his dark, curious eyes while they waited for the ale to arrive.

"So?" he said after a good swallow. "Have you ever been there?"

Eric gazed out at the river and the road beside it. Stratton just waited. That was why it was Stratton who came. Langford would never be able to wait it out.

"I have not been there in many years, but I was there when my father was alive."

Silence from Stratton. Eric eventually turned his attention to his friend. Stratton's expression said there would be no more questions because Stratton had drawn some conclusions. Possibly erroneous ones.

"It was my inheritance, after all," Eric added.

"Of course. Only you must have been quite young, because your current coachman does not remember. And I could not help but remember that time after university when you retreated from friends for almost a year. You were not in town for some of that period. Is that when you went north?"

Stratton was so amiable and smooth that men often underestimated him. Two had done so to their eternal regret. Eric respected this friend, especially his mind, but he wished at the moment that Stratton were not quite so sharp in his wits.

He looked out the window again. *Sheep dotting the hills to the horizon. A bewitching madness.* "Yes."

"But you aren't going to tell me about it, are you?"

Fire burning the heavy clouds. "No."

Stratton drained his ale. "So be it. I believe the advice I shared is even better than I guessed. Unless you want half the world investigating that place and that time, come to terms with this woman one way or another."

"The king wants me to marry her. That is a hellish solution."

Stratton did not laugh. "If you are hiding something, that may be the best solution. Now, I am riding back. Are you joining me or wandering farther?"

Eric followed him out. Stratton had been right about one thing: It was time to come to terms with Miss MacCallum.

The dust in the chamber lay densely on the records and tomes, and every movement sent it flying like tiny snowflakes. Whenever Davina turned a page, a thin cloud formed in front of the window.

"It should be here." Mr. Hume's thin, long finger slid down the page. "Ah. There he is."

His finger stopped at a name in a list of those who died at Culloden. Her great-grandfather's name, Michael MacCallum.

"It does not refer to him as a baron," she said while she stifled a sneeze. "It could be any Michael MacCallum."

"Only one died there. I checked."

"You have done this before?"

"I took it upon myself to do so, lest someone say even the source of your claim was false. Had another Michael

MacCallum perished that day, someone might say you are that one's great-granddaughter."

"If you had told me what you found, I would have trusted you and been spared all this heavy air." She also would have been spared the way Mr. Hume leaned in close while they examined the huge bound manuscript. He still hovered too closely, increasing her discomfort. She considered allowing the sneezes to erupt right in his face.

"Let us go, then, so your health is not affected."

They left the War Office and began the walk home. Mr. Hume did not like to hire carriages. He said nature had given people two legs for a reason. Davina could not disagree with that, but an hour walk in each direction for no purpose did not amuse her.

"I am glad we are having this time together," Mr. Hume said. "It gives me an opportunity to talk to you about something that has been much on my mind."

"Is this conversation the true reason for this outing? Because while the records chamber was fascinating, I did not need to visit there."

"You should see what evidence there is in any direction, so you can say you did when you are questioned."

"Then perhaps you can find a way for me to see whatever records Parliament also has about that title and estate. I was thinking there may be other information, regarding his family and heir, for example."

"I can find out if such records exist at the College of Arms. Now, regarding the matter I want to talk about." He returned to his overture with deliberation. "It has come to my attention that there are suitors attending on you. You almost caused a scene at the theater, where they lined up, and now some are becoming bolder in their attempts to enthrall you."

"Only two have called, if that is what you mean by

bolder. I assumed Mrs. Moffet would inform you about them, but I can't imagine how you learned about the theater." Neither caller had been what Davina would describe as *enthralling*.

"You accepted the introductions at the theater. You received the two who called."

"Like any woman, I am not opposed to flattery and diversion. Do not be concerned. The calls were after three o'clock and did not interfere with my duties to Nora, nor would I let them."

"You should not encourage these men. Receive them once and they will return. Keep receiving them and they will form hopes and expectations that will never be realized." He spoke with surprising force.

"I will take your advice to heart and give it every consideration."

"Consideration? I am sure you do not entertain the slightest idea of marrying one of them."

"My dear Mr. Hume, if the notion is as appalling as you seem to believe, I will conclude as much, no doubt. *When I consider it.*"

Being red-haired, he had snowy white skin. It now flushed a deep pink. "Do you find it amusing to vex me? The notion is beyond consideration. It is impossible. Would you wrest your family lands back from Brentworth only to hand them over to some other Englishman? Would you have yet more tenants answer to a factor who reports to London? Isn't enough Scottish territory all but annexed to England through the English lords who own it and have absorbed it into their own holdings? With such an inheritance comes a duty, and you must acknowledge yours."

Davina glanced from side to side to see if anyone was noticing this lecture. Mr. Hume had become the image of a man incensed, and she had become a child being scolded.

"Becalm yourself, sir, or the whole world will know our business," she hissed. "It is not for you to instruct me, least of all about marriage."

He caught himself up, looked around, then walked on for five minutes without a word.

"I do not seek to instruct you," he finally said. "I merely seek to remind you of your duty lest your head be turned by the *flatteries*, as you put it."

"My first duty is to my family, past and future. As for marriage, if it gives you any comfort, none of the men who have flattered me are promising in that area. I am not so ignorant as to think their interest is in *me*."

He looked relieved. He even smiled.

They walked in silence most of the rest of the way, but Davina felt him there. An energy came from him, one that begged to be released. She feared he would declare himself, or launch another argument, this time about why her duty was to marry *him*.

"I will part from you here," she said when they neared Bedford Square. "I have things I must do at the journal."

"I will accompany you, and wait in the park so you do not have to make your way back on your own."

"That would not be wise. This could take me some time. I will be back at the house before dusk, so you need not worry."

He fished in his waistcoat pocket. "Let me give you—"

"That is not necessary. As you said, nature gave us strong legs for a reason."

Chapter Ten

"This is all very sly," Langford said. "I promise you will be impressed. You couldn't have planned it better yourself."

High praise indeed. Eric idled in a chair in the library while Langford all but rubbed his hands together. There was nothing Langford loved more than a plot afoot.

This plot was a very small one. In order to speak with Miss MacCallum alone, he had to see her outside Hume's house. Either he needed to follow her when she left the house and accidentally come upon her on the street, or he needed to arrange to accidentally come upon her somewhere else. Like Langford's home.

"Your wife is aware, I assume." Once married, a man's discretion went to hell, at least when it came to his spouse, and this friend had never been discreet to begin with. Eric pictured Langford and his duchess chatting about everyone's business over dinner, in bed, in the carriage—all the time, in other words.

"She is. Don't worry. She can play her role. She and the ladies believe that if you come to know Miss MacCallum better, you will be sympathetic, so she thinks this is a splendid idea."

Eric wondered who the ladies were. The two duchesses, of course. Others who were involved with that journal perhaps. Stratton said there was a club of some sort at Clara's house on Bedford Square, though. There might be dozens of ladies offering opinions.

It was exactly the kind of public airing of his affairs that he had avoided over many years. Now, thanks to the king, he could not avoid it.

Langford walked to the garden doors and spied out. "They are coming. Time for the plan." He opened the door a bit.

Eric pulled himself up and followed Langford over to one of the cases on the wall. Like many town libraries, it replaced some breadth with height. The books near the ceiling could be accessed by one of the ladders that ran on a railing three feet below the top of the cases.

Langford climbed one ladder. He grabbed four heavy tomes and dropped them to the floor. "Damnation!" he shouted while he scrambled down and threw himself on the floor amid the books.

Eric looked down at him. He had been promised a clever plan, not these histrionics.

"Oh, no! What happened, darling?" The duchess rushed in, her face a mask of worry and shock. She fell to her knees beside him. "You fell! Are you all right? Is anything broken?"

Langford sat up and rubbed his shoulder. "The weight of the books unbalanced me. Stupid to go for them all at once. Help me get to that divan over there, Brentworth."

"Should you even try to move on your own? Maybe I should call for several footmen to help me lift and carry you," Eric said dryly.

Langford glared at him. "No, no. I think I can manage it with only a bit of help from you."

With much fussing on the duchess's part, and tentative moves and a few groans on Langford's, Eric moved his friend to the divan. While he did so, he noticed Miss MacCallum angling her head to read the title on the front of one of the books on the floor.

"It is a good thing you are here, Brentworth. Davina and I were just taking a turn in the garden, and if we had been by the back portal we might never have been aware of Gabriel's accident." The duchess fussed more, this time over that shoulder. Or maybe it was the other one.

Eric could not remember which one had been injured.

"If you would allow me, I could tell you whether you need to send for a physician or surgeon," Davina said.

"Surgeon!" The duchess gave her husband a desperate look.

"If a shoulder breaks, it is very serious. All breaks are," Davina said. "Will you permit me to see if there are any?"

Langford and his wife shared an unfathomable look. Langford shrugged. With the *hurt* shoulder. His wife stood aside. Eric folded his arms to watch Act Two.

Davina advanced on the divan. She placed her hands on the injured shoulder. She made a series of firm presses, each time waiting for something. Probably for Langford to howl in pain, which he neglected to do. Indeed his lack of reaction was such that by the last press Miss MacCallum wore a frown.

"Please raise your arm straight out in front of you."

Langford obeyed.

"Now to the side, then above you."

Out the arm went. Then up.

Miss MacCallum stood back. "After the way you cursed and cried out, I feared you were seriously hurt. Instead, I doubt you will even have a bruise in the morning."

"Perhaps you had hoped for more damage. I am sorry to disappoint you. That was a far enough fall for me."

"Why, the shock alone would make a man curse," the duchess said. "Isn't that so, Brentworth?"

"Apparently so."

"I think I will forgo our outing," Langford said to him. He rubbed his shoulder again for good measure. "It may not be broken, but I am quite sore."

The duchess sat beside him and rubbed the shoulder too. She ruffled the dark curls on his head in reassurance. Rather suddenly, no one else existed for the two of them.

"Miss MacCallum, I have my carriage here. I will take you back to the City," Eric said. "I was going in that direction myself."

The duchess heard. "Oh, would you, please? I invited Davina to go with me to some warehouses, but now, with Gabriel injured—" All her attention returned to Langford, who somehow managed to appear pale but stoical.

"I suppose I can take advantage of your offer."

"Let us go, then, so Langford can rest."

As soon as the door closed behind them, Miss MacCallum smiled to herself. By the time he handed her into the carriage, she was grinning.

"Are you going to tell me the reason for that farce?" she asked after he settled across from her. "You were there, so you must know he did not fall, let alone from the top of that ladder. That would be a good fifteen feet, and I assure you, had he done so and landed on his shoulder, he would not easily move it, let alone hold it straight out to his side."

"Well, as you said, it was not broken."

"Even if it were not broken. Nor was he in pain. Not really. He did not flinch at all when I examined him."

"He is very fit. And uncommonly brave."

"The books on the floor dealt with agricultural practices. They looked to be at least a hundred years old, so not *modern* agricultural practices. Did you and he have some argument over how barley was harvested in the last century and he needed to consult the authorities of the time?"

"You are too clever for the average ruse, I can see."

"Please do not forget that."

"I was not consulted about the how of it, but the goal was to arrange for me to see you without having to call at Hume's house. It appears the plot, even with your excessive cleverness, succeeded, because here we are."

She barely reacted. "Why not simply write and ask to meet me in a park? That is what Haversham did."

"Would you have come?"

"Of course. Curiosity would have bested any sense that said not to."

"What did Haversham want?"

"He merely wanted to apprise me of the efforts being taken on my behalf."

"He needed to meet you in a park for that? At least he did not declare himself another suitor. There are enough of those already."

"I could do worse than Mr. Haversham. After all, he has the king's ear all day long. With some persuasion, I might have all I seek."

He assessed her in that light, as if he never had before. He pictured her working her woman's wiles on such as the king's lackey. "I expect you could be most persuasive if you chose. Poor Haversham would not stand a chance. Speaking of suitors, has Hume proposed yet?" It was none of his business but he wanted to know.

"Is this why you wanted to speak with me? To find out Mr. Hume's intentions and to make sport of those suitors?

If so, I am dismayed a peer has time for such childishness. I assumed such as you were engaged most days with important governmental issues."

He almost colored himself but managed to keep his face acceptably cool. That he needed to fight that battle, let alone because a woman had dared scold him, was so unusual as to fascinate him. "I wanted to speak with you about documents and evidence. I am told you and Hume visited the War Office."

"You know about that? Have you set spies on me?"

"Miss MacCallum, when the world knows your business, the world sticks its nose into your business. I do not need spies because anyone with information is gleeful to tell me everything. Did you and Hume find anything useful?"

"Why should I tell you?"

"To add to the evidence on your side of our dispute. There is no point in finding more if you keep it a secret."

She came as close to pouting as he guessed she ever did, but soon gave it up. Which was too bad because it turned out she had the perfect mouth for pouting and she looked adorable.

"Unfortunately, I found no new evidence, only my great-grandfather's name in the lists of the deceased. Mr. Hume said there are also records kept by Parliament regarding the lords, but he can't get me in to see them."

"I can."

Her gaze turned quizzical. "Would you?"

"We will go there now, if you want, and examine any record pertaining to him together. However, it is not Parliament we must visit, but the College of Arms."

"This is very good of you to explain and help. Suspiciously so."

"Not at all. The sooner I convince you there is no evidence, the better."

* * *

It was an understatement to say that doors opened for Brentworth. They swung wide as he approached. Davina looked for peepholes or windows that might be used to identify visitors before they arrived so appropriate deference could be shown to a duke.

No one questioned why he brought a companion. She assumed they didn't dare. Even the most supercilious functionary would be intimidated by the arrogance that Brentworth wore even more comfortably than his coats, and his garments fit him very well indeed.

They made their way to a gentleman prepared to assist them. Brentworth explained that they wanted to examine the records regarding inheritances. "Scottish peers," he added.

"We have a copy of the records from the Lord Lyon. I will bring them."

Ten minutes later, Davina stood by his side while he paged through a large book of bound sheets of parchment on which were written the history of various titles down through time.

Some had next to the last name listed *Title in abeyance* or *Title attainted* or *Title extinct*.

"Here it is," Brentworth said.

Davina read the row of names. She'd had no idea the title was four hundred years old, or that the first baron had come from the Highlands. Around two hundred years ago, a MacCallum had purchased the estate, and hence the barony, as could be done in Scotland. The ancestors of the last baron ran down the page. Below his name, someone had written *predeceased by James, his son and heir, who died in 1745, recorded and buried St. Thomas Church.*

"That is the parish church near Teyhill," Brentworth said.

"That must refer to my grandfather."

"It says his death was recorded by the church."

She battled the disappointment dragging down her heart. "I don't think that means much. It was put out that he died. It may have been recorded that way, so the story made sense."

"It says there is a grave."

His tone, almost gentle, caused her to look from the page to his face. Their joint examination of the tome meant they stood very close to each other, and now she noticed how he warmed her side. His expression arrested her attention. Not so hard now. Not triumphant. He almost appeared disappointed too.

She gazed again at the page in order to break the peculiar connection she felt with him. What an odd moment for that little bridge to appear, in this dusty chamber of all places, while searching out evidence to disprove each other. Yet she could not deny that for a few moments she had experienced his presence like that of a friend. And also something else. The short span of air between them trembled with a rare vitality.

"It is odd he was buried at the church. There is a family graveyard on the property," she said.

"You know that, do you? Have you been there?"

It had been an unfortunate slip. "Once. With my father. We were nearby and ventured to see what it was."

"When was this?" No longer so friendly. Not gentle at all. Yet, oddly, that tremor did not cease so quickly. If anything, it grew stronger.

"I was perhaps seventeen. Maybe a year or so younger."

"You trespassed, no matter when it was."

"Because it should have been ours, trespass is the wrong word. We disturbed nothing and did not dally. We did not enter the house." Memories of that day came more clearly. "My father wanted to, but he realized the house was inhabited. Visitors, he said, or members of your family."

Silence fell beside her, an utter void of sound, as if he had disappeared. She looked over and realized he had, in a spiritual way. All his sight turned inward. The firmness in his face had slackened. No tremors between them now. Utter stillness instead, as if the air froze in place.

He appeared . . . lost.

"Anyway," she continued, pretending she had not noticed, "we left quickly and never entered the graveyard. Yet, if the son and heir died, that is where he should be, I think. Not at the church."

"I will go to see." His voice sounded normal. She looked over and saw he was himself again.

"He will not be in either place, because he did not die."

"More likely he will be. It is time to find out. I will set out at week's end. Let us depart this dusty place. You have seen all there is to see."

Once out in the open air, she declined his offer to bring her back to the duchess, or to her own home. "I could do with a good walk." She took her leave, but paused after a few steps. "If you are going, I am going too."

His gaze narrowed. "Are you implying I can't be trusted to tell the truth about what I find?"

"Not at all. However, this is my quest, and if it is to end in failure, I want to see and hear the evidence that dooms it. I think I am entitled to that. Also, leaving London might be wise. Mr. Haversham intends to play matchmaker."

"At least he will do better than those fortune hunters at the theater."

"No matter whom he finds, the problem remains. Someone who seems to know the male nature warned me not to tie myself to a man who might later blame me for thwarted expectations." She turned to walk home. Fifty yards away, she glanced back and saw that the duke was still watching her.

"The ladies are most annoyed with you." Langford offered the news while he threw himself into a chair.

Eric ignored him. He had asked to meet Langford and Stratton at their club to speak of important things, not the mood of the ladies, especially because by *the ladies*, they meant their wives. The way Eric saw it, Clara would always be annoyed with him, and it would be years before Amanda would ever express it, what with what he knew about her.

"Now that you are both here, I need to know if you are going to support the bill on abolishing slavery in the colonies. As far as I know, neither one of you have interests on the islands at least."

"You are implying that if we did, we would not support the bill out of self-interest," Stratton said. "That is rather insulting."

"If you had interests, you would have already either divested yourself of them or freed the slaves on your property, in which case I would have heard of it. All of London would have," Eric said. "It is not insulting to attribute basic human morals to a man. Now, will you stand with us on this? Unless we get a certain number, there is little point in trying this year."

"Of course," Stratton said. "Although I don't think you will get the number you want."

"I'm with you," Langford agreed. "Now that we have settled that, I repeat: The ladies are very annoyed. Vocally so. Aren't they, Stratton?"

"That they are," Stratton muttered within a slow sigh.

"His tone of resignation means that when the ladies are

annoyed, it is their husbands who suffer their lengthy scolds at the world," Langford said.

"Then it is good I called you here, so you could gain a respite," Eric said. "Now, because you are with me on this, I need to ask a favor of you."

"He doesn't care, Stratton. Our domestic peace is in shatters all because of him and he doesn't give a fig. Instead, he asks for a favor."

"How do I get blamed for your domestic affairs? If your wives are unhappy, find out why and fix it, or go rusticate until they calm down, or do whatever husbands do when wives harp on something."

"A wise husband blames someone," Stratton said. "In this case, that would be you."

Eric looked from one to the other, exasperated.

"Miss MacCallum is leaving London," Stratton added, by way of explanation.

"The ladies blame you," Langford said.

"I can't imagine why," Eric said innocently. "Did you tell them to?"

"They think you have bullied her, and frightened her, and glared at her, and in general been Brentworth with her," Langford said.

"On the contrary, I have been gracious and helpful. I deserve a medal for how I have controlled myself. Not once have I accused her to her face of being a fraud trying to steal from me."

"I should hope not," Stratton said.

"Well, I am a gentleman. If she were a man, however—"

"Which she is not. She is a woman, and a helpless one at that."

Helpless? *Helpless?* Did Stratton see the same female when he looked at Miss MacCallum. That woman was anything but helpless. "I have not bullied her. Nor has she ever seemed frightened of me, which is somewhat refreshing. And I do not glare. Go home and reassure your wives of that and all will be well."

"Do you know why she is leaving?" Langford asked.

"Do you?"

"No, nor do the ladies. That is why I asked if you do."

"How would I know if the ladies don't? I am not Miss MacCallum's special confidante."

"I thought perhaps when you and she had that meeting I helped arrange, she told you. She made the decision soon after, or at least informed Amanda the next day. The ladies find it all precipitous, as if she is running away from something." Langford eyed him. "You didn't try to kiss her that day, or do something else that—"

"I did not. If that is what *the ladies* are conjuring up within their ire and ignorance, please make it very clear to them that I swear as a gentleman that I have in no way imposed on Miss MacCallum in that manner. The very suggestion is laughable."

Langford shrugged. "It might have been an impulse."

"I do not have impulses like that with women."

Stratton grinned. "Come now, we all have those impulses, even you, even if you never give in to them."

Eric gave Langford a hard look. "You will please make sure the ladies are disabused of such a notion."

"I will, but I think they may be disappointed. I overheard them talking, and the word *comeuppance* was spoken. I think they have worked out an elaborate plot with you as the pining swain and Miss MacCallum as the spurning woman."

"You did not say anything to encourage such nonsense, I trust." Comeuppance indeed.

"Of course not."

Of course not, hell. Langford talked too much. Eric pictured him and Amanda in bed, with Amanda probing for gossip and Langford, in his sated bliss, nattering away.

"You say you do not glare, but you are glaring now," Stratton said. "Perhaps you should let us know about that favor you want."

"Things are moving along about the bill. I have to leave town for a spell and would like each of you to sound out these peers for their positions." He reached in his coat and handed each of them a short sheet of paper.

Stratton studied his. "I will do it, but I doubt I will receive firm answers from half these names." He tucked it away. "The only way that bill or any like it will pass is if the slave owners are compensated. Perhaps when the economy is better—"

"The economy will never be better enough. It will cost millions," Eric said. "We might as well face the numbers now as later."

Langford had not looked at his paper. Instead, he looked at Eric. Intently. "You are leaving town?"

"For a brief spell. I leave tomorrow next."

"Alone?"

"I always travel alone."

"Not always. You have on occasion brought mistresses to some of your properties."

"This is business, and I travel alone when I travel for financial reasons."

Now both of them were looking at him.

"It must be very important to drag you away right when you need to shepherd this bill," Stratton said.

The two of them were spinning webs of nonsense now, all because he left London when that woman did. Not that she needed to go anywhere. She was just being obstinate. "It is important enough."

A twinkle entered Langford's eyes. "Perhaps you will come across Miss MacCallum while on your journey. At a staging inn or some such place."

"Unlikely. If it happens, however, I will be polite and ask if she is faring well. Now, are you going to talk to those men?" He pointed to Langford's list.

"Oh, absolutely. They should all fall in line. After all, how awkward for them to be less moral than I am, of all men."

"So where are you going?" Stratton asked casually.

Eric had expected the question to come from Langford if anyone. Friends could surprise you at times. "West."

"West," Stratton said to Langford.

"I heard. It appears we can tell the ladies that while he is also leaving town, he is going in a completely different direction from Miss MacCallum."

Eric would have taken satisfaction in a lie well told, except it was obvious neither of them believed him.

Chapter Eleven

Davina rose from the bed. She had arrived in the afternoon and taken a nap, which she almost never did. The journey had been long and tiring, however, even making use of the coach and four Amanda had insisted she have.

That coach had left already, to return to London, after bringing her here to her childhood home in Northumberland. She stood in the center of the chamber, steeling herself for the nostalgia that had almost drowned her when she first walked in the door. It waited for her when she left this bedroom, used by the housekeeper back then.

Leaving London had not been easy. Mr. Hume had expressed displeasure that she abandoned her duties to Nora. She found another woman to take her place for a fortnight, so the child would not be left to her own devices. She explained to Mr. Hume that any evidence would be found in Scotland, not London, so she needed to go find it. He had finally acquiesced and, except for an unfortunate overture at bringing her north himself, had wished her well.

Prior to leaving, she had written to the duke, explaining her plans and demanding he join her in Northumberland so any visits to the baron's property would be made by them at the same time. If he did not respond at once with his agreement, she had written, she would go on her own and not share whatever she might learn in this place where her grandfather had lived.

She slipped on her shoes and straightened the sheets on the bed. Amanda had sent the mattress in the coach, and the sheets and coverlet, because, she said, after so many years, the house was sure to be in poor repair. Davina, upon entering, was grateful her duchess friend had not always been a duchess and proved to be so practical. Before the coachman left, she had him take the old mattresses and linens out and burn them.

She ventured into the kitchen, found a bucket, and went out for water. Upon returning, she eyed a large brown stain and hole on the ceiling. That was what had sent her to the housekeeper's chamber rather than upstairs when she decided to nap. The damage indicated water had been entering, probably from the roof. Above this was a chamber her parents had used when her mother was alive. If the roof had gone bad, it would not be habitable. Perhaps none of them up there were.

It took her two hours to wipe down the kitchen so she could use it, and another to wash the dishes and implements. Night was falling by the time she finished. She ate some food she had brought, fetched fresh water, then took her damp cloth to the sitting room and wiped more dust away. Taking a chance the chimney still functioned, she used some coal left in the bin to start a fire.

I will agree to your plan so you are not wandering the countryside unprotected, the duke had replied to her letter. *Better if you remained in London. In other words, I will allow you to complicate this more than is reasonable because I have no choice, but you are a nuisance.*

He had then written that he would take lodgings in

Newcastle and come to Caxledge the afternoon after she said she expected to arrive. Her direction to this house had not been the best. It had been so long since she lived here that she might have gotten some of it wrong. Still, she expected him to arrive as indicated. One of the benefits of being a duke was that you probably could find any place and any person you wanted.

After a final wipe of her little chamber, she put herself to bed. Rain woke her in the middle of the night, but its sound and drips lulled her back to sleep. Happily, sunshine greeted her in the morning.

So did a large puddle in the middle of the kitchen floor. She looked up at that hole. Perhaps her father had paid a caretaker when he was alive. If so, he had neglected to inform her, and she had not seen to it after his death. Blaming only herself for the state of the house, she tied up her dress above her knees, retrieved her bucket and a mop, and got to work.

The duke said he would be arriving in the afternoon. After she finished this, she would walk into the village and do a bit of investigating before he came.

Eric watched the outskirts of Newcastle give way to countryside and villages. He resented the inconvenience of this coach. He doubted Miss MacCallum had a horse, however, or even rode one much, so this had become a necessary inconvenience, like too much else about this journey.

His coachman had the directions she had provided, but a few words at a coaching inn on the way provided better ones. They pulled up in front of the cottage before noon, which was a few hours earlier than he had told her.

Politeness dictated he not call yet. Expediency said

otherwise. He hopped out of the carriage and paused while he examined the house. Not large, it would be handsome if better maintained. Unfortunately, the plaster needed skimming and paint, and birds had made free with the eaves for their nests. The garden showed years of neglect. Nature was busy reclaiming this plot of land. If left alone for a few more years, the cottage would be well on its way to being a ruin.

He tried the door knock to no good purpose. Perhaps she had not arrived yet, or had already left. He strolled around the house, through a gate off its hinges, and sought the back door. The path, long lost to weeds, took him past a well to a flagstone terrace.

The door back here was open, but no sounds came from within. He stuck his head over the threshold, then stepped inside.

Miss MacCallum sat in what was a kitchen. She did not see or hear him. Her chair faced a cold fireplace. She stared at it almost sightlessly. A bucket stood beside her chair, and a mop had been propped against the wall.

Her legs stretched out in front of her. Bare legs. Nicely formed legs. Quite lovely legs, ivory tinted with a blush of pink. She wore no shoes or slippers either, so her pretty feet sat just so on the plank floor.

He noticed her dress had been tied up between her legs at the same moment when she realized she was not alone. She looked over abruptly, the shoulder-length locks of blond hair swinging like a drape disturbed by a breeze. She gazed right at him, then at his coat, then down at his boots.

"Welcome, Duke. I would be more pleased to see you if you were not tracking mud on my clean floor."

Indeed he was, but the damage was done. "I tried tracking mud on your floor in front instead, but no one answered my knock."

"I was in a daze, I suppose. Remembering times spent here with my father and mother. Come in and sit down, and I will redo that section before I give up."

He stepped outside and scraped most of the mud off his boots, using the edge of the threshold stone, before returning. He took long strides to get to the chair at the work table. With nary a comment, and with her loins still girded and her legs very visible, Miss MacCallum grabbed her mop and plunged it in the bucket. Then she bent to wring its long strands.

Which meant her rump rose up to his face. Bare, shapely legs and delicate, narrow feet. Narrow waist and flaring hips. Nicely rounded bottom. Eric prided himself on not being impulsive, but there were several almost overwhelming impulses at this moment.

The first was to ungird that skirt and lift it so he could see just how nicely rounded that bottom was. The second was to insist that she mustn't do this labor; he would hire a woman to come and do it for her instead. The third was to reach out and caress that womanly form all but being offered to him. The fourth was to do much more than caress.

She straightened, as if she knew what he contemplated. "You are early," she said while she gave another sweep to the muddy footprints. "You said afternoon."

"I rose early and did not know how long it would take, so we started out." That was true, but not all the truth. He could have whiled away an hour or so after breakfast before coming. Only he had not wanted to.

"*We?*"

"The coachman."

"Did you bring your valet too? A few footmen?" She smiled impishly.

"No valet or footmen."

"What? Whoever will do for you?"

She enjoyed teasing him. He enjoyed looking at her, standing there, leaning against the mop handle, oblivious to how she still flaunted those legs. The fabric had been hitched highest on the left side, which faced him, making the bottom of her thigh visible.

"I assumed you would, of course," he said. Impulsively.

Her face fell in shock before she laughed. However, he had made her self-conscious because suddenly she did remember her naked legs. She fussed with her skirt, untying it until it fell down in a wrinkled flow.

"Actually, I am capable of doing for myself and normally prefer that when I travel," he said. "It is a nuisance to have servants in tow, and the ones for hire at inns are rarely useful."

"How odd and unusual." She walked to a shelf, opened a wooden box and removed some bread. She placed it on the table, then brought down a cheese basket and put it there too. "How did you even learn? I would think there were those doing for you from the day you were born, and you wouldn't know how to dress yourself, let alone shave and do whatever else gentlemen must do."

"I will tell you, but you must never tell anyone else."

She slid into the chair across the table and cut some bread and cheese. She took some, then pushed the food toward him. "I promise."

"When I was first at university, a friend and I slipped out and went someplace we were forbidden to go. Our plans were dashed when we both fell asleep. Morning came and there we were. No valets. No one to do for us. So we figured out how to do for ourselves, slipped back in and no one was the wiser. But for one cut on my jaw, I was as put together as if my valet had done his duties." He shrugged, and helped himself to some bread. "Granted, it took me a lot longer. So much longer that the slipping back in part was almost thwarted."

She bit some cheese, her fine white teeth emerging from her lips for the nip. He tried mightily not to imagine that little bite landing elsewhere. Several elsewheres.

"That is an interesting story. I think you and your friend visited a brothel."

"Why would you think that?"

"You needed to dress in the morning. Also, if you had slept in your garments, you could never have turned yourself out well. You would have been too rumpled. So you slept naked, or almost naked."

Damn, she was clever. "I refuse to confirm your outrageous conclusions."

"I also think the friend was Langford."

"Now you are just guessing."

"Amanda said you have been friends for years and years, and that he was always wild and bad."

"No more than most men. He is, however, indiscreet in the extreme, so the whole world knows just how bad he has been."

She lifted the bucket, stepped outside and threw out the water. When she returned she set it and the mop into a long cupboard. Then she crossed her arms and frowned at the ceiling.

His gaze followed hers and saw the hole between two beams. "Ah. It rained last night. You have been mopping up the result."

"The roof is leaking for certain, and it is coming right through to down here. It has been happening for a long time. See how the wooden floor here is stained and warped? I have refused to go see how bad it is in the upper chambers. To witness the evidence of my neglect would be too disheartening."

"I will do it." He stood and strode out, found the stairs and mounted them.

He examined the chambers, then went back down. "It is not good news, but it could be worse. The roof is bad in two places, but it can be fixed for now."

"I will put the bucket beneath this one here until we are done with our business, then see to hiring a man before I return to London."

He gazed at that hole. "It will only get larger with the autumn rains. Nothing will ruin a house faster than water."

"Except fire."

Her words made his spirit pause, as his heart skipped a beat. "Yes."

"It will have to wait."

"I will bring you back to the inn and get a chamber for you there. You can't live here with the house in this condition."

"The bed I used last night is back there, and is dry enough. A bucket is all I need, so I am not mopping up rainwater."

There had been a light hesitation before she refused, but her refusal had come through firmly.

"It is far more sensible to stay at the inn."

"I will stay here, thank you."

"Then let me see what else can be done." He left her and walked through the house, then outside to the coach.

"You have some tools with you, I assume," he said to Napier, his coachman.

"Of course. Never know when there will be a problem with a wheel or what have you." Napier walked around to the back of the coach and opened a box there to reveal a hammer, some pegs and an iron bar. "Can I ask why you need them, Your Grace?"

"The roof of this house has been damaged. I don't need

it fixed. I just need it patched until someone who knows roofs can see to it properly."

Napier bit his lower lip. "I'd gladly do it, except that my bad leg has been giving me trouble of late. Can't be climbing on roofs with that, can I?"

Napier's bad leg always gave trouble when its owner did not want to do something.

"Then I will do it. There must be a barn here or an outbuilding where salvage slates were stored." He went looking for it.

Some distance from the house in the back garden, he found the structure that served as carriage house and stable. With a little searching, he discovered the stock of salvage tiles. With several in one hand and a ladder on the other shoulder, he went back to the front. He shrugged off his frock coat and rolled up his sleeves.

"Move the coach close to the portico so I can use it to get up there. Then you will have to hand me the ladder, tools and this slate so I can get them to the roof proper."

Shaking his head, Napier climbed into his seat and maneuvered the horses so the coach seat was right below the eaves of the portico. "If you break your neck, I hope no one will blame me."

Eric climbed up and stood on the seat. Damned if he knew what he was doing. He might well break his neck. He had even less idea *why* he was doing it. Yet here he was, hauling himself onto the portico's roof. If he could figure out how to do for himself after a night in a brothel when he was seventeen, he could figure out how to do for Miss MacCallum today, was how he saw it.

He was only being practical. The roof needed to be patched or the house was unlivable. None of this had anything to do with those naked legs.

* * *

When the duke did not return quickly, Davina sat down and finished her breakfast. She had forgotten to buy coffee, so she had only well water to drink, but after her labor, it refreshed her. She took the rest of the water into her chamber and washed and changed her dress. Then she took the bowl outside to pour out the water.

It had been over a month since she had taken care of household duties, and her time in Mr. Hume's home had spoiled her. If a duke could do for himself, she certainly could too, but she had never liked such chores. Of course, the duke would have water brought to him while living at the inn, and food cooked for him, and a servant would mop up any water on the floor, so his doing for himself was not at all the same.

She should have accepted his offer that she stay at the inn. She almost had. It was a very sensible solution. Only a second of consideration had her refusing. She did not want to be beholden to him, for one thing. For another— she admitted to herself that the very notion of sleeping under the same roof as Brentworth evoked a very odd reaction in her. A thrilled warning had throbbed through her like a plucked harp string, as if the idea presented danger. Stupid, of course, but it was enough to have her condemn herself to living here.

Realizing that a good half hour had passed, she ventured outside to see what he was doing. To her surprise, his coach all but blocked her way off the little portico. His coachman stood at his seat, looking up, grimacing.

She found her way down and turned to see what arrested the coachman's attention. Up on the roof, the duke walked, his coat discarded, carrying some slate tiles. It was a wonder he didn't simply slide off.

"What is he doing?" she asked the coachman.

"Fixing it," he said. He shook his head.

The duke settled down on the roof, worked at something, then cast pieces of slate down into the garden.

"Does he do this often?"

The coachman looked down at her, aghast. "Why would he do that? No point in being a duke if you have to fix your own roof, is there?" He looked up to the roof again. "Will be ruining his hands with this."

If he had never done it before, she wondered what possessed him to do it now. She also wondered if he had any idea how to fix a roof, but she expected most of it would be obvious once one was up there.

Suddenly, he slipped a little. Not much, but enough that he had to brace himself with his legs. The coachman gasped audibly. Davina's heart skipped a beat.

"Not for me to scold, Your Grace, but I would be most appreciative if you did not fall off," the coachman called up.

"Have no fear, Napier. I am safe, and almost finished. Pity there were no copper nails in that box of yours. It might be fixed for good if I had them. These wooden ones won't last more than a month or so, and are a bit too small for the holes drilled in the slate."

Davina decided she would wait inside, so if he did fall, she would not see it. She returned to the kitchen and rehearsed everything she knew about setting broken bones.

Chapter Twelve

"You did not have to fix the roof."

Miss MacCallum had waited until they were in the carriage, rolling toward the village, before she said it.

"You are welcome."

"Your rebuke is well taken. I should have thanked you. So, thank you for fixing my roof, even though you might have broken your neck."

"Instead of *even though*, try *especially because*. Then it will be a proper thanks."

She looked embarrassed, then realized he was teasing her. "If you had broken anything besides your neck, I might have been able to help you. A neck, however—well, there is no help for that."

"Should I ever break my neck while fixing your roof, please do not allow the newspapers to know how I died. Say I fell off my horse."

"Of course. I suppose it would stain your reputation to die while performing such menial chores."

"It is not the how but the who that would get the papers interested. Now, where are we going today?"

"First, we will visit Mr. Portman. Mr. Jacobson wrote to me with his name when I in turn wrote to ask for a reference to someone old enough to have memories of value to me. After that, I intend to visit an old friend of mine. You are welcome to go back to the inn once we are done with Mr. Portman. I will walk home."

The walk would be a good three miles from the look of it. He voiced no disagreement, but she would not walk home.

Caxledge was a good-size village with three main lanes and an assortment of others. On its outer edges, some homes looked newer than those in the center. The industry of Newcastle had begun altering the village because it was close enough to partake of that prosperity.

Miss MacCallum had the direction to her old man, and they pulled up outside his small house soon enough.

"I hope he will receive me," Miss MacCallum said.

"Don't worry. He will receive us."

Indeed he would. The *us* ensured it. One look at the duke's card and the woman who came to the door ushered them inside. "My grandfather is in the garden. Just go through if you like." She pointed to the back of the house.

They walked through a sitting room and a dining room, then a kitchen. An abundance of furniture, along with low ceilings, cramped the space so that the duke appeared over-large for it. A child's laughter chimed down from above as they exited by a back door.

"What a charming garden," Davina exclaimed. She paused to take it in. Small, like the house, it had been planted with an artist's eye. Vines covered the walls, and one nice fruit tree stood in a corner. The rest showed flower beds with a few last blooms backed by bushes of various sizes and shapes. A stone walkway wound through it all.

The artist, it seemed, was Mr. Portman. He heard them and stood from where he worked some soil while on his knees. He came toward them, peering through spectacles while he pulled off his work gloves.

A short, spindly man of at least eighty, he held his ground while the duke towered over him and introduced himself and Davina. "A Mr. Jacobson advised Miss MacCallum to call," he explained.

"You know Jacobson, do you? How is the boy doing? Very well, if he has come to know a duke."

"He appears contented. He is still making boots," Davina said.

"Makes the finest. It is why he left. No one to pay what his are worth here." He pointedly looked down at a pair of boots owned by someone who could pay for good ones. "Don't look like his, though."

"I have not had the good fortune to meet him yet," Brentworth said.

"I have, however," Davina said. "He thought you might be able to help me. I am seeking information about my family."

She received a strong scrutiny. Mr. Portman rubbed his chin. "I thought you looked a little familiar. So, you are of the MacCallums who used to live down south of the village, are you? You resemble the woman the son married."

"I am their daughter. My father and I left some years ago."

"Not too long after his father died, as I remember. I knew him, though."

"Was he born in these parts?" Brentworth asked.

Mr. Portman shook his head. "He came as a lad. That was well known. Fostered he was, by the couple who had no children. Restless sort, as if he knew he was in the wrong place. I was told he was a bit of a troublemaker when he was a youth. Not what you want to hear, probably."

"I want to hear anything at all that you can tell me. Did he have a nickname of some sort?"

"Not that I can remember."

"Mr. Jacobson said he was at times called the baron."

"Ah, well, that wasn't a nickname. No one addressed him like that. But the older ones, like my parents, sometimes referred to him that way when speaking about him."

"A reference to his bearing, perhaps," Brentworth said. "A private criticism of airs he assumed?"

"I don't remember it being like that either. No joking or criticism to it, seems to me. Just a word that was used among them at times. A simple thing, as if maybe when he was young that label was put on him and the old ones remembered."

Mr. Portman was as vague as Mr. Jacobson. Davina decided to poke at the memories more sharply. "Did you ever hear anyone say he really *was* a baron?"

Instead of scoffing at the suggestion, Mr. Portman turned thoughtful. "No, but now that you mention it, he said it once. Was at the tavern one night. He'd been gone— just up and left, and we all thought he would never come back, that he had abandoned his family—there's men who do that when they get older and are looking downhill in their years. Go off to grab a bit of life before it is too late."

"What did he say? Were you there?" Brentworth pressed.

"I was there. He showed up late, drank two pints, then said to his mates something like *I should not be here. I was born to be a baron.* More than his mates heard, and everyone made sport of him, and he even joined in. Well, a man in his cups says lots of stupid things."

"Was there anything else similar?" Brentworth asked.

"Nah. He went home and that was that." He looked at Davina. "Your father took it hard when he died. He insisted that had a physician come, he might have made it."

"We left so he could study to become one," she said.

"We went to Edinburgh and he became a physician himself, so he could help others."

"A noble calling. We still don't have one here, just an old sawbones, but he's no good for what ails you inside sometimes. Have to send to Newcastle for one, and there's none who come all this way without the fee being paid. So mostly we make do with the old remedies." He slapped his chest. "I was born with good blood, though, so I do fine. There was a bad fever late summer that lingered, but I was spared. Some still falling to it, it was that bad, but I'm still working with my friends." He gestured to the garden.

"You've created a little paradise here," Davina said.

"We will take our leave now, so you can continue," Brentworth said. "You might help us in one other way, though."

"I'd be glad to, though it is hard to refuse a duke who is twice your size." He chortled at his own joke. "What do you be needing?"

"The name of a man who is very good at fixing slate roofs."

"We will see this roofer, Mr. Bates, before we leave the village," Brentworth said once they left the house.

"You can see him if you like. I am going to visit my friend Louisa." She gestured down the lane. "Her family home is right past the churchyard. If she does not live there now, someone will know where she is."

"I will escort you, in case you need the carriage."

They strolled down the lane, past houses that looked like Mr. Portman's. Davina had not realized how small many of the homes were. As a girl, they were what she knew. After spending several years in Edinburgh, village homes and cottages shrank considerably.

They passed the stone church, and she called at Louisa's

house. She learned that Louisa had married a farmer and lived about a mile east of the village.

"It appears you will be needing the carriage," Brentworth said.

"It is only a mile."

Too late. The carriage had been trailing them and now approached more quickly when Brentworth raised his arm.

She climbed in and was surprised when he stepped in too.

"You were going to see a roofer."

"I will first see you to your friend's home. Then I will visit the roofer, and we will return for you."

The duke had decided how it would be, and she doubted all the reason she could muster would change his mind.

"Is this how ladies live, with gentlemen escorting them to and fro everywhere they go?"

"It might be a footman, not a gentleman."

"How sad."

"It is only for their protection."

"That is not true. It is also to deprive them of freedom to do as they choose."

"What a cynical idea. What can't a lady do if she has the protection of an escort?"

Davina gave it some thought. "Visit a friend who is not approved of by her family or husband. Or an area of town where she normally would not go. Or—or, a man. She could not simply call on a man without it being known to those who seek to protect her."

His lids lowered. "That is because it is from such as he that they protect her."

"Depending on who he is, that could be sad too."

He cocked his head. "Do you seek to be relieved of my company so you can visit a man? Perhaps an old beau from when you lived here?"

"Of course not."

"Then indulge my old-fashioned notions of my duties as a gentleman."

"If we are going to be particular about my protection, shouldn't there be someone else here? A chaperone?"

He just looked at her.

"Another woman," she continued, managing not to falter under that intense gaze. "To protect me from you. Not that I need protection from you, of course, but then, I do not need any protection to speak of from anyone. It has just been your sense of obligation and duty. However, it is a fine line, isn't it?" She kept talking, trying to backstep from the implications of what she was saying but discovering she only walked in deeper. "I am just speaking about where strict propriety lands one in such situations, that is all, not that I in any way am in any danger from you, goodness no, but if one follows your way of thinking, one finds oneself admitting that this is not exactly acceptable, even if I am no child. Not that I would say that you do unacceptable things . . ." Her last words drifted out into the silence across from her.

"Your point, which was in there somewhere, is well taken. I cannot disagree with anything you said except one small part."

"Which part is that?"

"The part where you said you do not need protection from me." He looked out the window. "It appears we are here."

Miss MacCallum almost jumped out of the carriage. Flush-faced, she did not look at him. He had flustered her, finally, with that last comment.

Her gaze swept the farmhouse and garden. "I expect she is much changed. I am. It has been some years."

"Have you written?"

"I have. After a few letters, however, she stopped writing back. Perhaps once she married she was too busy."

He sensed she debated whether to make this call at all. He let her take her time to decide.

The farmhouse looked to be a fair-size cottage with a well-tended garden in front. Past it, in the back, one could see another garden, probably for the kitchen, and outbuildings. Past those, the fields began. In the first one, a horse grazed. Her friend's husband must be a yeoman farmer and not a tenant if he owned a horse.

The door opened and a tall, sandy-haired man stepped out. He eyed the carriage, then turned a curious expression on them.

Miss MacCallum marched forward. "You must be Mr. Bowman. I am Davina MacCallum. I grew up in these parts and knew Louisa when we were girls. I came hoping to see her for a short while."

He met her halfway up the path. "That is good of you, but you'll not be able to do that. You should not enter the house either. She caught that fever and is in bed."

Miss MacCallum frowned. She looked at the house. "Who is tending to her?"

"I am, such as she will allow. She won't let me in, and told me to keep our son away, so he is sleeping in the sitting room. I bring her food and such, but then she sends me away. She fears for the boy."

"And for you, but that will never do." Miss MacCallum sidestepped Mr. Bowman and walked to the house.

Mr. Bowman watched her, then turned back to Brentworth. "What is she doing?"

"Going to see your wife, I assume."

Mr. Bowman looked at the coach. "We don't see such as that around here. Who are you?"

"Brentworth."

Mr. Bowman did not seem to know just which lord that was, but he did know from the coach and the title that it was some lord or other. "The lady may get sick if she goes in there. You may want to stop her."

"I may want to, but I doubt I can." All the same, he followed Miss MacCallum into the house, with Mr. Bowman in his wake, wishing that on hearing an illness lay within he had picked Miss MacCallum up and dumped her back in the carriage.

The son sat in the sitting room, tapping a stick against the floor. Blond like his father, he looked to be about eight or so. "That woman asked where mum was, then went upstairs," he reported.

Eric decided he wanted very much to keep Miss MacCallum from spending time with her sick friend. He began mounting the stairs after her.

"Do not come up."

He looked up to see her head sticking out an ajar door.

"If you were to take ill, I would probably be exiled from the realm," she added.

"And if you take ill, I will not forgive myself."

She made a shooing gesture. "I rarely take ill."

"Your hair says differently."

She felt the hair dangling next to her cheek. "Well, that once I did. I am saying there is no reason for more than one to risk it, and I already have. You can help, however. I can tell she needs water. Quite a bit of it. She has not been drinking enough. It can make all the difference. Ask her husband to draw some fresh water and bring up a jug to me. Then I could use more of it, warmed by the fire, not too hot, and some rags."

Her head disappeared. Having issued her commands, she returned to her charge.

He retraced his steps and told Mr. Bowman what she wanted. After bringing up the jug, he set more water on the hearthstone and built up the fire a bit.

He looked up the stairs while they waited. "Does she know what she is doing?"

"I am told she does."

"Don't you know?"

His response had sounded disloyal. He corrected it. "I believe she does."

"I'm thinking, what with you here, I should get my horse saddled and ride to Kenton. It is only five miles away and there is a surgeon there. I'll pay him whatever it takes to come back with me."

"I would ask Miss MacCallum if she thinks that is necessary. If she does, we will stay here with your wife and son until you return."

Mr. Bowman took a few steps toward the stairs, then stopped. He looked back over his shoulder sheepishly. "She doesn't seem to be a woman one would like to cross. She may be insulted if I suggest I should get a surgeon."

"I will ask her if you want."

He stood aside.

Miss MacCallum opened it on his knock. Through the crack, he could see a woman lying on a bed half naked.

"He wants to take advantage of our presence to ride for a surgeon."

"Good heavens no. A surgeon is sure to bleed her, and nothing good will come of that. In her state, it might kill her."

"Is it as bad as that?"

"She has had a fever for some time. Days. I can tell from her eyes and her skin that she is sorely lacking water, and that has made it worse. I am spooning it in her, and washing her down to cool her. Bleeding is the last thing she needs. Tell him no surgeons."

"What about a physician?"

"You heard Mr. Portman. There are none for many miles around."

"I will send the carriage to Newcastle and tell Napier to come back with one."

She hesitated. "He won't know where to go."

"He'll find one. I'll make sure it is worth the man's while to come."

She looked back into the room. "Yes, please do. I think . . ." Her voice broke, and she blinked at tears forming. "I think it may be too late, but I'll keep at what I am doing and hope that a physician can do more."

His gut twisted at her sadness. He wanted to comfort her. He turned away, to do the only thing that might help her.

Davina sat beside the bed and wrung out another cloth. She used it to wipe down Louisa's arms and chest. The skin felt hot beneath her touch.

She set the rag back in the pail, took the cup of water and sat beside her friend. She lifted her up with one arm and used the other to hold the cup to her lips. "You must drink, even if it is just a sip. Yes, like that. A little more now."

Louisa obeyed until about two ounces went in, then sank back onto the pillow. She blinked and looked at Davina, then frowned. "I know you."

They were the first words Louisa had said. Davina had not been sure there had even been an awareness of her presence before. "It is I, Davina. We were friends as girls. I was traveling by and decided to call on you."

"My son—"

"He is below with your husband, and quite healthy."

She laid her palm against Louisa's cheek. Still hot. Too hot. Dangerously so. "It was wise to separate him from yourself, but I fear that you did not eat or drink enough while alone."

"I mostly slept, I think." She looked ready to do so again. Davina took the opportunity to get more water into her, then put down the cup.

"You are well, Davina? Happy in Edinburgh?"

"Very happy. Do not try to speak. I do not need a social visit today. Another time we will sit in the garden and tell each other about the years that have passed."

"I married Mr. Bowman. He is good to me and our son. Not like Papa."

As a girl, Louisa had feared her father and tried to avoid him. Davina always suspected he beat her. "I am glad. You deserve a good man."

Louisa nodded drowsily. "Good man."

"He has a fine farm here. I suppose it was his family's. I did not know them, but I remember the name."

"Neil was in the army. Came home after the war, and I began walking out with him." She twisted under the sheet. "I am so hot now. Hot, then cold, then hot, then . . ." Her words drifted and slurred.

"Sleep. I will be here when you awaken. Do you want to see your husband?"

She shook her head. "I don't want them to get ill too. Promise you will not let them come in here."

"I promise."

She waited for Louisa to fall asleep, then went below to the sitting room. The boy held vigil with his father there. Brentworth was nowhere to be seen.

She found the kitchen, and the remains of the food Louisa's husband had tried to cook the last few days. A chicken was his most recent effort. She found a big pot, threw the carcass in it, then called for the boy and asked him to bring water from the well and some roots from the kitchen garden.

"I can do it," Mr. Bowman said from the door. "I'm better if I keep busy."

"Perhaps you should do that by tending to your farm. If you don't go too far, I think it would help you. Your son can get me what I need, and it will give him something to do."

Mr. Bowman shifted from one foot to the other. "Is she any better?"

"She spoke to me, so I think so. She still needs to drink more. I'll make a broth to give her. If you have beer or ale, set it out and I'll use that too."

"That carriage has been gone several hours."

"Only three. Have faith, sir. If the duke said a physician would come, one will arrive soon."

"I will pay the fee, of course, if you tell me what it is."

She stopped her preparations and gave him her full attention. "I do not think the duke will allow that. Nor do I think you can afford it. The physician who comes will probably have very high fees. I will offer for you, however, so there is no risk that you will insult His Grace without intending to."

He nodded, and realized that his son stood right beside him. He stepped aside so the boy could enter the kitchen. "I'll be in the barn for a spell, then."

Davina told the boy what she needed. She had only her thoughts to keep her company while she waited for him to return.

Louisa, despite her malady, appeared much as she remembered her. Her brown hair and plump face were the same as the girl who had laughed with her so often. She regretted sorely not returning before this, so they could laugh again.

She faced squarely what might happen in the next few hours. Sometime soon, perhaps very soon, either the fever would break or Louisa would. She doubted the physician would make much difference.

At least it had not been cholera. She had seen its effects. Indeed she had experienced them herself. On first entering that sick room she had died inside because her friend's sunken eyes and wrinkled hands suggested just that. But there had been none of the severe purges caused by cholera, from the evidence in the chamber. The lack of fluids to her system had only mimicked the symptoms.

Louisa had wanted to spare her family and locked herself in, but she may have doomed herself. Davina had seen ill people die before. When she accompanied her father, the results were not always good ones in those cottages. She had nursed her father herself, and not been able to save him. It was always very hard when the person was a friend, and she would have to steel herself for this.

She wiped her eyes and found a bit of solace in knowing that her visit may have made a difference in Louisa's comfort, if nothing else.

The boy came in with the water and a handful of carrots and parsnips. Davina used some of the water to clean the roots, then chopped them and added them to her pot. She hanged the pot on the hook in the hearth, then called for the boy again.

"What do you normally do at this time?" she asked him.

"Lessons." He pointed to the worktable. "While Mum cooks."

"Have you a slate? Go and get it, and do the same lesson you last did with her. Don't look at me like that. You must do something besides worry."

She waited until he returned with his slate and got busy,

then let herself out the garden door. The evening had cooled substantially.

She strolled toward the kitchen garden. Lush now, as the last of summer's growth went wild to cast off seeds, it boasted fat cabbages and even some greens. She allowed herself a few minutes surrounded by autumn's abundance. She permitted memories of playing with Louisa into her mind. She turned so no one in the barn or house could see her, and tears of sorrow and frustration flowed.

Chapter Thirteen

He did not often feel worthless, but he did now. He paced in the gathering dusk, looking to the road too often, hoping Napier returned soon. Had anyone else but Davina said a sick woman might die soon, he might have been skeptical. One look in her eyes, however, and he believed she knew what she was talking about.

It did no good to tell himself that people died of fevers all the time, that like everyone he accepted that. He did not know them most of the time, of course. But he did not know this Louisa either. All he knew was that Davina cared a great deal about saving her. They had loved each other once, and perhaps still did, despite the years and distance.

He began another circle of the house but stopped when he neared the back garden. Davina stood there amid the plants, taking some air, which she sorely needed by now. She looked to the sky, then her head bowed, and a curtain of short locks obscured her face. She turned away, facing a fence across from the barn.

He would leave her in peace. A subtle shift in her posture stopped him. Her shoulders and back sagged just enough to reveal her composure had broken. One small, quiet sob reached his ears.

He strode toward her on impulse. She heard him and looked over her shoulder. The soft light made the tears in her eyes glisten. She rushed to wipe them.

He took her hands in his so she would not work so hard at being brave. "Weep if you need to. No one will think the less of you."

She looked up in astonishment. Her lips parted, as if she meant to respond, but instead her face fell into an expression of such sorrow that it broke his heart. She broke then. Large, loud sobs shook her until her chest heaved with them. He pulled her into his arms and held her while they racked her body.

"I should not—I don't know why—" She gasped out the words when she could catch a breath.

"You should. As for why, you are tired and worried and no one can be strong all the time."

She let him support her while she gave in and the tears flowed. He patted her head, the short locks giving way to her nape and shoulders under his fingers.

It was sympathy that led him to press a soft kiss to her crown, but more than that stirred in him when he did it. She did not seem to notice.

The tears tapered off, but she remained against him, sighing out their remnants. He should release her now, set her away. He didn't, but instead submitted to the reckless impulse to hold her longer.

She stirred, as if wakening from a dream or a daze. She looked up at him. Her eyes still glistened and her face appeared luminous in the dusk. Not thinking or caring about consequences, he did what he should not do. He kissed her.

Warm lips pressed hers gently. The kiss expressed kindness and care, just as his embrace had, but—She could not deny it was more than that. For her, at least. It affected her deeply. It banished the worry and blotted out sorrow. Its warmth and sensuality seeped through her like water does dry sand.

It lasted too long to be a kiss of comfort, or so it seemed to her. Perhaps not. Maybe it was very brief, but she so totally experienced it that time slowed in her awareness.

Only when the kiss subtly changed, only when she sensed a rising passion in him and herself, did the truth press on her. *The Duke of Brentworth is kissing me.* Surely that was not a good idea. She should not have permitted it. The moment had made them both people other than they were.

He stopped the kiss. She looked up at him. He looked different. Harder and softer at the same time. His gaze arrested hers, and she did not resist the way his demanded a kind of submission to him seeing inside her. She realized she had been wrong about those eyes. Yes, they absorbed one, but one did not seek a way out. She didn't, at least. She explored, much as she guessed he did. Not all was darkness in him, but more was than she expected.

A sound, distant but distinct, entered her awareness. Not in the house or barn, but on the road. He looked in that direction. "Napier has returned."

They released each other and strode toward the front of the house, walking back into their true selves even as they left the garden. Within five steps, that kiss might never have happened.

But it had.

The carriage pulled up in front of the house. The duke got to the door before the coachman could climb down. A very tall, thin man in a dark coat stepped out. He took one look at the man who served as footman and bowed. "Your Grace, I assume."

Napier inserted himself. "This be Dr. Chalmers, Your Grace."

While Dr. Chalmers ingratiated himself with Brentworth, Davina pulled Napier aside. "Where did you find him?"

"At his club. I was told he is among the best."

"By whom?"

"The best hotel. I asked who they call when they've someone of note who needs a physician. His name was given to me."

"Was he drinking at that club?" She gave Dr. Chalmers a critical inspection.

"Might have been. But I was told that him half-foxed was better than all those who care for the king. Oh, and it seems he knows of you."

"I am sure I have never met him."

"Well, that is what he said when I mentioned you were tending the woman."

Dr. Chalmers and the duke walked over. Brentworth introduced him.

"I was just telling His Grace that I know Sir Cornelius Ingram, who told me about you. He speaks highly of your late father, and your own medical interests." Dr. Chalmers's smile, indulgent but hardly approving, implied what he thought about women in medicine. "I am relieved to know that if you were here, no harm was done. Now, Your Grace, if your man could bring in my case, I will see the patient."

Davina walked beside him toward the house. "I allowed no bleeding. No surgeon." She waited to hear how he reacted to that. If he thought her decision wrong, and wanted to bleed Louisa, he would be on his way back to Newcastle at once.

"She was fortunate you were here to stop it. Barbaric custom."

Davina immediately had more confidence in Dr. Chalmers, half-foxed though he may be. "When we arrived at first I thought it might be cholera, but there had been no excessive purging. She had refused help and care, so she had not taken enough fluids. I have mainly just endeavored to have her drink, and wiped her body with water so it would cool a little."

"What made you think of cholera?"

"Sunken eyes. Dry sweats. Very dry skin, wrinkled, on her hands."

"Ah. You know it well, then."

"I have had it."

He turned and eyed her head. "But did not have someone as enlightened as yourself at your bedside, I see."

She fingered her hair. "Nor would he listen to me when I told him it was pointless."

Dr. Chalmers followed her into the house. "Well, if we shaved heads completely it might cool them down a little. But just cropping hair—it makes no sense. Now, where is the woman?"

Louisa's husband had come in after Brentworth. "I'll take you to her."

Davina sorely wanted to go up those stairs with them. Instead, she watched the dark at the top of the stairs swallow both men.

Which left her alone with Brentworth. She turned to face him, and immediately memories of that kiss returned. It was there between them, like a veil that changed how she saw him. She wondered if he was going to apologize.

"It appears he approved of your care," he said.

No apology. "It reassured me that he did."

"Reassured your confidence in your care, or in him?"

She had to laugh. "In him. Louisa should get the best care available, for what it is worth."

"That is not very encouraging."

She sat down, finally. Her whole body groaned with relief. "We are all rather helpless with maladies like this. We don't know what causes them and can do little else but pray and try not to make matters worse. We are still almost uncivilized when it comes to medicine."

He smiled. "We, you keep saying. You think of yourself as a doctor."

"I am painfully aware of my limitations in training and gender. The *we* referred to my father and me. I helped him when he went into the countryside to try to make a difference there, and I learned much in doing so, but I will never be allowed to learn all he did."

He thought about that. "It seems a waste to me."

"That is a remarkably open-minded thing to say. I think so too. How sad that we had to send a duke's carriage to a city in order to find a physician for Louisa." She looked around the sitting room. It was nicely appointed but not generously so. "Her husband does well enough, but I do not think he can afford Dr. Chalmers's fee, especially because he came all this way."

"I sent for Chalmers. I am responsible for his fee."

Just then, the doctor in question came out of Louisa's chamber and began down the stairs. He looked at Mr. Bowman, who followed him. "Is your well water good?"

"It is."

"Then get me several clean pails of it. Warm the water— not hot, warm—and bring them up. I will need you to help me with your strength, so compose yourself. She is not entirely unconscious, and if you are not becalmed, she will notice. We don't want anything to agitate her."

"I could help," Brentworth said.

Dr. Chalmers advanced into the room. "No, Your Grace, you cannot. Nor can the lady. What I am about to do is indelicate in the extreme, and I daresay if either of you are there, it will only make a bad situation worse." He turned to Davina. "It is good you noticed her dehydration at once. The coachman mentioned it, so I brought something that might help. A clyster syringe is normally used to administer medicine, but it can also be a way to get water into a person. A lot of it, quickly. The body will absorb far more this way than spoonfuls by mouth."

Davina knew that. She had been debating how to create a makeshift clyster if necessary. In ancient times, they used cleansed animal bladders. She doubted Mr. Bowman had any of those around.

Brentworth appeared impassive. If he knew what a clyster was, he was not showing it. However, he did not offer to assist the doctor again.

"Once the water is ready we will proceed." Dr. Chalmers removed his frock coat while he spoke. "I will sit with her tonight. I expect the crisis to happen before morning and the final result to be apparent, one way or another." He turned to Davina. "You most likely kept her alive. Know that, no matter how it ends. Now, I advise you to get some sleep. You are of no use to anyone if you become ill too."

"I will take you back to your house," Brentworth said.

"I really should stay—"

"No. There is nothing for you to do here. Come with me now."

She did not want to go. It felt like an abandonment of the family. Yet, as she stood, she noticed that Mr. Bowman was busy in the kitchen warming the water and talking to his son. There was a point where helping became intrusion, and she might have reached it.

Back in the carriage, exhaustion settled on her like a damp blanket. She gazed out at the last light and tried to ignore that she sat across from a man who had kissed her today. A very nice kiss. Under other circumstances, if it had not been a kiss of pity, really, she might become girlish about it.

She slept at once. Her head nodded and she was gone from the world. Eric was both relieved and disappointed. Mostly the latter.

When he kissed her, he had realized that kiss had been a long time coming. Langford had seen that at once, but then, Langford had a special instinct when it came to sensual matters.

He watched her now, barely visible in the rising moon's glow and the vague light from the swinging coach lamp in front. The qualities that impressed him were invisible now, with her vibrant eyes closed and her expressive face stilled. The self-confidence that had gone into that chamber to aid a woman she had not seen since girlhood—anyone who saw it would believe at once she would make a difference. As soon as she closed that chamber door, both father and son had displayed improved spirits.

He readjusted himself so he could stretch out his legs. He was tired too, even if he had done nothing all day but pace. He should have gone with Napier. He had not even considered doing so. He supposed he had thought he might be needed if Louisa passed. Not by Mr. Bowman and the boy, but by Davina. The way she had wept in the garden, not with grief but with regret and frustration, said he had been right.

Not that he had any idea how he might help her. Not by kissing her; that was certain. That had been an impulse and a mistake. So often, those two things went together. Tomorrow, or the next day, or sometime in the future, he would have to speak of that with her. He was not sure what he would say.

Something emerged in me that I have buried for years and I was not myself. He would sound like a fool if he said that, true though it might be. Nor did he mind that he had succumbed to impulse. To passion. To recklessness. After ten years of controlling that part of himself, he had reveled in its victory over his better sense. But for her sleeping, he might have done so again here, in the dark. Instead, he rode in silence, listening to her calm, deep breaths, while memories pressed on him of how destructive true passion could be.

He had Napier stop in the village as they rode through, and sent him to a tavern to buy a basket of hot food and some wine. Davina dozed through it all. When they reached her house, he needed to jostle her awake and enjoyed that brief touch more than he should.

She blinked and straightened, then looked out the window. "We are here so soon?"

"You were sound asleep."

She wiped her eyes. "What is that?" She pointed to the basket.

"Food from the tavern. I cannot promise it is any good, but it should still be hot enough. You have not eaten all day."

"Nor have you."

"I will dine when I return to Newcastle."

"That is a long way. We can share what is in there."

He should decline and start on that long way. He didn't.

He carried the basket into the house. She found a flint and lit a lamp, then led him back to the kitchen.

"I hope this will do. The dining room is not clean." She found another lamp and lit it; then knelt and built up the fire a bit in the hearth.

The basket contained hen stew with potatoes in a crock, some bread and a decent bottle of red wine. She saw the last and pawed through a drawer until she discovered a corkscrew.

They sat to the simple fare and he poured some wine. The stew tasted wonderful. He had been hungrier than he realized.

"Perhaps we should give some to your coachman."

"He ate at the tavern while they prepared the basket. He is probably napping now."

She ate heartily, then sat back and looked at him. A private smile turned up her lips.

"What?" he asked.

"I am noticing that even after a day in which you climbed a roof and spent hours in a rustic farmhouse, you still look like a duke. Your cravat is all but unblemished and I could cut this bread with your collar. All of this after you did for yourself in the morning. Do dukes have a dispensation from showing the effects of life?" She set her chin on her fist and propped her elbow on the table and examined him more. "Perhaps it is not your dress that does it, though. Even rumpled, you would still look like Brentworth."

It did not sound like a compliment. "Thank you."

"Are you insulted?"

"I can hardly be insulted about looking like myself."

She began to respond but stilled. She looked down at her plate, then at the wineglass, then finally at him. "Aren't you going to say something about the garden?"

Brave woman. Right to the heart of the matter, with no nonsense. "Yes. As a gentleman, I am bound to apologize, which I now do."

"Somehow that does not sound like an apology. You hardly sound sorry."

"That is because I am not sorry. Unless you felt importuned, in which case I am abjectly sorry. Did you?" *Just how brave are you?* If she said yes, he would accept that and retreat totally. He had known many women, however, and his experience said she had not minded that kiss and embrace.

She thought about her answer before giving it. "If I am honest, I was not importuned. However, considering who we are to each other, it might be best if we forgot it happened."

"I understand. You are correct, of course." He stood. "Now I must leave. Tomorrow, I will come for you before noon, after fetching Dr. Chalmers and sending him home. Once I have come for you, we will see your friend, then continue on to Edinburgh."

"I intended to take the mail coach."

"I will bring you. I will ride up with Napier."

She stood to escort him out. "All the way to Newcastle, then back here for Dr. Chalmers, then back to Newcastle, then back here. Yesterday, I would have said you and Mr. Napier could stay here, but not only is it not fitting for you, we probably should not—that is, after what happened—but if we are to forget it—"

"I could not stay." He ventured a small caress of her face. "The truth is, Miss MacCallum, while we agreed it would be best to forget about that kiss, I will not."

He left then, while a primitive voice in his essence thundered, *Stay, you idiot. Stay.*

Chapter Fourteen

Davina carried a bowl of soup up to Louisa. Back in the kitchen, a fowl roasted for the midday meal. The apron she wore bore the stains of a morning of domestic labor, undertaken gladly because her friend had survived the crisis and greeted the dawn cool to the touch.

Brentworth had sent Dr. Chalmers back to Newcastle. He sat now in an armchair reading a book he had taken from his baggage before the carriage left. He seemed lost in it, which suited Davina. She had work to do. She also had grown more aware of him than she liked, so the retreat of his presence in any way relieved her.

She propped Louisa up, making small talk, and began feeding her the soup. Her mind dwelled on other things. That kiss had most definitely been a mistake if the duke would not forget it. It had been one even if he blotted it out of his mind. How did one remain an enemy of a man with whom you had shared an intimacy like that?

"What are you thinking about?" Louisa asked. "Something serious."

"I am just contemplating my return to Edinburgh. I have been in London a month now, and it will be good to see old friends." She smiled. "Not as old as you, of course."

Louisa reached out and squeezed her hand. "I am sorry I did not write. Your letters came to me, even after I married and moved here. I thought it so kind that you paid the postage so I would not need to."

"Why did you not reply?"

Louisa shrugged. "Once I married, there was always work to do, especially after our son was born. You wrote of such a grand life, too. I had so little to say in comparison."

"Hardly a grand life."

"You were in the city, and your father was at the university, and you wrote about people who sounded grand to me. Friends who were knights and such. And now—Neil told me that a duke brought you here. A duke, Davina. Neil says he sits below even as we talk now, in this house. I'm almost glad I am too sick to meet him. I would not begin to know what to say."

"He is just like any other person. It is only a title." But he wasn't like any other person, and Louisa would probably be more tongue-tied than she guessed. With this particular duke, most people were.

"Give him my thanks for the physician and for allowing you to stay with me, but do not allow him to see me." She reached instinctively for her hair, which needed a good washing. That made her look at Davina's hair too. "Did that happen because you were ill too?"

"It did. Be happy I am too enlightened, or you would have woken this morning with a crop worse than the king's."

"I expect it is easier to care for. I rather like the way it looks."

"I am impatient for it to grow. I can manage to appear normal now, but four months ago it stuck out every which way." She spooned more soup. "Eat."

"I can do it myself now."

"I know, but it gives me pleasure to serve you while I

can. We will leave after our meal, and you will probably
insist on believing you are healed when you should rest
another few days."

She had spent the morning cooking, and she explained
what she had prepared so Louisa might indeed rest. They
reminisced for half an hour, then Louisa drifted to sleep
and Davina returned to the kitchen to finish preparations
for the meal.

They all sat together, boy, farmer, duke and herself.
Brentworth drew Mr. Bowman into a conversation about
land management and new farming techniques. He had
removed his coat when the farmer did, and sat in shirt-
sleeves and waistcoat, still looking most ducal but also
more approachable than he normally did. He seemed to be
going out of his way to make Mr. Bowman at ease with the
most unexpected guest at the table.

Then he began the words of taking his leave. Davina returned to Louisa to say goodbye. Mr. Bowman walked out
to the carriage with them.

True to his word, Brentworth settled her inside, then
climbed up beside Napier. Was that relief she saw on Mr.
Bowman's face?

*"They are traveling alone together, Louisa. He didn't
ride inside with her, though, so it is possible it isn't what it
seems."*

"Davina is not like that, like what you are implying."

*"He is a duke, my dear. I could hardly blame her if she
allowed liberties. Better than her have, from the telling of
it. He is unmarried, and even if he had a wife he probably
keeps a woman besides. It isn't like it is for such as us."*

Of course, he might share more with Louisa. He might
mention that while in the barn, he had seen the duke and
Davina kissing in the garden.

Her face warmed at the thought he might have. That

was how oblivious that kiss had made her. She had not even wondered, for an entire day, if anyone had seen.

Traveling in a duke's coach on a long journey turned out to be an experience in luxury. Not only did she have the entire inside to herself but also she sat on a velvet cushion and peered out through silk drapes. The equipage surpassed the mail coaches in function as well as appointments. Instead of being jostled, she barely felt the road. At stops, she took as long as she needed instead of worrying about regaining her seat in minutes. At the first one, Mr. Napier came out of the coaching inn with two baskets of food and placed one beside her.

Left to herself, she turned her mind to her mission. The evidence she had gleaned from Mr. Portman in Caxledge gave her heart, even if Brentworth put little value on it. She did not expect him to capitulate unless undeniable proof were found, and after all this time, that was unlikely. However, she did not have to convince him of the rightness of her claim. She needed to convince Mr. Haversham and the king and, eventually, Parliament.

She tried to plan her next steps. Clearly, she needed to go to the property, so it was wise to have undertaken this journey now. She considered how to find the proof she needed.

She chose to forget about that kiss, just as she had recommended they both do. Only she did not forget it. The memory was in her head, at times distracting her down a path best not trod. After one long reverie that was far too vivid, she scolded herself and bent to find a book in her valise. This was why it had been a mistake. Here she was, planning her campaign, and a stupid kiss diverted her from clear thinking. A kiss from the man determined to thwart her, no less.

Brentworth's coach and four could travel as fast as the mail if he chose. He did not. They stopped more often than a mail coach would. They rolled more slowly, although still at a high speed, in Davina's opinion. Most significantly, at nightfall they did not continue but sought out an inn.

She had no say in the arrangements. Mr. Napier disappeared into the inn the first night and returned quickly to speak with Brentworth. The duke then came to her while she stretched her legs. "Two chambers have been hired. This inn is passably suitable, so you should be comfortable, I hope. I intend to dine in half an hour, if you would care to join me. Or you can have something in your chamber."

It would be cowardly to cower in her chamber. She needed to show him that she was the same formidable enemy she had always been. "I will come down, thank you."

That gave her time to wash and pace off her stiffness. At the appointed time, she went below, and the innkeeper brought her to a little private dining room where Brentworth waited.

He tasted his soup. "I remember the fare here being better than typical, and it seems they have continued the standard."

Davina had to agree. She was hungry, and it looked as if he was too. They partook of most of the meal in silence.

"I assume you have made arrangements for your stay in Edinburgh," he said when forks moved slowly.

"I am staying with Sir Cornelius and his wife."

"We will give Napier the direction and take you there at once. We should arrive tomorrow next midday."

"You know the timing well, and the inns on the way. Have you visited Scotland more than I realized?"

"When I was younger I came here a few times. I have a good memory, that is all."

She did not think that was all, from the somewhat clipped way he responded. "If you take me to Sir Cornelius directly, you will be imposed upon to visit at least a brief while. Perhaps you should have Mr. Napier take you to your rooms first, then deliver me to them."

"I do not mind visiting a brief while. I know of Sir Cornelius and expect he is an interesting person to meet."

"I should warn you, Sir Cornelius's wife is a free thinker."

"Do you think that will shock me?"

"I think nothing much shocks you. I merely thought to prepare you. She is outspoken in her views too, and is sure to take advantage of the ear of a peer."

"Yet you speak warmly even as you warn."

"She is a wonderful woman and I admire her. She is like an aunt to me. The warning was for you, because you might not share my esteem of her."

"I do not dislike outspoken women. At least you know what you have in them. I might not want to marry one, but if given the choice, I would rather sit beside one at a dinner than beside an empty-headed beauty."

"What an odd thing to say. You would rather spend time with such a woman but would not want to marry one. What kind of woman do you expect to marry, if you marry at all?"

He shrugged. "One like my father, and his father, and the duke before him."

"An empty-headed beauty?"

"Not too empty, if I can help it. Nor all that beautiful, for all I care. But . . . appropriate."

She wondered if he had disapproved of Langford marrying Amanda. He probably considered Stratton's marriage to the daughter of an earl far better. But even Clara was not truly appropriate.

"You do not sound as if it appeals to you at all," she teased. "You have not yet availed yourself of this wonderful opportunity to be just like all the dukes before you, so I think it does not."

"I had time to wait a while. It is not the union I avoid but the imposition on my time of arranging it all. Next season, however, I will do the dance and find a partner and fulfill my duty."

"An appropriate partner." She leaned in. "Do you know what I think? I think you have avoided it because you do not relish being appropriate all the time. I think maybe you would prefer not being the most ducal duke in this matter, or in many others."

He looked at her, first in surprise, then with an interest that made her uncomfortable.

"Miss MacCallum, I am not the most ducal duke. That is a public face. I was raised in a tradition of extreme discretion, trained in it, and discovered it creates considerable freedom to live the way I choose. The difference is, the world does not know about my private doings. Because my life is no one's affair but my own, that suits me." He in turn leaned in until they faced each other squarely across little space. "I am not appropriate all the time, as you well know."

She fought being absorbed into that gaze. "I doubt discretion alone gave you that name. You could not live in London, in society, and secretly be some wild rake or dissolute peer."

"I admit I am not a rake. I am glad I am not dissolute. As for London, however—it is not the whole world. When I leave it, I leave all those eyes, and gossiping mouths too. For example, had I taken one room for us up above, and not two, no one here would have cared or much noticed.

It is so common an occurrence that I doubt the servants even comment about it to one another. Do not pity me my appropriate life. I daresay it is less appropriate than yours in the sum."

She resented the way he had turned things around. "No doubt. I am a woman. I am not permitted to be free without being ruined. I would think if a man had your privileges, he would explore his freedom fully, not live behind a public face except when he left Town. Have you never been stupidly indiscreet and inappropriate and . . . and *mad*? What a shame if you have not, considering you are one of the few people who can be so without consequences."

He altered subtly right before her, becoming the Brentworth she first met. Something in that public face nudged at her. An explanation of the reaction Amanda said he inspired in women. She felt its power. Fear was the wrong word. It was too alluring to be called that.

"You do not know what you are talking about." His vague smile of tolerance hardly softened his face. "There are always consequences to madness and passion. Often serious ones." He pulled out his pocket watch. "I intend to retire now. You should too. We leave at eight o'clock."

Damn the woman.

He sat in the dark in his chamber, hearing the muffled sounds from below as Miss MacCallum prepared for bed. He had not wanted this particular chamber, but of the two it would have been rude to take hers instead. Another flight of stairs for this one. It was smaller and poorer too. Not that Miss MacCallum would care about that. Still, he had wanted her to be comfortable.

The reasons why did not interest him right now. Instead, her probing insights echoed. *You should have told her that*

*you have been mad, drawn into it like a moth to a flame.
Hopelessly so. You should have put her in her place by
saying she was an ignorant innocent when it came to the
madness of all-consuming passion.*

As for consequences—hell, he knew about those. Not
the petty little ones she spoke of. Real consequences. The
kind that made you curse the world, and yourself.

No more of that, he had sworn. No more. And yet—
here he was with that stirring in him again, after all these
years, with another inappropriate woman. Far different
than the last time, but still a mistake. Langford, damn him,
had noticed first. *The interest*, he called it. The curiosity.
The fascination. His own essence had slowly seen it too.
His attention to detail. His worry for her friend, a person
he had never met. Hell, he had climbed a damned slate
roof for her.

That kiss they should forget.

Damnation.

It would not be the same. She was not mad herself. She
did not want to consume him. She did not want his soul.
She saw him as an enemy. And yet—

The sounds from below ceased. She had gone to bed.
He realized he had been listening for that, before he
rested himself.

"I should take Davina above and settle her in, then let
her rest," Lady Ingram said to her husband, leaning low
and giving him a kiss and an embrace. They both had red
hair, so in that kiss they all but merged together. "You can
catch up on all the London news at dinner. Come with me,
dear, and I'll show you your chamber."

Davina had been enjoying her time with her father's
friend and wished she could continue. However, she left

Sir Cornelius and followed his wife out of the library. It was only late afternoon, and she really did not need rest. The sight of Edinburgh alone invigorated her, and she had intended to go for a walk now that Brentworth had departed.

He had indeed been pressed to sit a while, as she predicted. Lady Ingram had indeed bent his ear about her reform interests. Sir Cornelius had told some amusing stories about the university. Brentworth had been gracious and friendly.

That was a change. Ever since their dinner that first night, he had been most unfriendly with her. Last night, there had been such frost in his manner, she took her meal in her chamber. She had gone too far in her words, she knew. She doubted a duke thought it *appropriate* for others to criticize him.

Not that she had done so. Not really. She just found it strange, almost perverse, that a duke should have less freedom to be true to his nature than she had, or Sir Cornelius. Yet that was how it seemed this duke had been raised and trained, and he believed it a good thing. So next season he would find that appropriate wife who hopefully was neither wild nor empty-headed, and they would have an appropriate marriage and life and bring forth appropriate heirs.

It all sounded very dull to her.

"Here we are." Lady Ingram opened a door. "I thought you would like to use this chamber instead of the one you had the last time."

"That was thoughtful." Sad memories lived in that other chamber, from when the Ingrams had given her safe harbor after her father's death. This chamber had nice prospects of the crescent on which the house was built, one of many new and identical, tall, pale stone houses lined up side by side in a long arc. Its long windows filled it with light, and the chintz drapes displayed happy festoons of flowers.

Although they had servants, Lady Ingram herself helped Davina unpack. When they were finished, the lady did not leave. Instead, she set her stout body down in a chair and looked up quizzically. "Have you and the duke come to a meeting of the minds about your claim? I ask because you journeyed here with him. Alone, I believe." One pale orange arched eyebrow accompanied the last sentence. "From the conversation as he left, I think the plan is to do so again when you visit Teyhill."

"I had planned to take the mail coach from Newcastle, but after the ordeal with Louisa he insisted I travel in his coach so as not to be overtired." She explained the situation she had found at her friend's home. "He was above with the coachman the whole way. Nothing inappropriate happened, I assure you." *Except one kiss*. "We have no agreement on my claim. Far from it. He has no sympathy at all on that matter."

"None at all, you say."

"Yes. None."

"Well, he has sympathy about something concerning you. It was in how he spoke to you and how he looked at you. In fact, I think it important that you no longer travel with him. Such a man can turn a woman's head. Even I felt giddy."

"If he goes to Teyhill, I must too. I suppose I can hire a coach. More likely a wagon, with my purse."

"Do you not trust him to report what he learns? Is he so dishonorable?"

"I do not trust him to hear what is being said. You know what I mean. We tend to hear what we want to hear, unless someone is so clear and certain that we cannot deny the truth."

Lady Ingram's brow furrowed while she thought.

"If you are determined to go, and he intends for you to go with him, I will have my husband's aunt come as a chaperone."

"I understand your concern for my reputation and how it will look, but I don't think—"

"Allow me to be clear and certain, Davina, so *you* hear the truth. I do not care how things look. I am saying that Brentworth has a man's interest in you, no matter what you are claiming about your family and that land." She stood. "You must not travel alone with him again. I will not hear any arguments on the matter."

Sir Cornelius's maiden aunt arrived at the house two mornings later with two valises. One held clothing and the other contained a variety of books. It was the latter she insisted stay in the carriage at her side.

She proved to be the best travel companion, which meant Davina barely knew she was present. The same concentration her brother brought to bear on his experiments, Miss Ingram gave to her reading.

Other than some pleasantries when the door closed on them both and the coach rolled, they spoke little. Miss Ingram's half of the short conversation alerted Davina to the woman's failed hearing, as well as her somewhat scattered perceptions. Davina suspected the old woman of having one foot into her second childhood. She doubted Sir Cornelius would agree, but it was something, in her experience, that family members were not quick to acknowledge.

Soon, the peculiar conversation, such as it was, ended, and Miss Ingram pulled one of those books from the valise. Spectacles perched low on her nose and her cap hiding most of her pale, wrinkled face, she tilted the book to the light of the window and immersed herself in a world Davina guessed still made good sense to her.

Davina had her own book but spent a good hour chewing on her brief visit home. Lady Ingram normally was not a stickler for propriety, especially with a woman of mature years. She believed the marriage laws must be changed, and that women were burdened with too many expectations set by men. Her insistence that Davina have a chaperone, therefore, was out of character.

If it had not been Brentworth, but some ordinary gentleman of little note, would Miss Ingram be sitting with her now? A duke would draw attention in ways other men did not. Perhaps Lady Ingram merely wanted to spare her from gossip should word spread about this journey.

She did not think it would, however. They had left town, heading west, and already the environs of the city thinned and the countryside asserted itself. Soon they would pass many more sheep than people.

She discarded Lady Ingram's belief that Brentworth had an interest in her. He might have kissed her once, out of sympathy or—well, he might have done that, but an interest implied much more. She hardly needed some other woman to protect her from dastardly intentions on the duke's part.

Miss Ingram chuckled at something she read. Davina considered how ineffective a chaperone this would be. Maybe that was Lady Ingram's intention. To fulfill the letter of the propriety's law, but in reality spare her from the full effects of it.

They stopped at an inn so Mr. Napier could rest and water the horses. Davina climbed out of the coach when he opened it. Miss Ingram remained inside with her book, unaware the coach no longer moved. Davina felt obliged to reach it and jostle her and say bluntly that now was a good time to use the necessary.

Together they found it, then Miss Ingram returned to the coach. Davina strolled around the inn's yard, tucking her wrap close to warm her in the chilled weather. She inhaled deeply through her nose, so she could smell the Scotland she and her father had traveled so often.

"Is Miss Ingram as given to confusion as Sir Cornelius warned?"

She turned. Brentworth walked up behind her.

"He took me aside while the baggage was loaded," he explained. "He apologized for burdening me with his aunt, because her mental condition is not the best. She was the only one they could find quickly, however."

"She will not be trouble, if that is what you fear. I daresay you will not even notice she is with us."

"The perfect chaperone, then."

"For my purposes, she is. I feared I would have to entertain another woman, one I did not even know. I don't think I could bear to make small talk for hours on end. Inside a carriage, one is thoroughly trapped."

They continued their stroll around the inn's yard.

"Did you request a chaperone?" he asked.

"Why would I do that? If I did not have one on a very public road from Newcastle, it would be strange if I decided I needed one for show now."

"They are not only for show. They are supposed to be protection."

"I need no protection besides Mr. Napier and you."

"Do not pretend you don't understand what I mean. You are not good at dissembling."

They had reached where the walls of the yard met, far from the busy activities of carriages and guests. A tree grew in the corner, its leaves now gold and red. She pivoted to retrace her steps and found her nose almost in Brentworth's waistcoat. She retreated a step, and her back rubbed the wall. She darted a look to her right, to see if she could slip away. His arm stretched and blocked her. He pressed his hand against the stones right next to her head.

"I ask again: Did you request that Lady Ingram find you a chaperone?" His voice, low and quiet, flowed over her like a caress.

He seemed very close, so near that his warmth affected the air between them. She dared not look up at him. Those eyes of his would probably turn her into a tongue-tied fool. She kept her gaze steady on his cravat, with its perfect creases.

"I did not. I said it was unnecessary. Silly, really, considering my age and my mission. Lady Ingram insisted, however."

"She did not seem a woman bound by propriety, so her insistence is curious." A light touch on her chin, dry and warm. He lifted it so she had to look at him. A mistake, that, just as she feared. Her senses swam under his gaze. A delicious shiver trembled down her body. "Did she think you were in danger from me?"

"Not danger. Not really. She just thought—that is, she did not trust—" She heard herself babbling on short breaths, like the fool she feared she would be.

"She did not trust me with you?"

"She did not imply you were dishonorable. Do not think that."

"The lines defining honor can be very vague sometimes for some of us." He still held her chin, and now grazed his thumb over her lips. "Perhaps she did not trust you with me, as much as me with you. Not so dishonorable on my part, then."

A whirlwind gusted inside her, but the world surrounding them seemed utterly still. Soundless. "Something like that, I think."

"A perceptive woman. Do you fear yourself with me?"

Oh heavens. Right now, yes. In the garden, yes. Did he really expect her to admit it? "You toy with me to feed your own conceit. What does it matter, as long as I do not fear *you*?"

"Not even a little? How insulting." His face came very close to hers. "And how untruthful."

He was going to kiss her again. "We should return to the coach," she said haltingly. "We really should."

His arm dropped. He stepped away, retreating from her and into himself. They began walking back. She fought to achieve some steadiness. "Anyway, Lady Ingram insisted on a companion for me. She is not a woman to be denied when she sets her mind to something."

"That sounds a lot like you. No wonder Sir Cornelius thinks of you as a daughter."

"He does?"

"He said as much while we talked."

She had seen them retreat into a tête-à-tête. She had assumed they spoke about Sir Cornelius's scientific work.

"He spoke of you most admirably, and expressed the opinion that it was a crime that you could not study medicine. He said you hoped to still help the sick to the extent you are able. I think he sought to influence me to help you do that."

"Unless you can purchase a university, that is unlikely."

They had reached the coach. Miss Ingram's profile showed her still reading.

"Not that part. The other plans you have." He opened the coach door and handed her in, then spoke to her through the window. "Why did you not tell me about your plans for the property?"

"That is not a plan. That is a dream, and one unlikely to come true even if I retrieve the land."

He subjected her to a long consideration. She hoped Miss Ingram did not choose this moment to put down her book, because no one who saw that look in his eyes would doubt what he considered.

He glanced at her companion. "We will stop tonight north of Sterling and go the rest of the way tomorrow. I will see that Miss Ingram has her own chamber so she does not impose on you."

"That is not necessary," she hastened to say.

He had walked away before she finished the sentence.

Chapter Fifteen

"Some call me a witch."

Miss Ingram announced this in the middle of their dinner at the inn. Her voice broke an awkward silence. Eric had been surprised and displeased to see the older woman descend the stairs beside Davina. She had not even brought her book.

Which meant that the dinner took on a formality he had not wanted. Not that he *expected* informality. A dinner of increased intimacy might play out like a theater piece in his head, but he doubted Davina would be agreeable. He had not expected her to force her companion to join them, however.

Perhaps he frightened her in the inn's yard. Short of controlling his impulses regarding her, which increasingly he could not do, he doubted that could be avoided. His situation confounded him. Normally with women, he did not have to be subtle or tread a path from enemy to dear friend. He started at the latter point, and the only move necessary was to bed. No subtlety needed at all.

"Maybe I am a witch. I don't think so, but who knows?"

"I think witches, if they even existed, would know they are witches," Davina said.

"It is because I have two cats. For some reason, people think cats mean a witch."

"It is not common to keep cats as pets, but hardly only done by witches," Eric said to help out the conversation. Anything to slice through the thick cloud of expectation hanging between Davina and himself. She felt it too. It was why she managed not to look at him. "Have you had them long?"

Miss Ingram pondered that, angling her head and frowning beneath her white cap's significant lace brim. "Let me see. Lucifer has been with me for seven years and Mischief for five."

"Let me guess," he said. "They are black, aren't they?"

"How did you know?"

"Miss Ingram," Davina said gently, "if you insist on keeping black cats named Lucifer and Mischief, you can hardly blame the unenlightened for thinking you are a witch."

"What else can you name a black cat? George?"

"George would be a splendid name."

From her expression, Miss Ingram thought the name not satisfactory at all. But her consternation melted and her eyes turned dreamy. "I was reading about Scotland today. I should like to go there next summer."

"We are in Scotland now," he said. *You live in Scotland*.

"Oh. I thought we were in Brighton. I could have sworn I smelled the sea." She looked down at her meal, of which she had partaken a decent amount. "I think I will retire now and read a while before sleeping."

She stood to go. He did too.

So did Davina, who had not finished her own dinner. "I should see her to her chamber."

He gestured for the servant waiting silently near the

door. "Please see that Miss Ingram is escorted to her chamber, so Miss MacCallum can continue her meal."

The young man shadowed Miss Ingram from the small dining room. Davina watched them leave, hesitated, then sat again. "A witch, no less. It is good she lives in the city. Out here that rumor could still take a bad turn."

Alone, finally. How ignoble for that to be his first thought. "It was disconcerting that she did not remember where she is, or where she lives."

"As we age, memories move around. The oldest ones seem to gain more prominence. She will probably need to be watched closely soon, however. I am relieved that Sir Cornelius told you he is aware of her condition." She lifted her fork, poised to continue her meal, then paused. "That is the hardest part about being alone, I think. When we age, we need care again, and without family who will give it?"

"Is that why you want to turn my property into a hospital? To give that care?"

Her response was to eat. His question had vexed her, from the evidence of her severe expression.

"I think of it as my property, of course," she paused to say. "I have no illusions I can staff a hospital such as one finds in the cities these days. However, a dispensary would be useful there. Perhaps an infirmary with a few beds. It would be a place where the poor and sick could come to have someone with medical knowledge tend to them."

"Would you be that person?" *If you win our little battle, would you live out your life there?* He did not care for the images that conjured, of this vibrant woman devoting herself to nothing other than the care of others. She should be enjoying life and being young. She should be loving and being loved, not only as a caretaker.

"I would find a true physician to live there, of course."

Her voice had grown testy. "The income from the land would pay him."

"Did you think I mocked you with the question?"

"We both know my limitations regarding giving medical advice."

"Sir Cornelius does not. He told me that three hundred years ago, physicians were trained in apprenticeships, much as you served with your father. In his opinion, the medical schools today often are inferior. What is such a school but an apprenticeship, after all, but perhaps a less intensive one?"

Her hard expression melted. "It is, of course, useful to have more than one teacher, so they are superior in that way. However, I approve of the new view that all physicians should spend time in a hospital while training, and not only take notes at lectures. Seeing maladies is far different from hearing about them."

"Were you never allowed to listen to any of those lectures?"

A smile broke. "One day my father had me dress as a man and snuck me in. A young man sitting beside me in the theater kept falling asleep instead of taking advantage of this wonderful opportunity. I confess, my foot jabbed his leg each time he did."

"I find it difficult to believe no one was aware of the ruse. You could never pass for a man."

"Well, I bound my—um—I bound myself and wore a coat. My hair was the hardest part. I kept a low-crowned hat on the whole time and let others think me rude. This was before . . ." She absently fingered the ends of her hair.

"I have grown fond of your hair, Davina. It becomes you."

Acknowledgment passed in her eyes that he had addressed her with familiarity. He waited for her correction.

"You are just being kind."

"Not at all. Although I confess, I have pictured it longer, like a waterfall of spun moonlight." Where the hell had that poetic nonsense come from? It blurted out, breaching his reserve in one big jump over common sense.

She colored. Her eyes subtly widened. Her lips parted, as if she intended to say something but forgot what. They remained like that. He began picturing other things besides spun moonlight.

He poured more wine.

It was becoming a peculiar dinner. That the duke had addressed her by her given name had made her pause. That he waxed poetic about hair she did not have astonished her.

His gaze no longer appeared steely. Fiery, but not steely. It reminded her a little of the way Mr. Hume looked at her sometimes. Only Mr. Hume's warmth never made her insides curl and tighten like this.

Perhaps the duke was drunk.

She glanced at the wine bottle. He mistook her interest and poured her more. He smiled. A truly friendly smile. Gracious and amiable, not merely tolerant.

"You should have told me about your noble intentions for the property," he said.

"Would that have made you amenable to my petitions? Would you have stood aside?"

"Perhaps I would have said you are welcome to use it for your charitable purpose."

"Then it would still be yours, and I would be beholden to you. I prefer to secure the property myself before trying to make my dream a reality."

"That will take years, even if you find the proof you seek. My way would mean you can start right away."

He dangled a tempting compromise. She rebelled against the logic of it, however.

He must have noticed. He leaned in. "You do not only want it for saintly goals, I think."

"No, I don't," she blurted out. "I want it because it should be mine."

Humor entered his gaze. Goodness, he looked handsome right then. Her insides twisted more. She drank some wine to give herself something to do. She should take her leave. Yes, she should tear herself away from the enlivening sensations he evoked—

"Perhaps if you continue fascinating me, I will just give it to you," he murmured.

Fascinating? What did that mean?

"Your Grace—"

"Call me Eric."

Eric! "I will not."

"Then use Brentworth, as most of the world does."

Even that sounded too familiar, but so be it. "Brentworth, forgive me if I am either forward or foolish in my question, but . . . are you flirting with me?"

She received the biggest, most genuine, and most charming smile she had ever seen on his face.

"Davina, I do not flirt."

She should correct his use of her name. She would too, if she could think of a clever way to do that without sounding like a spinster scold. "Never?"

"Not in years. I doubt I know how anymore."

"Come now. Everyone flirts."

"Do you?"

Now that was an awkward question. "You do not flirt because dukes don't have to. Am I right?"

"Some enjoy it. Langford, for example. It was his favorite sport."

"If you do not flirt, how will you manage this marriage you anticipate making next season?"

"I expect I will dance with her at balls a few times, call on her a few times, then propose."

"How dreadful you make it sound. Poor girl."

"Dreadful? *Poor* girl? She will be a duchess. Her family will be delirious with joy."

"She will have to agree, I expect, even if she would rather not. Dreadful for you too, then." She found his blasé acceptance of this duty irritating. "Don't you want more than that? Don't you want passion, if not love? Your friends both are ecstatic in their marriages, so it is not as if you have never seen it among dukes."

The cool reserve attempted to descend, but did not quite make it all the way down. "Not only do I not want that in a marriage, I intend to avoid it. Passion is disruptive and makes us other than ourselves. Langford is being a saint, which he was never born to be. Stratton is turning soft, and I assure you that while he is amiable, he is not by nature the way you see him with Clara. They have both lost control of their true selves, and passion is the reason."

He sounded very sure about all of that. As if he knew what he was talking about. It happened to him once, she realized. He had lost himself that way.

"I hope that at least you will make sure this poor girl you marry is contented."

"My wealth will be at her disposal, so she will be contented."

"I was not speaking of worldly goods. I meant in bed." Goodness, where had that come from? She eyed her wineglass, not feeling nearly as appalled with herself as she should.

"Excuse me?"

She looked up to see him appearing astonished. She

rather liked that she had done that. "Perhaps you are aware that women can have orgasms too. Medicine has documented this, and physicians have written about it, in case you wonder how I know it."

"I am aware, thank you."

"Then you may know that a woman having that experience is very dependent on the man being so aware, and taking steps to ensure it. All I was saying was that I hope that you at least allow this poor girl that much." She swallowed more wine.

"Do not worry about the poor girl, Davina. I pride myself on being enlightened in these matters." No longer off balance, his gaze all but dared her to go on with the topic.

She decided that might not be wise. For one thing, by anyone's account it was a scandalous subject that she should never have raised. For another, talking about such inappropriate things proved more fun that it should, and oddly stimulating.

She set her wineglass a good distance from her. No more of that.

"If not in your match, do you not flirt in your friendships?" she asked, to turn the topic sideways.

"It is much the same. I dance with a woman at a few balls, I call on her a few times."

Then I propose. He did not say it, but it was there. Only it was not a proposal as much as a proposition.

"You did not answer my question," he said. "Do you never flirt?"

He would remember she had sidestepped that question.

"Don't you know how?" he pressed.

"I tried it once but was not successful. Perhaps it is no more in my nature than in yours."

"Every woman should know how to flirt. Let us put this

journey to good purpose. You can practice flirting with me, and I will let you know if you are successful."

"I am not going to flirt with you. Besides, according to you, it isn't even needed."

"Not by me, but the ladies must know how to do it. Otherwise how will I know that they will welcome my calls? Don't you see? It is all decided before I arrive at their doors. It is all communicated wordlessly."

She knew what the *all* was. His eyes communicated it. Wordlessly. Which was very inappropriate. So why was she still sitting here, allowing that? All but inviting it with her own frank talk? And where was that servant? Perhaps he had returned but left after seeing the look in the duke's eyes. She would not have noticed because every part of her attention was on him, not the chamber and not propriety.

"As for your never flirting, that is not true," he said, holding her gaze. "You have been subtly flirting with me all evening. Your outspokenness is a type of flirting. You know I like it so you never retreat. I think you do not try flirting outright because you fear where it will lead."

"I have no illusions that flirting with a duke will ever lead anywhere."

He reached across the table and *took her hand*. "My dear Miss MacCallum—Davina—how very wrong you are."

He was on his feet then, lifting her onto her wobbly legs. In the next second, she was in his arms.

"It leads here," he said. "Twice now."

"That first time was different. An impulse. This is . . ."

"Again an impulse."

"It is not always wise to succumb to those. It could lead to insulting someone."

"I assure you. I do not embrace women unless I know they welcome it."

"Are you sure I do?"

"It appears so, because you are still here." He lowered his head. "I think you were right and I should seek more passion in my life."

He was going to kiss her again. Right here, in this little dining room, with the remnants of their meal awaiting a servant. With the less-privileged guests shouting and laughing on the other side of the wall. If anyone entered—

His lips touched hers carefully but decisively, and she no longer debated whether she might be ruined. The jig her heart had experienced for hours suddenly broke into a more primitive dance. It seemed she stopped breathing, yet she did not faint.

The kiss was delicious. The embrace firm, comforting and dangerous all at once. She let both continue and submitted to their power. *His* power. Wonderful sensations flooded her over and over, warming her, arousing her.

Even as her passion ascended and his own grew more aggressive, a corner of her awareness noted her physical changes with medical interest. The tipsy balance that forced her to embrace him too. The way she lost control of her physical reactions until they conquered her will. The sensitivity of her lips and mouth and all her skin, so that her body felt his through her garments and ached for more closeness.

He palmed her face, holding it while his tongue invaded her mouth. That startled her, but the intimacy caused new excitement to pour down her center and pool very low near her vulva, which now had a vitality that could not be ignored.

It was too wonderful to end it. She no longer heard the noise from the public room. She did not care that this was a terrible mistake. Even her mission and his opposition to it ceased to concern her. All of her, body, mind, blood and essence, only wanted to dwell in this pleasure.

He sat in her chair and drew her down onto his lap. Easier, then, to kiss without wobbling. The position gave him better purchase to her neck and ear and the skin atop her chest. He explored with hot kisses and bites. They remained close like that, but not as close as before, and her body ached for the contact it had lost, for the warmth and hard body and pressure against her breasts and hips. She placed her palm on his shirt, under his coat, but it was not the same.

He knew. His hand slid down her body to her knees, then up again in a caress that answered her desire for more contact. Each firm stroke created a path of new sensuality. Soon that was not enough either, and her need maddened her. She was helpless against the way her body urged her on.

Pleasure overwhelmed her. It enhanced her senses so she felt every touch and inhaled his scent and heard his heart beat. It blotted out her awareness of everything else. A new touch barely grazed her breast. A voice, low and quiet, barely broke the silence. *May I?* He asked for permission to— He wanted her to answer, to allow it, to put her frantic hunger into words. Yes, yes. Only she could not say it. She only tucked her face into the crook of his neck and nodded.

The first caress on her breast created a charge of pleasure that left her breathless. The next ones, subtler but more focused, devastated her. The power built in her until she was kissing him madly, trying to release it, dying from the torture but not wanting it to end.

Savage kisses, grasping holds, unbearable caresses. Their passion escalated until she almost cried from the way her body throbbed. More; there had to be more, her insane mind insisted.

That voice again merged into her mind. If it made a

sound she did not hear it, but only absorbed the words. *Come above with me.*

Yes, yes. Only slowly, the meaning sank in and found a thread of rationality. Go above to a chamber, his or hers, and finish this. That was what he wanted. She wished he had not asked. She wished he had picked her up and carried her through the door and up the stairs and—

She buried her face in his neck again, trying to think. Why shouldn't she? It was what she wanted. She had told him to find passion. Why shouldn't *she*?

"I suppose so," she murmured.

He stopped caressing her breast, but those long strokes resumed on her side and hip. "You suppose?" He turned his head and kissed her cheek gently. "You are not sure?"

She turned her head too, so he might be able to kiss her lips, and so her voice would not be so muffled. "I should experience this at least once in my life. Now seems an excellent time."

She expected him to rise, grab her hand and pull her to the door. Instead, those caresses and soft kisses continued. She wanted him to touch her breasts again. She almost reached for his hand and moved it there.

"You are still a virgin." A long exhale.

"You thought I was not?"

"You have lived an unconventional and worldly life. I can be excused, I hope."

"It is a small thing."

"Hardly. Gentlemen do not ruin innocents."

"Nonsense. I'm sure they do all the time."

"Not this one."

She straightened and looked at him. He meant it. His expression still bore the signs of passion. His eyes still burned and his face's planes remained tight. But he was not going to take her above. Enough of the most ducal duke had returned to his face for her to know that.

"Well, damnation, Your Grace. It is rude to seduce a woman, to get her into such a state, and then not—not—" Several scandalous words popped into her head, but none of the medical ones.

She scooted off his lap. "We will wait a short while so that you can get yourself in order." She gestured at his lap. "You do not want to leave in high salute, I am sure. Fortunately, women do not give evidence of their arousal so easily."

"You don't think so? I wish there were a looking glass here." He laughed out loud, then pulled her closer and reached to stroke her head. "One good thing about hair that length is that it does not appear disheveled after such an indiscretion."

The playfulness died away, leaving them looking at each other wistfully.

"Was I supposed to tell you about my inexperience?"

"The misunderstanding was all my fault. I allowed myself to believe what I wanted to believe, so I could continue being a scoundrel."

"Not a scoundrel. Do not think that. True, you gave no quarter, but I—well, I didn't mind nearly enough for you to call yourself a scoundrel." It had been wonderful, and she would not be a coward and pretend it hadn't been. She suspected the woman in her would feast on the memory for months. Her body, not yet becalmed, still sent sparks into her blood. She wished she had never given him cause to become noble with her.

He stood. "That is good to know." He cupped her face with his hands and gave her a final kiss, then released her. "Now you should go above on your own. I will wait a short while."

She went to the door, hoping he would follow. Of course he didn't.

"I suppose now we return to being enemies," she said.

"That might be impossible. Let us be friends with different goals."

Oh, how handsome he looked there, his gaze still warm and the corners of his eyes crinkling a bit with his vague smile. She looked long enough to keep the memory, then left the chamber and made her way to her empty bed.

Chapter Sixteen

When a well-ordered life veers off its cleanly marked path, there is normally a good reason. Eric decided it was all Scotland's fault. He might have succeeded in releasing his frustration with that idea, except he had to acknowledge that he had kissed her first in England.

He should be proud of his restraint. Instead, he argued all night against the rules that demanded it. It seemed to him that Davina had been more rational than he. She perhaps felt life owed her the experience. That he was the convenient man for the purpose did not flatter him, but it damned well suited his own purposes.

Which were—what? That was the devilish detail that kept him from sleeping, and, as she so adorably put it, saluting. She was not typical of his women at all, which probably was her appeal. He could not simply dance a few dances, make a few calls, bring an expensive gift and require discretion. Everything in his world and hers said he should never have touched her, let alone driven them both to a point twelve stairs away from an irreparable blunder.

Yet he had. Nor did he regret it. He could not even swear he would not do it again if given the chance. It had been a long time since he had known mindless, driving passion. His sensuality luxuriated in having been given free rein for a while. It beckoned him all night to find a way to have a wild, adventurous rut with someone, if not Davina than anyone else would do.

She thought they could keep turning back time. That they could forget about that first kiss and now, after this, after being damned close to having each other on the floor of an inn's dining room, they could go back to being enemies. That spoke to her inexperience as much as her artless embraces did. Which, if he were honest with himself, had told him she was probably an innocent, but hope and hunger conquered that notion in a blink.

Nothing much was resolved in his mind when dawn broke. When Davina came below with Miss Ingram, he received one warm, almost nostalgic smile before she guided the old woman to the coach. He climbed up beside Napier and took the reins. Driving the horses would give his mind something to do besides ruminate about Miss MacCallum, at least. Besides, Teyhill waited down the road, and he needed to prepare himself for a visit he did not want to make.

"You will stay here." Brentworth announced the plan as soon as Davina stepped out of the coach. "The top floor has an apartment kept for me. You and Miss Ingram should be comfortable there. It has several chambers, and the windows look out on a little kitchen garden to the south. The smells from the yard are not bad up there."

Mr. Napier removed all the baggage from the back of the coach, even the duke's.

"Will you be staying here too?" she asked. "I would think you would stay at Teyhill."

"If I were staying there, you would be too." He did not even look her way, but watched Napier. Then he turned to her with one broad step. "I choose not to live there. That is why I let the top of this inn, so it is available should I ever visit."

"Which you never do."

"I will stay here," he repeated evenly. "I will take a chamber and leave the top floor to you, unless you mind the stairs."

"I do not mind, and Miss Ingram is not infirm physically."

"Napier will arrange everything. Take your meal where you will. I will see you in the morning." With that, he unleashed his horse from its tether at the back of the coach, mounted and rode away.

It had not been a promising conversation, and it had been the first of the day. She assumed he sorely regretted what had happened. Perhaps he was even embarrassed, although as a man he would never admit it. He had lost control. It was that simple. Then he had encouraged, even lured, her to do the same. It was not the kind of behavior for which Brentworth was known.

Mr. Napier handed their baggage to several servants, then brought them inside. She heard him mention Brentworth's name several times. He insisted a woman be given over to the ladies for the length of their stay, to serve them exclusively. The innkeeper left the chamber and returned with a young woman who invited them to follow her up the stairs.

Miss Ingram turned her head this way and that all the way up, "Someone has changed everything. The panels on the wall used to be much nicer."

"I don't think you have been here before."

"Haven't I? Well, one inn looks much like another, I suppose. Will we be here long?"

"I don't know." It could be a day or so, or it could be a

week or so. It all depended on Brentworth. She had no choice but to have him take her around. If he chose not to bring her somewhere she thought she needed to go, she would have to hire a conveyance. She wondered if this inn, which was so beholden to his largesse in permanently letting an entire floor that was never used, would help her do that.

By the time they arrived at the chambers at the top, she had half-convinced herself that Brentworth was putting her here so he could keep her from learning what she needed to learn. They may not be enemies anymore, but they were not of one mind either.

The chambers proved to be luxurious enough for a duke. Fine fabrics and furniture graced the large sitting room and three bedchambers. As he said, two of them overlooked the little kitchen garden and some trees. Miss Ingram, however, decided she preferred the third one, a small nook of a room on the other side with one window in the rear.

"It will get the northern light," she said. "That is best for reading. No glaring sun during one part of the day." She bent down to pick up her valise. The servant snatched it first, carried it into the chamber and began to unpack the books.

Davina chose her own chamber, one that had a small entry before it spread along the exterior wall. The afternoon sun did glare in, but the trees kept it from being too harsh. The bed felt soft, and the white walls made a cheery contrast to the red fabric draping the windows and bed.

She opened the windows, although the weather had cooled, and moved a chair near one so she could look out on the last growth in the garden below. She settled down to make plans for the days ahead. Memories of Brentworth's seduction tried to invade her mind. She concentrated on her mission in order to keep them at bay, as she had most of the day. This time, however, as the lowering sun made mottled patterns on the windowpanes, she found she no longer had the strength of will to succeed. She closed her eyes, crossed her arms to hold herself and succumbed to echoes of that delirium.

He could not stay here forever, on this rise of land, looking at that house and the mountains looming not far behind. Yet he did nothing to move his horse any further.

The damage was not too apparent from this angle, but charred stone could be seen on one corner. When viewed from the front instead of back here, he knew the whole west wing remained a black ruin of walls.

Fire. Screams. Horrible fear and finally devastating reality. His fault. He had never been able to argue away his culpability. Ignorance did not excuse him. He had not known because he did not want to know.

He had been so blinded by passion that he had not known what he had in her. Had not recognized that mercurial temper for what it really was. He had not wanted to, because he had been freer than he had ever been in his life. No rules, no borders, no restraint. He thought of Davina's scold last night, that he needed more passion in his life. *Once I knew passion untold. Primitive, scandalous passion, and it almost consumed all that I am.*

Down below, a rider appeared, growing larger as he galloped toward the rise. An arm waved as the horse came closer. Roberts, his steward here, reined in the horse twenty feet away. "Your Grace. I thought it might be you and so I decided I would come and see." His accent marked him as native to the area, as did his blond Celtic appearance and strength. Brentworth would recognize him anywhere, even if it had been almost ten years since their last meeting. But then, of course, Roberts knew everything. No one else did.

Roberts looked over his shoulder at the house. "It has been some time."

"A long time." He had intended it to be much longer yet, but Davina had changed those plans, hadn't she?

"On receiving your letter that you would visit, I had the good chambers prepared." He meant the ones in the part of the house that had not burned. Not the ducal chambers. Those were ash now.

"I will be staying at the inn. I came with guests, and even the good chambers would not be suitable for them. They are ladies." He added the last to make his case, even though the chambers in question would suit Davina fine, and Miss Ingram would never notice.

The truth was, he did not want to stay here. Not even one night.

"Will you come down and see how things sit, Your Grace? The servants, though few, would be honored."

Damned if he wanted to go down there, but some duties, though small, mattered to others besides himself. "We will go now and you can call them together."

Roberts smiled broadly and turned his horse. Brentworth moved his mount to a canter. Through sheer force of will, he did not see the flames reaching toward a night sky.

The coach rolled over hills and through shallow dales. Davina gazed out the window, beset with excitement. She had been here with her father once, and she was sure she recognized this road and the low cottages visible across some fields.

The road widened as they went up a low hill, then turned at the top. From her window, she saw Teyhill below. The

ancient ruins of a tower house served as a sentry to the
approach to the current building. It would be handsome,
even impressive in its stone four stories, if half of it were
not a ruin too.

A fire, they had been told by their servant girl. A huge
fire one night, one so hot it cracked stones and gutted the
entire interior of everything there. Only a heroic effort by
the servants had spared the eastern half, but even there the
smoke had ruined most of the furnishings.

She stretched her neck so she could stick her head out
the window. Up ahead, Brentworth rode his horse silently.
They'd had a row last evening, when she insisted on seeing
the house, and accused him of trying to keep her from it
because he did not want to admit it had burned and he had
simply left it that way.

There is nothing of use to you there, Davina.

Perhaps not, but she demanded to see it anyway. It was
hers, after all. Or should be. Did he really think she would
come here and not even gaze upon her ancestral home?

Steel and ice, that was what he had become when she
had pestered him on the point. He'd left dinner in the upper
apartment abruptly in his pique. Then, this morning, a
servant had brought the note that said they would leave at
ten o'clock to visit the estate.

She feasted her eyes on the building she had only seen
once before, sneaking about with her father. There was
nothing fancy about it. A big block of gray stones, it rose
high over the treeless land. There had been a garden in the
back when she last visited. She hoped that had not been
left to ruin too.

The road became a drive and curved toward the house.
She scooted to the other window so she could watch. The
fire's devastation became visible soon. No roof and black
stones and splintered, long wooden beams sticking every

which way. No one had even cleaned it out. Brentworth had left it the way it was when the last embers died.

Despite its state, her heart warmed just on viewing it. A new contentment settled in her heart. She knew then that any misgivings she might harbor about her cause were misplaced. She belonged here. She knew it in her soul.

Mr. Napier opened the door after the coach stopped. Brentworth was handing over his mount when she stepped out. He strode toward her just as a big blond man appeared outside the entrance.

"That is Mr. Roberts," Brentworth said. "He is the steward. He cares for the estate."

"From the look of things, he has not cared for it well. Half of the building is still a burned-out derelict."

"He, of course, must obey my commands about what is done."

"So the fault is yours."

He gazed at her steadily and silently.

"Why did you leave it like this, Brentworth? When I accused you of neglecting the property, I had no idea it went this far."

"I chose to. That is all you need to know. It is mine, and I chose to. Now, let us go in. I am sure you will insist on a tour, so I will be agreeable on that from the outset."

He introduced Mr. Roberts. She liked this man. Not only was he quick to smile, and so very Scottish in his form and speech, but he looked at Brentworth more man-to-man than she expected. She admired him for that. He did not defer much, and actually carried some warmth in his eyes when he gazed upon the duke. She did not think that whatever loyalty he felt was merely a servant's gratitude for a good situation.

"Miss MacCallum would like to see the house," Brentworth said.

"I am more than glad to take her around myself, Your Grace. And the cook has some refreshments prepared for later. Would Your Grace be joining us as we take a turn through the property?"

Brentworth had actually taken a few steps away when that question came. He paused. "I think I will."

After that, Roberts gave her all his attention. "There's no need to explain that we won't be going that way, Miss MacCallum." He pointed toward the ruined side. A large, heavy curtain hung at what must have been the entry to that wing. "We will start in the library, on this side."

Entering the house yesterday had been hellish. Today, Eric discovered he did not mind as much. He had ridden here beside the coach as if his body was a taut bow, and braced himself yet again when he dismounted from his horse. But actually walking inside did not affect him the same way.

He had chosen not to stay long yesterday after being greeted by the servants. He certainly had not paced through every room. He did so now, in Roberts and Davina's wake. Into the library, replete with new furnishings he had paid for but never seen before. Back to the morning room, where he had eaten many morning-after breakfasts in the early afternoon light, temporarily sated but already anticipating more. Up to the drawing room, now decorated in a somewhat medieval style that suited the structure better than the forced classicism of before.

The ease with which he experienced it all fascinated him. Had he dreaded this place too much, for too long? Were the new furnishings enough to blunt memories? Had time worked its magic and absolved him?

Their party halted near a window outside the drawing

room, while Davina took in the prospect. "I can see farms in the distance. Are those tenants?"

"They are," Roberts said. "The long, low building closer to us is a stable."

"Is there a garden down below?"

"There is, but it is quite wild now. More rustic than a proper garden, although there is a kitchen plot."

They moved on to the ballroom. Davina gawked and peered and peppered Roberts with questions. A smile animated her expression. Her eyes gleamed with excitement and avid interest. She viewed the appointments as if she owned the place. She did not miss a single vase or chair.

They paced down the gallery that flanked the ballroom along the front of the house. Eric had never bothered to learn if any of the paintings were significant. He doubted it. The barons were no Argyles in wealth or worldliness. Of course, the walls also bore the portraits of barons past. Davina pretended to examine landscapes and myths, but he saw her gaze narrow on the faces above.

Which led his own attention to those heads.

One baroness near the end of the line arrested his attention. He looked hard at the painting, then glanced at Davina, who had moved on. She had not seen what he did. A resemblance, it seemed to him. Subtle, but there in the eyes and nose. Possibly. Maybe not. You couldn't trust painters anyway. They always changed things to flatter their patrons.

"Would you like to go above to the private chambers, miss?"

"Oh, yes, absolutely. I must see everything, even the kitchens."

She saw it all, until Roberts left them in the dining room to partake of the cook's refreshments. As expected, the cook outdid all expectations and requirements.

"This is a lot of food," Davina whispered when the fifth platter was deposited in front of them. "It is early for such a meal."

"I would be grateful if you ate some. I think the cook is overcome with delight at cooking for me."

"I will partake of everything if it is all as delicious as this soup. Why would you make do with the inn's fare if you could eat like this?"

"Because I choose to stay at the inn."

Her full spoon paused on its way to her mouth. "Why? Does this house not please you more than an inn? This part of it is lovely."

He decided to do some eating himself.

"Of course, the other side . . ." She helped herself to the pheasant on one platter. "I suppose nothing is to be saved of it now, after years of rain and weathering. It will have to be rebuilt." She bit into the fowl and made an expression of appreciation before continuing. "What happened to it?"

And there was the reason he had not wanted her to come here.

"It burned."

"How?"

"A fire."

She lowered her eyelids. "Really? A fire made it burn? Who would have guessed?"

"You want the particulars?"

"I do, thank you. None of this delicious pheasant for you until you give them, too."

"One night, a fire started in the private rooms. As for exactly how the first spark occurred, I do not know." Lies, but he'd be damned if he gave the details.

"Well, such things happen. I thought perhaps it was lightning. It is a rare building that survives that if it hits directly."

"There was no storm that night." He wished he had thought of *that* lie.

"It is very bad of you not to have done something with what is left. You cannot be blamed for the fire, but you can be blamed for that."

"Do you think it devalues your supposed inheritance?"

"I think—you can have some pheasant now and really should taste it—I think it speaks poorly of you that it is a ruin, left to deteriorate. It has nothing to do with my inheritance."

"Let us not lie to each other." Bold, that, considering he just had. "You were not only admiring the house while you toured it. You were taking inventory of *my* property and belongings."

"Partly. Mostly, however, I was wondering, as I have already indicated, why you would stay at the inn when you have this house within a few miles at your disposal."

"Perhaps I thought I would have a better chance at seducing you if I were at the inn too." He said it to send this conversation away from the reason he avoided this place, but the notion had passed through his mind, often, scoundrel that he was.

That took her aback for a five count, no more. She lifted a cover to see what else the cook had made. "I'll wager this fish was caught within the last few hours." She moved a chunk of it to her plate. "If that was your plan, you could effect it just as well here. Even better is my guess. Just invite Miss Ingram and me to stay here too."

"You would like that?"

"Which? Staying here, or being seduced?"

"For now, you need only respond to the *staying here* part."

"Who wouldn't like that, except you? It is luxurious. The food is very fine, the mattresses are wonderful, I am sure, and I am guessing the linens are of top quality. Are there other servants besides the cook and this footman who brings us too many dishes?"

"Several. They are spying on us through the keyholes."

"As long as there is one woman to help Miss Ingram so I don't have to, I would say this is a marked improvement over any inn."

Could he do it? Stay here? Right now, he thought he could. While they toured the house, he could. Only he did not think anything had really changed about his feelings toward this house. All that had changed was Davina's presence, and the way that pushed old histories away for a while.

Still, she wanted to sleep in the house she thought should be hers, and be served by the servants she thought she had a right to command. He could indulge her for a few days. He could conquer his aversion that long. Perhaps it would blunt her eventual disappointment about the property.

"I will speak with Roberts. He will send for our baggage and Miss Ingram and move us all here."

Chapter Seventeen

For now, you need only respond to the staying here *part.*

He assumed they both understood and accepted that of course he would not seduce her, so he could joke about it. Little did he know she had almost blurted out that she would gladly be seduced.

She strolled through the overgrown garden while he went to give instructions to Mr. Roberts. One could still find the paths if one pushed away the bushes' tall branches. A few blooms poked through in one area, indicating there had been a flower bed there, now all but swallowed by the encroaching wilderness.

A back portal beckoned. She unlatched it and walked into a field of heather. A short distance away, on a little hill, she saw a copse. The trees looked young enough to believe someone had planted them here, forcing an unnatural canopy over what should have been pasture or fields. After walking another twenty feet toward them, she saw why. The family graveyard enjoyed this bit of nature, the headstones and small mausoleums showing through the bare branches.

She took her time walking among them, reading the names of her ancestors. She knew in her heart she was one of them, just as she had known upon entering the house that her mission was just and right. She had experienced the same contentment she knew when her father and she had returned from one of their journeys into the country. *Ah, home again*. It brought a special peace to return to where one belonged. She had not enjoyed that feeling since he died, until she entered their home in Caxledge. Today, stepping into that house, she had once more.

She read the names of those buried here. MaCallums, most of them. No Marshalls. None of Brentworth's ancestors had been laid to rest here. Perhaps if any perished here, their bodies were sent back to England.

One grave marker made her pause. Not a MacCallum. Not even a Scot, from the name. Jeannette O'Malley. Nor did the stone look very old. It showed no chips and not nearly as much weathering as the others. Not fresh either. Just more recent. A servant, most likely. She could see how one might end up here, if it were an old retainer without local family.

She turned to make her way back and saw Brentworth watching her from amid the trees. The branches sliced his form. She walked to him.

"There is no grave for the son of Michael MacCallum."

"The records show him being buried in the parish yard."

"The day is young, and I have eaten enough to last until morning. I think I will visit that parish yard." They re-entered the garden. "Is the church far from here? If you give me its direction, I will go now."

"Do you think to walk? It will be a rigorous four miles each way. Roberts has sent my coach to the inn, but I am sure there is a gig or wagon to be had. I will call for it and take you."

"I can drive a gig myself."

"We will do this together, Davina. It was your rule that

we both learn what is to be discovered, so neither of us misinforms the other."

"Are you saying I would lie to you?"

"Of course not. Just as you did not insist on coming north with me because you thought I would lie to you."

Together they went inside and waited for the gig to be prepared.

"A phaeton is hardly a gig. This is a most uncomfortable conveyance." Davina kept gripping the edges of the seat so she would not bounce around. Because when she did, she bounced closer to him, he had no incentive to slow down.

"What an impractical carriage for the country," she complained.

"I think Roberts indulged himself. It is far more fun to drive than a little gig."

He glanced over whenever the road permitted it. Her blond hair swung beside her cheek and her blue eye sparkled with her spirited good humor. Despite her objections, she was enjoying herself. The brisk breeze caused her face to flush, and he thought she looked very lovely.

It went without saying that he would take her to the parish church. Not only because he needed to hear what she heard and see what she saw, but also because he enjoyed her company. There was another reason, perhaps the most important one, however. Should she start prying into the events surrounding the fire, he wanted to distract her. He did not doubt there were rumors about that night. Some might even be true.

He would prefer she did not learn about it. Ever, and certainly not now, here, in the shadows of that ruin. No one could hear that story and think well of him. He realized her opinion of him had come to matter.

"Ah, that must be it," she said, pointing to the small stone structure up a short lane to their left.

He slowed and turned the carriage. Inside a stone fence, he stopped, stepped out, tied the horse and helped her down.

A smaller building flanked the church. An old man came out of it. He wore the clothes a farmer might, loose trousers and a linen shirt and a long frock coat many years old. He placed a low crowned hat on his white hair and approached them.

"Are you the vicar?" Davina asked.

"No vicar here. Just me. If you've come to marry, you'll have a properly ordained Church of Scotland minister not some vicar." His light blue eyes peered from a face so wrinkled it looked like crushed parchment. "Are you Brentworth?"

"Yes, he is," Davina said. "How did you know?"

The old man chortled. "Well now, that is the silly carriage from the big house, and this one is looking a lot like a lord, so I just guessed. Been a while since you've been in these parts, Your Grace."

"Yes."

The priest looked at Davina. "Man of few words."

She nodded. "We have come to look at the parish records. To see if there is any information about the barons or their families in them. The ones before . . ." She made a vague gesture toward the current owner. "The Scot ones, I mean."

"Come in, then. I'll pull out the books and you can look all you want. There's probably at least a few marriages noted and whatnot else. You can use my dinner table." He turned and walked inside with the careful, slow steps of the aged.

Brentworth followed Davina into the little cottage. Stone like the church, already it held the damp of winter.

A low fire burned in a large fireplace. The whole lower level was one big chamber, with the dinner table close to the hearth. Beams overhead made for a low ceiling, and he had to duck to avoid hitting his head.

He sat beside Davina. The priest placed two very fat, large books in front of them. From the condition of the leather binding, it was easy to see which was more recent. He opened that one and saw that *recent* meant it began in 1685. "This is the one we need."

She leaned over so they both could read the pages in the overcast light. The priest brought a candle, which helped, but she still hovered right over his arm, her face no more than five inches from his, her breast all but pressing his side. The impulse to give her soft, luminous cheek a kiss almost overcame him. Only the minister's presence stopped him. The old man kept looking at Davina.

She paged through, curious.

"We should move forward in time or this will take many hours," Eric suggested.

"I know. It is just interesting to see these names follow through over the years. I supposed if I had lived here my whole life, I would recognize them as the ancestors of my neighbors."

It no longer irritated him when she spoke as if she might have lived here her whole life because, of course, she was a descendant of the MacCallums noted on these pages. Thus did desire alter a man's opinion, he supposed.

She permitted him to find the page for 1730, at which point they examined each notation more carefully. Births, burials, marriages—all received their space, with the marriages showing the signatures of the couple, and some deaths describing causes.

"Here he is. Here is my grandfather. I am sure of it," she said, her delicate fingernail stopping on a birth notice in

1740. "James MacCallum, born to Michael and Elsbeth on 4 March. Now we know what name to look for, at least."

"Was he known as James in Northumberland?"

"He was."

"James MacCallum. It is such a common name."

"Which is why they did not have to change it."

She smelled so nice, he kept turning the pages. They did not see references to James MacCallum until the fateful year of 1745. At the top of a page, all but in the margin, came the brief notation that James MacCallum, age five, died on 17 December.

"That is odd." Davina narrowed her eyes on that line, then turned back several pages, then examined it again. "It is almost as if it were added there later."

It did look that way, at least a little. Furthermore, it had been inserted above a marriage documentation, with all those signatures and such. Usually those started new pages, in order to make sure everything fit together.

Not far after that page came the one with the last baron's death. That did receive its own page, and a bit of a flourish. *Michael MacCallum, baron, owner of Teyhill manor and lands, perished at Culloden on 16 April 1746, fighting for Scotland. Buried on the field.* A few other men's deaths followed on the next page, with similar statements.

The old man was gazing at Davina again. She did not notice when she turned to him. "We would like to visit the graveyard. I believe a relative is buried there."

"It's on the other side of the church. Goes on a way after all these years. The newer graves are over by the big tree at the far end."

They left him and walked around the church to the graveyard. No stone wall surrounded it. The big tree seemed to mark its current border. "I suppose it will be over there," he said.

"Not all the way, though." She kept her gaze on the stones while they moved down a row toward the tree. "Around here, I would think," she said, stopping.

She went in one direction and he in another. He found the grave first. He almost did not call to her, not wanting to see her disappointment. He experienced none of the triumph he should have felt.

"It is here, Davina."

She came over, her expression carefully set to hide her reaction. She looked at the stone with James MacCallum's year of birth and death.

He noticed the minister had followed them out. He stared at Davina hard, his eyes squinting and his brow furrowed. Something about her clearly arrested this old man's attention.

"If I wanted to protect a child, I would arrange for a grave lest anyone come looking," she said. "And why is it here, and not in the family yard, if he truly died before his father? I have not seen many other MacCallums buried in this plot."

A few weeks ago he would have disabused her of the twisted scheme she wove around this boy's life and death. Instead, he kept noticing how the minister watched her.

"Davina, we can argue the finer points of new identities later. Right now, I think the minister wants to speak to you. If I go, he may not hold back as he does now. I will wait at the phaeton."

He walked away, wondering if he had just handed her a sizable chunk of the estate his father had entrusted to him.

* * *

Davina walked toward the minister. "His Grace thinks you may want to talk to me."

He palmed the air as if pushing the idea aside. "Nothing to say, really. Just wondering is all, if my mind is right or not on the memory."

"What memory is that?"

"My eyes aren't what they were, so I'm probably wrong. Only it seems to me that you look like him."

"Like who?"

"Years ago, a man came to these parts. A stranger. Shared a few ales with him, and a bit of whiskey too, so I came to know him a bit. He helped the local folk for a summer, then disappeared one day."

"My father has visited this region. I even came with him once."

"Oh, it was long before your time. I wasn't much more than a lad. Just taken my orders, as I recall. It was long ago." He peered at her face. "Something about you that reminds me of him. Your smile, for sure. And this." He drew his fingers down either side of his face. Then he chuckled. "I'm just an old man with an old memory. They're stronger than the new ones these days."

She judged him to be around seventy-five. The old memories had a way of moving around in time, stretching and contracting. What was remembered as five years ago actually was twenty, and vice versa. "If he was a relative of mine, I'm glad he helped the locals however he could."

"Seemed a good man to me. I was sorry to see him go."

"I thank you for your help today. You have been very kind," she said by way of taking her leave. She walked through the yard and back to the carriage, where Brentworth lounged against its side.

"Did he want something?" he asked.

She let him help her into the seat. "He thought I looked like a stranger who was here some years ago. I think he meant my father, who visited this region a few times in the summers. I do resemble him."

He appeared relieved, which she thought odd.

"It was not an encouraging day for you," he said, settling beside her. He did not sound smug, at least. Perhaps his tone even carried a shade of sympathy.

"I was not able to place any proof in front of you, but I am no worse off than before."

"We found his grave, Davina. He did not grow to manhood in Northumberland, and father a son who then fathered you."

She tucked her wrap closer around her and fixed her gaze on the lane. "As I said, there is no proof a body is in that grave, Brentworth."

Chapter Eighteen

That evening, after dinner with the ladies, Brentworth took his port to the terrace outside the ballroom. He gazed down on the garden. It appeared even more neglected and wild in the twilight.

Its condition was inexcusable. He must have ignored requests from the steward to be allowed to deal with it. He would tell Roberts to hire a gardener. And a few more servants. He might not visit this house again, but it should not go to total ruin.

He pictured the blackened husk of a wing. It was perhaps time to see what could be done about that too. He sipped his port, marveling that his mind even permitted these considerations. A year ago, he would have found something else to think about if such notions entered his head.

It was Davina's doing, he supposed. Not only her scolds, which were well deserved. Even now, with her above in her chamber, her presence changed his outlook. Last night, he had woken from a dream in which the whole house burned down around him. No sooner had he opened his eyes than he saw her in his mind, and the remnants of the dream and its horrors disappeared.

She had a rare influence on him, one he resisted acknowledging, but that was becoming harder to do. His decision to leave her with that minister in case there might be more to learn—that had been inexplicable as anything other than one friend doing what was right for another, even if it cost them something. It was the sort of thing he might do for his closest friends, and no woman had ever been one of those.

He liked her. He admired her. He wanted her. That last impulse complicated everything. He had never wanted a woman he could not have. He never retreated from a woman he *could* have. Had Davina been a different kind of woman, if she were sophisticated and experienced and worldly in the ways the ladies he pursued always were, he would have proposed an affair by now, and not accepted the torture he experienced.

He had watched her like a green boy's first infatuation at dinner tonight, trying not to be obvious, imagining scandalous things while Miss Ingram chatted on about some lieutenant she had known decades ago. The port he held now and the crisp air would hopefully enable him to stop gritting his teeth in frustration.

"Is there a family Bible to be found here?"

He heard her voice behind him. His reaction was not that of a gentleman. The devil rose in him. His better side whispered, *Tell her to leave at once.*

To hell with that.

He turned to see her just outside the French doors. The low light made an ethereal cloud of her hair and put stars in her eyes. "My family Bible is not."

"I meant mine, and you know it."

He set his glass on the terrace bannister. "It should be in the library. Let us go see."

Brentworth had not argued with her about whose family the Bible belonged to. He had not tried to disagree it was her own. Perhaps he was growing accustomed to the idea that she should have this estate.

Down the gallery they walked, down the stairs to the entry hall. The long curtain that hid the scarred wing's access forbade their turning that way, of course. Someday she would tear that down and watch those chambers rebuilt if she had the means to pay for it. Not that she would need more space for her plans. The part of the house that remained habitable would serve her purposes well enough. She had spent hours laying it all out. Here the pharmacy, there the physician's consultation office, upstairs the beds for those too ill to send home right away. A surgery too, with a good surgeon who had studied in a hospital. She had not yet decided where that should be.

Brentworth must have said something or made a sign, because the footman who scurried toward them to be on service suddenly pivoted and retraced his steps. Together, she and the duke entered the library.

"It will be good to use this chamber," she said. "The furnishings are in want of some humanity."

"An odd thing to say."

"It all feels so new in here, is what I meant. As if no one has ever sat in the chairs." She ran her fingertips over the carving at the top of one. "It is new, isn't it? This gothic style is in favor again."

"Roberts chose it. The old furnishings carried the smell of smoke and soot. Most of the house was refurnished by him."

"You had no say?"

"I left it to him." He used that tone that said he had nothing else to say on the matter.

He went to the bookcases. "We should look for religious books. I can't think where else a Bible would be put. These are all grouped by subject, as is typical."

"It could be in a desk or case."

"If it had been, Roberts would have put it up here when they changed the furnishings." He moved slowly down the case, surveying the rows of books. "You might help. It is your family Bible, you claim."

She took position on the other end of the case and sought any religious books. After a few minutes, she found them. "Here they are."

Brentworth came over, and side by side, they read every binding, even those of books far too thin to be Bibles. She pulled out any that had no title on the spine. She found a Bible and snatched it out triumphantly, but on opening it discovered it was not the one she sought. No names had been inscribed in its front. No births or deaths or little notes about important events in the family history.

"It appears it is not here," Brentworth said while he reached high above her for the books on the final shelf. His position brought him so close to her that his side brushed against hers.

"Well, it is somewhere in this house, unless someone disposed of it."

"Are you accusing me of destroying a Bible? I suppose I did that because I foresaw that someday a vexing woman would appear claiming she should have this land, and I wanted to destroy all the evidence she might find."

It has been an insulting thing to say, as well as a fairly stupid one. "I suppose if anyone came upon it over the years they would have put it somewhere, not destroyed it as a relic of a prior owner. As you point out, it is a Bible, not a common book."

"I think that is safe to say."

"I suppose it might have been in the chapel and burned in that fire."

"I would not expect it to be left there by my family, but since it is not here, that is the unfortunate conclusion."

They strolled to one of the divans and sat down while she pondered the alternative. "Perhaps one of your ancestors packed it away with other family items and put it in the attic. I should go up and check there." She began to rise to do just that.

He caught her arm and guided her back down to her seat. "It will be easier in the day, when there is light. Any search will be hard, even dangerous, in an attic with nothing but a candle."

"I suppose it can wait." But she did not want to wait. Having lit upon this idea, she was impatient to see it through. She needed to find that Bible, to see if it noted that the last baron's young son had died. She did not think it would.

She would chat a few minutes, claim she was retiring, then get a candle and go up to see if the Bible, or anything useful, was in the attic.

He rose and went to build up the fire. The embers caught. Low flames emerged. He stood there a moment, looking at them, his back to her. Then he turned.

Her breath caught. She forgot about the attic. Only a female born yesterday would not know what he was thinking.

She should take her leave now. At once. Go up to her chamber and bar the door.

She didn't. The way he looked mesmerized her. Hot and cool, hard and soft, all at once. Deliciously dangerous and completely focused on her. A primitive excitement spun through her.

Nothing will happen. Not really. It won't even be like last time. You can enjoy the flirting for a while. Enjoy this wonderful prickling, and how your blood courses quickly. He has already sworn off you, but you can enjoy his wanting you at least.

He came to her and sat, closer. He turned toward her, his left arm along the back of the cushion, his fingers toying with the ends of her hair. "You did not tell me what the minister said."

"I told you. I reminded him of a stranger who came here one summer. My father, I think, although he said longer ago than that, so it could have been my grandfather. He is said to have left home a few times, for months. He might have come here." She was speaking quickly, the words rushing out, hoping to sound normal but knowing she didn't. That light touch on her hair made her want to purr like a cat and snuggle in for more. "Maybe he found what he needed here somewhere, something to send to the king."

"Wouldn't he have done something about that grave? Disavowed it somehow?"

She tried to puzzle that out, but she wasn't thinking clearly right now. "Perhaps. One wonders what he could do, though," she murmured, her gaze locked on his handsome, wonderful face. What woman could stand against that face and those eyes and not become a fool in this situation? A better woman than she, that was certain. She could barely sit still.

"I don't know. It is probably a question for a clear mind," he murmured back. He placed his warm palm against her face. She wanted to move her head so it became a caress. "I should ask permission before I do this, but I am not going to." He leaned in and kissed her.

He did not ravish her mouth, but she almost swooned anyway. Soft, careful kisses lured her arousal to expand in sly rivulets of pleasure.

His mouth moved to her cheek, then nuzzled at her neck. She savored every nip and breath and how her skin tingled.

"I think Miss Ingram is a terrible chaperone," she said as she experienced the first signs of control slipping from her.

"I think she is a perfect chaperone." His voice, low and quiet and close to her ear, sounded unbearably sensual.

Perfect. Distracted. Absent. Happy to read above while her charge was seduced below. Not terrible at all. Wonderful.

That itching desire entered her bliss. The pleasure started pushing urges into her mind. The long, sweet kisses were no longer enough. She waited impatiently for the caresses her body craved. They did not come. His restraint held.

She couldn't believe he was going to torture her like this. She impulsively lifted his hand from her side and placed it on her breast. His kiss paused an instant, but she sensed that an hour's debate occurred in that moment.

"As you wish, darling."

Better, then. Comforting and exciting and a wave of brief relief. He touched her breasts, finding the tips and teasing until wildness beckoned. Invasive kisses, hot now, determined and hard, bound them in heightened intimacy. Sensuality submerged her until darkness claimed her consciousness. Her essence sought more pleasure, more closeness, more everything.

She slipped her hand under his coat so she might feel him too. He looked down at what she was doing, then managed to shrug off his frock coat without missing more than two beats in their savage dance. She fumbled at the buttons on his waistcoat while he tore off his cravat.

More buttons, on his shirt, until enough skin showed for her to press her lips against the skin of his chest.

He held her to that kiss, one hand on her head while his other worked the tapes of her dress. She frantically reached behind to help. Her body wanted to burst out of that dress.

He pushed the sleeves down her arms, then plucked at the lacing to her stays, all the while claiming her mouth with his in ways that sent shiver after shiver down her core. It seemed forever before her stays loosened enough for him to push them down. Her breasts pressed against the lawn of her chemise, wanting more yet.

He looked down while he slid the chemise down her arms, exposing her. The air on her breasts excited her even more. He skimmed his fingertips around one, then the other. "You are very lovely, Davina. Beautiful."

She looked down at that fine masculine hand barely touching her but causing such anguish and anticipation. She stopped breathing.

That light touch grazed one hard nipple. She almost rose off the divan from the sensation. Then the other. She wanted more of that, of everything. He gave her more while he kissed her again. Her desire became unbearable.

She thought it could not get worse, but it did, when he lowered his head and used his mouth, flicking his tongue and gently nipping with his teeth, when he finally sucked until she cried out, when his caress lowered to her hip, then pushed her legs apart and pressed against her mound.

The dress interfered again. She hated that it kept her from what she wanted. She reached down her skirt and began lifting it. He helped, skimming it higher with long caresses, until his palm found the flesh of her thigh. Higher yet, until finally that warmth rested right near the center of her need.

He touched her there and she cried out, loud. So loud

that she heard herself. The sound shattered the dark and fevered small world they had built. It seemed to echo through the entire house.

It stopped none of her hunger, but it stopped his touch. His whole presence stilled. Afraid of what that meant and desperate to continue, she took his face in her hands and kissed him hard.

He let her, and kissed her too, but not with the passion of before. Softer again, kinder. Careful. They were the kisses you might give before the very last one.

He turned his head. She did too. She gritted her teeth. She heard him mutter a curse.

Face set into hard planes of control, he smoothed down her skirt. "I am sorry. I should not—" He lifted the chemise so she was covered. "If you will turn, I will fix the rest."

She closed her eyes, trying to contain the chaos that plagued her. She could not believe he had stopped. She raised her hand against his offer to help with her garments and shook her head. "I will do it," she whispered.

One more kiss. The final one that was coming. He stood. "I am sorry. I was not myself."

Weren't you? "You were when you started this."

"Perhaps so." She heard him move. Walk away. She heard the door open, then close.

She collected herself, but it took some time. Then she managed her stays and tapes and made herself at least passingly presentable. With each minute, she grew angrier.

Did this man, this paragon of restraint, this person carved out of stone, expect her to believe he was *not himself*? He knew exactly what he was doing. What he was starting. To then become conscience-stricken *again*, after he had her all but tearing off her clothes— It was inexcusable. Unforgivable. Churlish. Ignoble. Outrageous. It was a good thing he had left, because she wanted to give him the longest, sharpest scold he had ever received in his perfect, ducal, lordly life.

Fuming, her head close to exploding, she strode to the door, cast it open and stomped to the stairs. The footman sitting near the door snapped alert, then veered back when she stopped in front of him. "Where are Brentworth's chambers?" she demanded.

The night air barely helped. He stood in front of the open window, breathing deeply, wondering just how he had allowed that to happen.

You ass. He could not claim any defense. He had not only hoped it would happen, he had planned much more. He had spent the day in anticipation. Oh, there had been a noble attempt to separate after dinner, but when she appeared on that terrace, the rest was a tale foretold.

You scoundrel. Wanting a woman did not excuse such behavior. He had insulted her in several ways, and no apology would do. He needed to accept that although he almost always got whatever he wanted, he would not get her. Unless—

Why not? It had been a solution from the start. One the king had proposed and wanted, and one that made more sense than he had admitted. He had to marry someone. Why not a woman he wanted, and also admired?

The reasons why not tried to line up in his head. He ignored all of them except one. She might not have him. He laughed to himself, not at that notion but at the likelihood of it being true. Davina MacCallum had been one of the few people who did not seem to give a damn that he was a duke, and the Duke of Brentworth no less. She might enjoy the luxury of this house and all the others he owned, but he did not think she could be bought by any of it.

He wished they were in London. He would not mind consulting with Stratton and Langford about this. Stratton could be very practical in his advice. Realistic. As for Langford, he rarely was wrong when it came to the way women reacted and thought. He had done a close study of them over the years.

Yet both had seen this eventuality long before he had. The interest. The fascination, as Langford said. Having both married inappropriate women, they no doubt considered it just fine if he did too.

The cool air had done its work, finally. He no longer battled the urge to go back down there, find her and drag her to a bed or even use the carpet there in the library. Of course, just thinking about it had him rumbling again. He took another deep breath.

A crash sounded nearby. Another. He turned, startled. There, just inside his bedchamber, stood Davina, her arm still out from where she had thrown open the door. She raked him from head to toe with a scorching gaze.

"You conceited, self-important, arrogant, spoiled, selfish toad."

Toad?

"You despicable man." She advanced toward him. "You coward."

"I will accept toad and even despicable, but coward is going too far."

"Give me another word for what just happened. Don't say noble and gentlemanly or I may scratch your eyes out."

Both words had been on the tip of his tongue. He swallowed them. "I can understand why you are angry."

"*I can understand why you are angry.*" She imitated him rather too well, although he did not look down his nose like that, he was sure. "No, you can't understand. The first kiss was an accident of the day. The last lovemaking was an impulse. This was deliberate, and it was cruel. Do you hear me? And do not tell me you suffered too. I don't want to hear it. Men always whine about discomfort more than women, but I am telling you now that to do that to me was among the most thoughtless acts of casual cruelty. And you did it twice. *Twice*."

She was right in front of him now, belligerent and damned magnificent, nailing him in place with her gaze. "Do not think to do it again. *Ever*. Never touch me. Never kiss me. I will die as I am at this moment before I ever allow you to treat me that way again."

It would be an excellent moment to grab her and kiss her, only she really might kill him then. She looked as if she wanted to, badly. He kept watching for a blow to come.

"See here, Davina—"

"*Miss MacCallum*, if you don't mind, *Your Grace*."

"Here is the thing: I am deranged by desire for you. You are more than willing. We have a common interest in this property. It seems to me that all these problems can be solved simply by our marrying."

She did not swoon with joy the way women were supposed to when dukes proposed. Her eyes narrowed. "Now you are mocking me. As if what happened down below was not humiliating enough, you now make a joke of me."

"I am not mocking or making a joke. I am very serious. If you allow yourself to consider it, you will discover it is a clever idea."

"Are you mad?"

"At least half so."

She no longer looked crazed. Her expression softened and her brow furrowed. Her gaze drifted away from him, to nothing in particular.

"You would do this because you want me in bed and are

too cowardly—I mean, gentlemanly—to do that otherwise? That is not a good reason."

"It is a better one than that it is the right year and you are the least-boring girl on the marriage mart."

"That girl will be appropriate. Remember? That would be her best quality."

"Who is to say you won't be appropriate too? If it is found that you are descended from the last baron, you could end up a baroness in your own right."

She strolled around the edges of the chamber, thinking. "What of my claim here?"

Now they were down to it. "If proof is found, it would still be yours. If not, you would still be of the family that holds it."

"Only if we are married, you would control it. You would decide how it is used, and everything else. If I have a son, the barony of this estate would be far down in his titles. We would be absorbed."

He did not agree, even if that was the whole point. "Think of it as a compromise. As half a loaf." He could not believe he was parroting Haversham and the king. He lit on his own brilliant argument. "And if we marry, everyone will assume that of course you were right and that is why."

"I *am* right." She gave him one of her direct, piercing looks. "But you still don't think I am, do you? That is why this is too odd. If I believed you even suspected I am right, that you needed a compromise as much as I do, then there might be one small bit of logic in this proposal. Instead, I am left to conclude that you, the Duke of Brentworth, a man so soundly sane in reputation, are proposing to me because it is the only way to have what you want. Once you do, of course, the marriage will seem a horrible mistake made in a moment of inexplicable madness."

"I want you, yes. I also admire you more than I expect to admire any other woman for a long time, if ever."

"I thank you for that. It is nice if at least a modicum of affection is part of a marriage proposal. I realize that is not how your kind do it, however. Admiration is a worthy substitute, I suppose." Her aimless stroll had brought her close to him. She looked at him wistfully. "I must decline."

"You would be a duchess. I can understand your rejecting me. I am surprised you are rejecting that. Do you even know what it means?"

"I know some of it. I have seen the deference and the luxury and the standing in the world. I am told at major banquets a duchess has one of the best seats and enters before all the other peers' wives. It is a rare privilege and status you offer me. The girl you choose next season will value it properly."

That girl would probably also bore him to death. He had two choices at this moment. He could try to persuade her with pleasure, or lie and profess undying love.

She smiled. "I know what you are thinking. I am flattered you still debate how to win me over. But I will know if you lie, and I will not allow you to touch me. I meant that. Now, I must leave before you compromise yourself because of this whim."

"It is not a whim."

"It *is* a whim. A sweet one. But that is exactly what it is."

She left, then. He threw himself into a chair to accommodate that he had been rejected in a marriage proposal for the second time in his life, in the same house, by a woman who by all accounts should have fainted with delight at such good fortune.

He could be excused if he hated Scotland.

Chapter Nineteen

She walked ten steps away from the door before the fullness of their conversation exploded in her head. *She had turned down the chance to be a duchess*. If anyone learned of it, she would be labeled unbearably stupid and hopelessly mad.

Nonsense. The proposal had been insane, not her response. She repeated that all the way to her chamber, but she noticed every expensive appointment in the house on her path. It could all have been hers. And this was not even one of his *good* houses.

Oh, how rational she had sounded. How selfless. As if he would be the first man to make a foolish match due to sexual desire. Somehow—and she had absolutely no idea how—a duke had come to want her enough to actually marry her to get her, and she had *turned him down*. Even she began to doubt her sanity.

Who was she to lecture him on his duty to find an appropriate wife? Or the way passion passes? On anything to do with men and women? His experience exceeded hers. Vastly, because she possessed almost no experience at all.

Of course that had not been at the heart of her reaction. She had not been thinking about his choice at all. Only her own. *How will this change my rights to this land?* Not her use of the land, as duchess. Her right to it. He'd known the answer, hadn't he? He'd thought all that out. It was one of the problems the marriage would solve, along with his inexplicable desire.

She found some contentment in remembering that part of their conversation. She concentrated on it, which was far better than thinking about the priceless Chinese vase set at the end of the corridor near her chamber, almost as an afterthought, as if it were not worthy enough to be downstairs in the library or drawing room with the truly precious items.

The whole episode distracted her enough that she was in the middle of her chamber before she realized someone else was there too. Miss Ingram sat in the chair set beside the fireplace, holding a book open, high and angled to the light of a candelabra she had set on the small table she had pulled over.

"Were you confused and found yourself in the wrong chamber, Miss Ingram?"

Miss Ingram peered at her book another few moments, then closed it and set it on her lap. She turned her attention on Davina. "I do not become confused about where I am. I know people think I have gone soft in my head, even my dear nephew, but I don't miss much, Miss MacCallum."

"That is good to know."

"No indeed. I don't miss much at all." She raised one eyebrow. "Were you just with him?"

"We had a conversation, yes."

"A chat, was it? How nice. I assumed by now he would have engaged in more than that."

If the woman claimed she was not dotty, Davina was not going to play childish games. "If you thought that, you have been negligent as a chaperone in leaving us alone so much."

"I told Cornelius to send someone else if he wanted you watched like a schoolgirl. His wife was there and dared to scold me about how the duke had nefarious plans for you so I had to be alert and aware. What nonsense." She struggled to her feet. "I wish a duke had insulted me with nefarious plans forty years ago. I would be sitting pretty now, instead of depending on Cornelius. He is generous, Miss MacCallum, but even from a nephew it is charity."

"Miss Ingram, are you saying you have deliberately been negligent in order to allow Brentworth to seduce me?"

"You do not sound nearly shocked enough."

"As you implied, I am not a schoolgirl."

"It was not the seduction I did not want to interfere with, although I assume that would have to be a first step. My thinking was that he might make a proposal to you. Not a proper one. The other kind that such men make to women they cannot marry." She began walking to the door, but paused. "Has he?"

"Made an improper proposal? No."

She sighed. "That is too bad. I really thought he might. I rather counted on your not coming back here tonight."

Davina stepped back and opened the door. "You know, Miss Ingram, you do become a little confused sometimes."

"Not when it matters, Miss MacCallum. Not when it matters."

Davina seemed to be avoiding him. By the time he went down for breakfast, she had already eaten. He shared the table with Miss Ingram who, for some reason, chose not to read but instead looked at him long and hard while she drank tea and ate toasted bread. Perhaps she was trying to remember who he was.

"Do you know where Miss MacCallum is?" he asked when he had finished. "She is not in the library or the garden."

"She said something about an attic. You should go and tell her to come down from there. It is probably dangerous."

"It could become too warm on a sunny day, but there are windows she can open. She is looking for something, and I should let her see if she can find it."

"If she is looking for something, you should help her. It is your house."

"She doesn't think so," he muttered.

"As host, you really should help her. What is the world coming to if a duke does not know how to treat a house-guest?"

What was the world coming to when a chaperone pushed a man to be alone with her young lady? "She would not want my help, I am very sure. She would not trust it."

He excused himself and took his leave. He trailed through the house to Roberts's office and found him at his desk, working accounts. "Do you want to see them?" Roberts gestured to the ledger and papers in front of him.

"I suppose I should every five years or so." He accepted the big ledger and scanned the pages, looking for signs of bad management or worse. His father had taught him how to do this, like so much else. *Five out of ten servants on the lesser properties will steal from you if you are not careful*, he had lectured.

"Your Grace, I am bound to ask, as I do every few years, whether you would consider having that ruin taken down. Not rebuilding, mind you. Just taking down the burned-out husk that is left. It is a scar on the land and clearly a recent destruction, not some ancient and charming old pile like the old tower house."

He met Roberts's gaze. The few other times Roberts had broached this subject had not gone well, and he could see his steward braced himself for loud, harsh expressions of displeasure.

"It may be time." Past time.

Roberts's expression brightened.

"I think I will go see just how bad it is. I will let you know my decision before I leave."

"You are going into it?" Roberts spoke with studied evenness.

"I think so."

"Would you like me to—"

"No, I will do it on my own."

Roberts played with a letter opener on his desk, studying it while he rolled it in his fingers. "I go in fairly often. I need to, in order to drive out the animals that have taken residence." He looked up. "There are no ghosts there, from what I can tell."

"I never thought there might be." No ghosts to confront there. Only his own stupidity. He handed over the ledger. "These appear in order, as I knew they would be. I appreciate your service to me, Roberts. The offer for you to come to the house in Kent still stands, should you ever want that. I could use you there."

Roberts flushed. "You must think it odd I don't take the opportunity. But—" He looked around, as if he could see beyond the four walls. "I like it here. Scotland is home. This house is home. Your father raised me up, from dog boy to this, step by step, and I've been here since I was ten. Besides, when you are not in residence, I am something of the laird, ain't I?"

"I expect you are." He laughed. "I will be leaving soon, so you can be laird again."

He left the office and walked back to the front of the house. In the reception hall, he sat in a chair and looked at the heavy drape blocking entry to the burned wing. Then he stood and went over and slipped behind it. Sunlight glared down on him from between a few charred roof timbers high above.

No attic here anymore. No roof to speak of. In the good attic behind him, Davina searched for her past. He did not have to search at all. He knew exactly where his was. Right here, in this empty fortress of blackened stone in which a wilderness grew.

Davina sat on the plank floor in the middle of the trunks. She had opened all of them, looking for that Bible. She had peered under the rough fabric guarding furniture and tried every drawer she could find. The Bible was not here.

She discovered other family items besides furnishings. Clothing, a doll, an old musket, even a broach of some value. One trunk held some letters from over a hundred years before, their ink oxidized to a light brown but the parchment still supple. One of the barons wrote them to his son. They mostly contained instructions on behavior and comportment. In one, a scold had been given about a special friend, and a warning to avoid an entanglement. She suspected that friend had been an inappropriate woman.

She stood and looked around once more, hoping to spy one more place to search. She had enjoyed handling a few relics of her ancestors, but that was not her reason for being here. She could not ignore that there had been no remnants of the current owner's life, nor of Brentworth's past. Not one of those dukes had cared about this land or spent much time here. They had stewards and factors like Mr. Roberts manage the estate and send them their rents.

Giving up, she made her way down the stairs. Perhaps it had been left in the chapel that burned, as Brentworth had concluded. She preferred to believe a retainer had taken the Bible for safekeeping, much as her grandfather was sent away for that purpose. If so, she doubted she would ever find it again.

The day looked fair, as so few did now, what with winter on its way. She decided to take a turn on the lane and road and enjoy the sun. She stopped in her chamber to don a bonnet and choose a pelisse, then walked down to the reception hall.

As she always did when she passed this way, she glanced at the tall drape that hid the damaged part of the house. She noticed its edge had moved so a gap showed. Although as thick as a carpet, she doubted that drape completely kept out the cold in January. This hall would be unpleasant then, even with its huge fireplace. Today, that gap allowed in a noticeable draft.

She went over to fix the edge. Curious, she peered through the gap first. To her surprise, she saw Brentworth standing within the ruins. He did not move. He did not seem to be looking at anything at all. He just stood there, arms folded, his gaze on the rubble at his feet.

He did not want to name the distasteful emotion filling him. It was not a sentiment that men acknowledged, and he was no better than the rest. Yet it pressed on him and demanded recognition.

Shame. After all the nightmares, after years of regret

and self-recrimination, that was not what he had expected to feel if he stepped inside these walls.

I was young and blind. It was not an excuse. He was the heir to one of the highest titles in England and *should not* have been blind. God knew he had been trained to use more astuteness than he had shown, and to never betray his duty the way he planned.

Mostly, however, he should have suspected that a mercurial temperament might thrive because of something darker. The excitement of freedom and passion had obscured his vision. He had lost control, lost *himself,* and reveled in doing so. He ignored any suspicions that inched into his mind and any warnings given by others. It had been enthralling. Heady. He'd behaved like a man let out of prison after twenty years.

Fire. Screams. He could smell it now, the stink while the flames consumed cloth, wood and eventually all within the stone walls. The scent still lingered on the remnants of the building. Even ten years of rain and snow, of nature reclaiming the floor tiles and fallen roof beams, could not clean the place of that odor. The bishops would like that. They would approve of the whole story. First sin, then punishment, but never total forgiveness.

Only he had not been the one to pay, had he?

The stones at his feet came into focus. He became aware of his surroundings again. He knew why. He was not alone anymore.

He did not look toward her presence, but he felt her there. *Go away, woman.*

"I told you not to come in here, that it was dangerous," he said.

"You are in here. It can't be too dangerous; there aren't even many stones or beams left to fall."

He sighed at her relentless rationality.

"What happened?" She asked as would a tourist wondering how Pompeii was buried.

"It burned." He looked at her in time to see her narrowing her eyes. They had trod this path before. "I was here."

She gazed up at the sky. "In this wing?"

"It was night and I was in my chamber. The family apartments were in this wing then."

"It is a wonder you survived."

I almost didn't. "Roberts gets the credit for that. He was heroic that night. The fire spread so damned fast. Up to the servants' quarters, down to the dining room. He roused me, and we did what we could, but we knew it was hopeless. Then it was just about getting people out." He was lying to her in a way. Leaving out the hard parts. It would be like her to know there were omissions.

"Did you get them all out?"

Ah, she did not miss anything. "All except one. I blame myself."

"You cannot be blamed. Fires happen. They are unpredictable and can level a city."

"It started in my apartment, Davina."

"You can't be sure of that. You said Roberts roused you, so you were sleeping."

He let that stand, coward that he was.

"I am glad you survived unscathed," she said softly.

"Mostly unscathed. I suffered some burns. The worst was on the back of my left leg. The scarring is unsightly, but I never see it. I should have warned you about that when I was proposing yesterday. I would have eventually, so you could change your mind if it mattered."

That was not how he normally informed his women, but he did warn them, right after he came to an arrangement and gifted them with expensive jewelry. *By the by, I must tell you that I have a disfiguring scar on the back of my leg. As with our affair, I expect unerring discretion about it. You are never to speak of it with anyone. You are never to ask me about it. If you do, I will ensure that you are never again received by anyone who matters.* It was not that he wanted to keep that scar a secret. His best friends were aware of it. He just did not want anyone prying into how it had happened.

"It would have made no difference to me," she said. "I have seen terrible scars. More damaging than anything you have, I am willing to wager, because you walk normally. I know what fire can do to human flesh. There are far worse scars to have than yours."

He did not doubt she meant it when she said it would not have mattered. In that moment, he regretted deeply that she had refused his offer. Such a woman deserved to be a duchess.

"Why did you come in here after all these years?" she asked.

"I am thinking of pulling it down." He looked around. "Either I do it now, or nature does it over the next half century."

"I think you should. I really do. Not to improve the view of the house, or even to rebuild. I think you have blamed yourself all this time, and this has become a monument to that blame. Take it down, I say. Remove it and remove the guilt."

"I will still have the scar."

"You said you never see it. Only your lovers do. If one recoils because of it, you will know what you have in her."

She turned to go back into the house. He fell into step with her. "You are being a little harsh, Davina. Not all women have medical experience and take scars in stride. I have been told it is very unsightly to females."

"I am sure you have seen it, using a looking glass. Did you find it unsightly?"

"Fairly so."

She pushed through the drape. "So, you are not perfect, Brentworth. Did you think being unflawed was part of your birthright?"

Davina took her walk alone. Brentworth occupied her thoughts the whole way.

He had looked so lost in himself out there. He had never appeared less ducal than in that ruin. She had wanted to gather him into her arms to comfort him, even without knowing what he pondered.

She had recognized his inclination to snarl at her when he saw her. Instead, he had told her about that fire.

Not everything, she was sure. She did not need everything, however. She did not even need to know what he had shared with her. He had honored her with that confidence. She did not think he told many people about that night.

No wonder he had not visited this house in all these years. She had been quick to think the worst, to assume he neglected his Scottish property because it did not signify much to him. Instead, he avoided it because it signified too much.

She had wanted to kiss him over and over and express how she understood. Her own words had kept her from doing so. *You will not touch me.* Spoken in anger and pride, they prevented her from releasing the emotion she had felt.

She wished he were not a gentleman. She wished she were not an innocent. What a stupid word to have branded on one's body. Untouchable Innocent. Unruined Innocent. She supposed it wasn't as bad as Virgin Spinster, but it was all of a piece in terms of how he treated her.

She did not regret refusing his marriage offer. That would be a mistake, she was sure. There had to be something binding two people besides signatures and pleasure. Nor did she think marriage would bring any recognition of her rights to this property. More likely no one would bother ever learning the truth if they wed.

She thought about Mr. Hume, whom she had not considered in days. He would be horrified if she married Brentworth. The lands should have a Scottish laird, in his view. She rather thought so too, but of all the reasons to refuse the proposal, that one had not entered her mind at all.

Back in her chamber, she called for her dinner to be brought to her there. She did not want to dine with Brentworth. She was not sure why. No, that was a lie; she knew exactly why. Being with him would make her sad and wistful. She would behave normally and chat, but the whole time she would be aching for him to kiss and caress her even though she had warned him off in no uncertain terms.

She picked at her food. She thought some more. She pictured him in the ruins. She felt his touch.

She made a decision.

Chapter Twenty

He sent away the footman who tried to serve as valet as soon as he washed his upper body. He could not bear how the young man shook in his presence, but he would not have wanted him around even if the youth were a citadel of stability.

Once alone, he removed his trousers to finish washing. When he moved the cloth on his leg, his hand felt the puckered skin even if he could not see it. He barely thought about it anymore, but every day there was this reminder. His own valet had nursed him through it all, and presumably was accustomed to it too. When he traveled, however, the servants he might use almost always paused long and hard upon seeing it.

Finished, he threw on his banyan and called the young man in to take away the water and towels. Finally alone, he left the dressing room.

A figure rose up next to the fireplace, startling him.

Davina. How long had she been sitting in that chair, watching the embers?

Enough light found her to show her hair tucked behind her ears and the determination in her eyes. Also that she wore a nightdress and a simple shawl. Perhaps she intended another row.

She walked toward him. Her luminous skin and bright eyes entranced him.

His body knew why she had come before his mind did. The hunger he had barely conquered these last weeks grabbed his essence and shredded his control in a blink. There would be no row tonight unless he insulted her again.

She stopped a mere arm span away.

"You should—" he began.

"I should what?"

You should leave at once.

"Don't tell me to leave. It took all my courage to come here."

His idiotic decency made a last stand. "Are you sure you know what this means to you? To your future?"

She nodded.

"Then you should remove that wrap and dress so I can see all of you."

She smiled shyly, but she let the shawl drop to the floor. She fussed with the buttons and ribbons on the nightdress.

He took the step to her. "I will help." So many buttons. Impatience battled the charm he felt at how she let him work at them, as if she truly needed help.

The fabric parted down her front inch by inch. She watched, then looked up at him. With more bravery than he expected, she stepped back and allowed the dress to fall off her shoulders and down her arms. It pooled at her feet. She made no effort to cover herself with her hands or arms. She displayed no embarrassment.

"Now you," she said with an impish smile. "Fair is fair."

"You are supposed to be shy and nervous, not demand I disrobe."

"You forget how many naked men I have seen."

He hadn't forgotten as such. He had never even thought about it. Of course, when she had accompanied her father, some of the sick had been men.

He cast off the banyan. She gave him a good look. Head to toe. He half-expected her to command he turn so she could examine him from the side.

Enough of this. He pulled her into his arms.

He held her there, with her body against his, skin to skin, while desire pounded through him like a hammer in his blood. He found one thread of sense remaining, and tied his mind to it. For all her courage, she was inexperienced. This could not be a ravishment. He would restrain his impulses.

Secure that he had found the control to hold true to that little vow, he turned up her head and kissed her. With the first touch of her lips, all hell let loose inside him.

A whirlwind. That was what he had dragged her into. Immediately and thoroughly. She could not have kept her balance even if she wanted to.

She had not known what to expect, but she had not anticipated this all-encompassing force surrounding her. Entering her. Urging her to find her own wind and fly on it. His kisses started carefully enough, but soon had a savage edge. His caresses did not touch so much as claim. His size dominated her, but so did his spirit and the madness he demanded she share.

She had no strength against it, so she accepted and submitted to her own ferocious impulses. She held and grabbed too. She bit and lunged and licked and tasted. When he held her close with both his hands squeezing her bottom and pressing her against his arousal, she did the same to his hard muscles.

He lifted her in his arms and carried her to his bed and dropped her there. Then he was on her, kissing and caressing and arousing her with his hands and mouth, with the warmth and hardness of his body, with all of him, she was sure, all of what was left of him at this moment.

He did not forget her pleasure. Not at all. As he took his own he brought her with him, higher and higher until that torture started and grew and she cried from it. He responded by touching her mound. Then deeper. She felt his hand caress her there and whimpered from the need it created. He made it worse until she groaned. She clung to him, and it seemed as if they entered the eye of a storm, with him becalmed and her totally focused on what he did and how she felt, and on the pulses and demands in her body. Only within that relative peace her pleasure grew and grew until with one deliberate touch it split apart, leaving her screaming.

He shifted. Moved. His shoulders rose and his arm braced the headboard. *This may hurt, darling.* He pressed inside her.

She knew about the hurt, about the tear. She did not know about the rest, and in her state she had no defenses against it. The power. The giving and taking. The saturating closeness. She did not care about the pain when it came because it meant an essential joining and a completion that her body and soul craved.

The rest awed her. His strength hovered above her, his chest near her face and his weight still braced behind her while he moved. He showed her how to wrap her legs around his hips so she rose up to his thrusts. She could tell he held back so as not to hurt her more. She did not care when his restraint finally broke because it increased all the other sensations and the sweet ache of knowing him this way. She would have accepted anything if it meant she could exist in this small world that contained only the two of them, sharing this incredible intimacy.

He fell to her side, spent and mindless, deep in the echoes of release. He let them course through him while he drifted in a satisfaction far more than physical.

Her body beneath his arm did not move. She did not speak. Her deep breaths eventually slowed. He rose up on his arm and pulled up the bedclothes so that now, with the heat gone, she was not chilled.

Her hand smoothed up his arm. He turned to see her smiling in a dreamy way. Her eyes still had the glistening, sensual lights he had seen while he took her.

He did not ask if he had hurt her. He knew he had.

He lay on his back and pulled her close so she lined his side and her head found a spot on his shoulder.

"This is nice," she murmured.

It *was* nice. Peaceful. Different. He could not ignore how different.

She turned into him and kissed his chest. While she did, her hand slid down his side and under his thigh. Her palm laid flat against the worst of the scar.

"Is this why you do for yourself when you travel? So strange servants won't see it?"

"It is not the seeing. It is the questions."

"Do servants question dukes? Bold of them."

"It is in their eyes. And, once they leave, in the ears of friends and other servants."

She nodded. "It would be annoying to have people wondering, talking. It is no one else's right to know how it happened and why."

It was the why, of course, that mattered. That he avoided speaking about. He noticed how she removed her hand, but not abruptly or out of revulsion. She had checked the scar and now was done.

She yawned. "I should go or I'll be found here in the morning."

"You can stay. I will bring you back before the household wakes."

Already she drifted. "Don't forget."

He wouldn't forget. He let her fall asleep. That was different too. He did not sleep with women. He visited, he shared pleasure, he left. He enjoyed her warmth beside him, however. Nice, as she said.

A few hours later, he put on his banyan, bundled her in the sheet and carried her back to her bedchamber. He would have let her stay till morning and the servants be damned, but he did not trust himself having her there. Already he ached to have her again, even knowing she was sore. He took her back, before he forgot he was a gentleman.

She woke slowly, accommodating in fits and starts to how differently she felt. Echoes of last night still affected her senses. Her body pulsed, as if it held him still. Even when she opened her eyes, she experienced the world as if through a thin gauze net. She saw that he had been good to his word and she was back in her own chamber.

Eventually, she realized she was not alone. She turned her head to see Brentworth sitting on a chair, watching her. He wore that long banyan and had not shaved yet. Seeing her alert, he came over and sat on the bed.

"Are we going to do that again?" she asked.

"Perhaps tonight, if you want. Right now, you need to rise and dress. Wear your best garments."

"Are we visiting someone?"

"Only the minister, but it is customary to look our best when we marry."

It took a moment for his meaning to penetrate. "I did not agree to marry you."

"Indeed you did, last night."

She searched her sated, foggy mind. Had she, in the throes of passion, actually said that? "I don't remember it."

"Davina, twice I left you because, as a gentleman, I could not, should not, take you. Do not pretend that you did not understand that if I ever did, I would be obligated to marry you. You came to me last night fully aware of what it would mean. I even found enough sense to ask you outright if you understood. Now, wash and dress and we will seek out the old man." He stood. "That is one good thing about Scotland. No bans, no license, nothing much except the exchange of vows."

"But I did not accept your proposal."

"Yes, darling, you did. You made your decision when you seduced me last night." He bent and kissed her, then left.

She stared at the door after it closed. She should probably be angry, or astonished. At least a bit of indignation was in order. Instead, the first thought that entered her still-dreamy mind was that she might have that amazing experience again. Or even a better one, now that the first time had been dealt with.

She rose and padded into her dressing room and began washing. When she saw remnants of blood on her thighs, she smiled. Memories invaded her mind so much that the washcloth on her skin became a sensual stimulation.

She might get with child. She might already have done so. The notion provoked neither fear nor panic, the way it should with an unmarried woman. She had seen them, those girls trying to hide the bulge, worrying that their families would cast them out. More than once, her father had played the role of mediator with girls and their families, because such things couldn't be hidden forever.

She would like to have a child. She had never expected to, but the idea warmed her. She could raise a child on her own, she was sure. No, wait, she would not have to. Brentworth said they would marry today. If she had a boy, he would someday be a duke. And she would be a duchess.

Did she want that? She wanted *him*, that was all she knew. Wanted that intimacy and the rare knowing that comes with it. The safety and comfort within his embrace had seduced her as surely as the pleasure. Of course she wanted more of that. Only a fool would not.

And the rest? She knew this required clearer thought than she had mustered, but she did not care. Still half-drunk from the heady experiences of last night, in a stupor of contentment, she dressed and went below.

He waited there. He had done for himself faster than she had. To her surprise, Miss Ingram also waited in the coach, and Mr. Roberts paced his horse around the drive.

"Witnesses," Brentworth said. He handed her into the coach. "Even Scotland requires them."

She settled in next to Miss Ingram. That lady gave her one long look of sly approval, then turned her attention to the view out the window. "Well done, Miss MacCallum. Well done indeed."

Brentworth rode with them. Davina had a hard time not staring at him. Was he real? Had she woken for certain or did she still dream? A thick disappointment formed at that idea, one that reassured her that if this was real, she did not mind at all.

At the church, Mr. Roberts dismounted and went in search of the minister. He came out of the house and waved them in just as the old man emerged and headed to the church.

Davina did not walk into the church beside Brentworth. She floated. Everything still felt different. The whole world seemed soft to her, like an invisible cloud cushioning her mind. A very comfortable cloud that made her happy and subdued.

Only while she took the final steps before the vows, did she think about the consequences of this match. The ones other than wealth, luxury and pleasure.

"Will you still help me to learn if the last baron was my ancestor?"

"Either way, we will learn the truth if we can."

She walked a few more paces. "If we learn that he was, will you interfere with my starting a pharmacy and infirmary here?"

"If your plans are sound, I don't see why I would. We will bring in physicians so you do not put yourself in harm's way, though."

Three more steps. They were almost there. The old minister smiled indulgently at her.

"Will I have to pretend I never cared for the sick, and saw things no proper lady should see?"

He stopped walking, turned to her and took her hands. "I do not expect you to be other than you are, Davina, or to play some role that is not in your nature so that society is appeased. The Duchess of Brentworth does not conform to the world. The world conforms to her."

He smiled and handed her forward, and they stood side by side. They spoke the vows that would change her life forever.

Chapter Twenty-One

The next morning, after another astonishing night, Davina woke up not the least dazed. In fact, she felt very much herself. While she had relished every moment in that stupor, she did not mind its passing. A woman could hardly live every day like that.

The changes in her life became apparent as soon as she went down to breakfast. Miss Ingram drank tea in the morning room. She set down her cup when Davina entered. "I would be honored if you joined me, Your Grace."

Davina almost giggled. Miss Ingram gestured for the footman standing idly near the door. "Her Grace prefers coffee, but I would like more tea. What do you want to eat, Your Grace? I am sure the cook will make anything you prefer."

Davina went to the sideboard. "I will help myself from what is here."

"The eggs are a bit runny. Perhaps you will have the housekeeper speak to the cook about that. I can't abide runny eggs."

Davina caught the footman's eyes after he served them beverages, and let him know he could leave.

"Now he is gone, so you do not have to *Your Grace* me every five words," she said while she filled a plate.

"And why wouldn't I? I don't sit to breakfast with a duchess every day, do I, Your Grace?" Miss Ingram cackled with delight. "Oh, how pleased my brother will be. He thought he saw something between the two of you, but did not dare to hope it might lead to this. I expect that wife of his to thank me excessively for being such a perfect chaperone." She gave Davina a big wink.

"About that, Miss Ingram. Rather suddenly, I no longer need a chaperone, even a conveniently negligent one. You are welcome to stay, of course, and return to Edinburgh with us. However, you no longer need to make yourself scarce in the hopes the duke will be naughty if you are not present."

"I would prefer to leave now, if that can be arranged. This house is too big for my liking. It is easy to become lost in it. I enjoyed this journey, however. I had a wonderful time abetting this match."

"I will see if you can be brought back to Edinburgh. It may be in a hired carriage. I think all that is here besides our coach is a phaeton."

"I would love to go in a phaeton. What fun that would be."

"It is hardly suitable for a long journey, or comfortable for a woman of mature years."

"Oh, tosh. Well, if you won't indulge me with the phaeton, any carriage will do."

Brentworth entered then. He greeted Miss Ingram, then went to the sideboard. Miss Ingram made a display of taking her leave. "I will leave the two of you alone," she whispered to Davina before slipping away.

Brentworth sat with his food and looked around for the footman.

"I sent him away," Davina said. "I wanted to speak with Miss Ingram alone. If you are looking for coffee, it is right there. I will get it." She hopped up, fetched the silver pot and poured. "She would like to go home."

"I don't know why. One chamber with good light is as good as another. However, if that is her choice, I will have Roberts arrange it." He reached over and took her hand in his. "I am going to be with Roberts much of the day. I need to ride the estate and see the farms."

The lord intended to survey his property. Only it really was *her* property. "I would like to see the farms too."

"I will teach you to ride, and you can join me another time."

"I can keep myself busy in other ways, I suppose. Perhaps I will start a new essay for *Parnassus*. I am thinking that women should know more about pleasure, and how to achieve it in their marriages."

He cocked half a smile. "You are joking, of course."

"Not entirely. Such an essay or book is long overdue. Why should women have their sexual natures subject to whether a man is enlightened or ignorant?"

He still smiled, as if she were not serious. "The journal will never publish it."

"I think they would. I will not be too explicit in my language, but I will make sure it is clear what I am explaining. I daresay it will improve many marriages throughout the realm."

"The bookshops will not sell it. There will be religious reformers breaking their windows and burning them down if they do."

"Then perhaps I should write it for men, not women. No

one breaks windows over men learning about pleasure." She leaned toward him. "Perhaps I will dedicate it to you."

"Maybe first you can think about this house, and what needs to be done here to change it to your liking. Also, Roberts said the housekeeper expects you to sit down with her and explain how you want the household managed."

"I will sit with her if that is expected, but I have nothing to say."

"Just give her one or two things to change, so she knows you are taking on your role."

"I'll tell her that the eggs are too runny. Will that do?"

He looked down at the remains of his breakfast. "They are somewhat, aren't they? See, you do have things you want changed."

He finished his meal, then gave her a long and rather arousing kiss. "I will be back in several hours," he said as he left. "I want to write to Haversham this afternoon to reassure him that our war is over."

Haversham? He intended to inform the king's man before he told his own friends, it seemed. Only it was not Haversham who would benefit from this sudden marriage. It had been most convenient for the king he served, however.

Quite convenient for the duke, too, if she wanted to face facts squarely, which, despite the mysteries unfolding at night, she could not help doing in daylight. Oh, he would help her learn the truth about her family, and he would see that the lands were returned to her, but it would not cost him anything at all. He would still ride *his* estate and collect *his* rents and rebuild *his* manor house. A parliamentary action returning these lands to the baron's descendants would change nothing for him now. Indeed, it would signify so little that she would not be surprised if such a bill were introduced and passed even if no more proof were found.

She let herself out into the library. She knew even less about decorating than she did about running a large household. It seemed eggs and drapes, however, were duchess duties.

Chapter Twenty-Two

She did not know how to ride, but she could walk the estate. The next day she did just that. While Brentworth and Roberts sequestered themselves in the library with ledgers and paper, she donned her half boots, tied on a bonnet, wrapped a shawl around her shoulders and carried her father's bag out of the house.

She had indeed sat with the housekeeper, Mrs. Ross, yesterday afternoon. Not to give lists of commands, but to learn something about the people here. First, she encouraged talk about the servants, because that sounded like something a new lady of the manor would want to know. Then, as Mrs. Ross became more comfortable and loquacious, she asked about the tenants.

Thus had she learned about Mrs. Drummond. "Dying she is, poor dear. Belly large with something. Stopped eating, I'm told, and in terrible pain. Her man has been staying by her side and his fields were not harvested, so no telling what will become of them."

Her spirit lightened as she trod up hills and down dales. Not because of Mrs. Drummond. She knew the sad news she might find there. Rather, it had been too long since she had put her knowledge to good use. She had helped a few poor people in the city, but mostly there she tutored. Education was a noble calling in itself, but her heart would always be in medicine. Even carrying her father's bag, heavy though it was with his bottles and instruments, gave her satisfaction. She had brought it for a reason, and this was it.

The land was beautiful in its wind-torn way. Few trees broke the view of the heather-strewn land swelling up and down all around her. She passed a few farmhouses and thought they appeared in decent condition. At least Roberts had not neglected them, even if his master had.

The Drummonds lived almost a two-hour walk away, but she barely noticed the time pass. Eventually, she found the farm she thought might be theirs and presented herself at the door.

A gaunt, graying man of middle years opened the door. He looked tired and worried and already in mourning. He looked her over from head to toe. "Who might you be?"

"I am the Duchess of Brentworth."

He almost laughed. He looked past her. "Where is your carriage?"

"I walked." She held up her bag. "I have come to see your wife. I hear she is very ill."

"Nothing to help her."

"Perhaps not, but let us see if we can't make her more comfortable at least. Will you invite me in?"

He stood aside. "I heard he'd just married. The duke that is. My friend John was by with some food from his wife, and she'd heard from her sister who lives near the church, who'd heard that he—you—just showed up two mornings ago and asked to be wed." He kept examining her, as if he expected something else. Something more.

"Where is your wife?"

"Back there."

"I will see her alone, if you don't mind. While I do, I want you to sleep. Even if it is only for an hour, it will do you much good."

Mr. Drummond did not argue. He let her go into that back chamber alone. As soon as she opened the chamber door, she knew that her long walk had probably been in vain.

"I think we've an excellent and practical plan, Your Grace." Roberts smiled in a self-congratulatory way. "Should be a fine new wing in a couple of years. There's plenty of men in these parts who will be glad for the work too. Not masons proper, but with good supervision they should be able to do some of it."

"Use the locals whenever possible." He looked over the black stones one last time. He might have never taken on the rebuilding if not for Davina. He probably never would have come back here. Or stayed here. He certainly would never have married here. Now this property represented more in his life than it ever had before. This wing stood now for nothing more than a ruin that a negligent owner had not dealt with for a decade.

"We can probably get the walls down before spring, and start new foundations once the ground thaws." Roberts spoke thoughtfully, working out the battle strategy, eyeing those burned walls like an enemy he would vanquish. "Need proper masons for those. Men around here will be busy with their sheep and crops then anyway."

"I will leave it all to you. As for the new wing, I will seek out an architect to plan it."

"It will be needing a chapel. Not right to have no chapel here anymore."

"I promise not to forget that chapel, Roberts."

He left the steward to muse about the future and to plan his attack. He wandered through the grounds to the garden, to see if Davina was there. He wanted to tell her of the day's results and see her expression when he shared his plans.

He checked the morning room, then the library. Davina was not in either, but Miss Ingram had taken a spot in the latter.

"Your Grace," she greeted. "Mr. Roberts told me he has arranged for a carriage to take me home tomorrow morning. I am very grateful."

"You are welcome to stay if you wish."

"I miss my own bed, and my cats. Mischief doesn't do well when I am gone."

He smiled down on her. "Be honest, Miss Ingram. You named your cats as you did in order to poke at society, didn't you?"

"I am far too old and confused to know how to do that, Your Grace. My days of poking society are long over."

"I think you should get one more cat and name him Gabriel. Everyone will think you reference the angel and feel better about the other two. However, you will really be naming him after a friend of mine, who has been known as a devil for most of his life."

"He sounds like someone I would like to meet."

"If your brother comes to London, join him and I will make the introduction. You are always welcome as our guest, Miss Ingram. Had you been even a middling chaperone, I don't think this marriage would have taken place."

She pretended to find that a confusing statement, but a bit of the devil entered her eyes.

"I am looking for Davina," he said. "Do you know where she is?"

"She went out some time ago. She was dressed for a

walk. I heard her asking the footman at the door for the directions to a farm." She paused. "She was bringing them something. She carried a bag."

"A sack?"

"A small valise of sorts. It was similar to what some physicians have when they visit."

Her father's bag. He barely got his gratitude out before he was out of the library, bearing down on the footman sitting in the reception hall. The lad saw him coming and shot to his feet.

"Do you know where the duchess went?"

The boy swallowed so hard it was visible in his neck. "She asked where the Drummond farm was. I think she went there."

Drummond. The name pricked his memory. Roberts had said something about Drummond. Suddenly, he remembered. The tenant's harvest had not been brought in because his wife was deathly ill.

A sick foreboding spread. "Where is this farm?"

"West, Your Grace. About three miles. One of the last farms with tenants."

"When did the duchess leave?"

"I did not note the time, Your Grace. I would say at least two hours ago."

Two hours. She would have arrived at the farm in that time, even walking, even carrying that bag.

He had told her she should not put herself in harm's way with her medicine. For several days after she tended to her friend, he had watched for signs that she was showing the same malady. To do that every time she walked out with that bag would be maddening. To perhaps lose her because—

She should leave it to the physicians. The real ones.

He strode out of the house and around toward the stable.

* * *

Davina sat on a bench outside the cottage. She did not have to remain here, of course. Mr. Drummond might need her, however. One never knew with these things.

She noted the clouds gathering in the northern sky. The sun still showed at times. She judged she had been gone over three hours. It would be raining on her walk back if she stayed much longer. She would have to start out soon.

She pictured her father sitting next to her, as he had the first time she held this vigil. She had not understood at the time why they stayed. He had much more experience, and knew the human heart better than she ever would. Only later had she realized the importance of that day, and what had happened, and how he had permitted it. There had been a few other times when they sat together outside a house, or in a sitting room.

Mr. Drummond knew she was out here. He had not come to ask why. She hoped he did not think she dallied as a criticism, or out of suspicion. She had said she would wait so he could let her know if the tincture had helped at all.

A muffled sound disturbed her thoughts. It became louder each moment. She turned her head to see a horse galloping down the closest swell in the land.

She stood and waited for the rider to reach her. He stopped and swung off the horse and strode toward her. "Perhaps I should have been clearer, Davina. I do not want you doing this. You put yourself in danger and I won't have it."

"I am in no danger here today."

"Roberts said this woman was deathly ill."

"She is. She has no disease of contagion, at least as far as is known. She has a cancer in her stomach."

He exhaled in relief, then realized how ignoble that was. "Forgive me. I was picturing you with someone who might make you sick too, and—"

"I did not know what it was when I came. The next time, it may be someone who has the kind of illness you fear."

"There will be no next time."

She heard the door of the farmhouse open behind her. "We can talk about this later, can't we? Mr. Drummond deserves that much from me. I can do little else."

Mr. Drummond took a few steps, then rubbed his eyes with one hand. "She is gone."

"Were you able to get her to swallow some of the tincture?"

He nodded, head down so low his chin beat his chest.

"Then at least she was not in pain at the end."

"Not in pain. That stopped for a spell. She even smiled. But then—"

"Be glad she is in a better place, and do not allow yourself to feel guilty if you feel some relief."

"The tincture. I may have—I'm not sure I didn't—"

"I am sure you did fine. Could I have the bottle back, please? I don't have much of it."

"Won't be needing it now." He returned to the house, then came out and handed her the bottle. "I should do what I can to lay her out, then walk to John's and let them know."

"Why don't you just go to them? I am sure his wife will come here and do what is needed."

He nodded dully, and started off.

Davina bent down and put the bottle in her bag.

"What is that?" Brentworth asked.

"Tincture of opium. She was in great pain for a very long time. Months, probably."

"Was it wise to give it to him? It can be dangerous."

"It can be bought in any apothecary. If there were one nearby he would have had it on a shelf in his home, and his wife might not have suffered so much. I was very clear on the small dose to give to keep it safe." She noticed that Mr. Drummond had left the farm door open. She walked over and shut it securely.

When she walked back, Brentworth was looking at the figure of the farmer, now tiny in the distance. He turned his attention on her. "What have you done here, Davina?"

"I did what my father would have done. What Dr. Chalmers would have done, and Sir Cornelius, and physicians since ancient times. I did no harm, and tried to help a woman die without too much pain."

He looked at Mr. Drummond again. "Do you think he—"

"Perhaps it was a coincidence. Or an accident on the dose. Or what you are suspecting. I do not know him well enough to guess." *I do not know how brave he is.*

She looked at the dark clouds, now thick on the horizon. "It looks to rain soon. I should start back."

"You will ride with me. I won't risk you out on these hills in a storm." He picked up her bag and bound it to his saddle on the side. Then he lifted her on, to sit sideways, before swinging up behind her.

"I don't like this, Davina. I don't want you going out to tend to ill farmers."

I forbid it. She waited for that to come next. It didn't, but she could hear him thinking it.

This was why women were not allowed to study medicine, or most things really. Not only because of the indelicate nature of the profession. All that risk, to their health, their bodies, their sensibilities, even their minds. *I will not risk you. I cannot risk you.* What a small life she would have if she lived without any risk.

She rested her head against his chest, welcoming the embrace his arms made while he held the reins. "You said you did not expect me to be other than I am. Well, this is who I am, Brentworth."

Chapter Twenty-Three

They filled the nights with warmth and erotic explorations that left Eric more contented than he had ever been. In the dark and the firelight, they were of one mind, one body and close to one soul.

During the days, however, a row was brewing. Twice in the next week, Davina openly defied him. She carried her bag out of the house after hearing about some sick farmer. The second time, he sent a footman after her in the phaeton. "Wait for her and bring her home when she is done," he instructed. "However, if upon arriving you learn that this person has a malady that can be passed to others, I want you to drag her out of there. No one will upbraid you if you must lay hands on her to do so."

Neither one had such an illness. The first, she told him later, had fallen off a wagon and down a steep ditch and suffered dizziness. Rest would probably be enough for him. The second, he learned to some discomfort, had been a child accidentally burned when some fuel fell from the hearth.

"What did you do for him?" he asked that night after some playful passion drenched with his relief.

"Wet compresses to ease the pain and heat, mostly. His

mother made a bath with some herbs and plants to soak the arm. Sometimes the old ways are more enlightened than a physician's medicine, and that may have helped."

"Will he scar?"

She turned on her side and looked at him. "Not badly. He is young, and as he grows the skin may well improve. The young are not fully formed yet, and that can make a difference." She gave him a little jab with her finger. "You did not have to send that boy after me."

"His name is Rufus. He would be insulted to be called a boy. He will take you whenever you go out from now on."

"I will not let him interfere, so do not tell him to."

"I wouldn't think of doing so."

But Rufus had his orders to interfere most seriously if necessary. Eventually, if this continued, he would have to. They wouldn't all be burns and falls. The farmers and local people now knew the new duchess was a healer, so more calls would come too.

It was time to return to London. There were plenty of physicians there, so Davina would not be needed. She could settle into being a duchess. Nor did he think there was anything more to be learned here regarding Davina's claims.

She stretched out on her stomach beside him. He had built up the fire and nothing covered her body. He admired the lovely curve formed by her back as it dipped down before rising along the swell of her bottom.

"I saw that part of one of the walls was down," she said. "Did that happen today?"

"It did. They are removing the stone much as it was put up, but in reverse. Roberts has wasted no time. Finally given leave to tear it down, he found some men and built a scaffold and set to it." Eric had watched the first stones fall from a hill where he went riding.

"Will you move the family apartments back there if you rebuild?"

He had not told her about his initial plans because he was not sure he wanted to encourage her medical interests. He no longer was sure how he wanted to use the wing. "I don't know yet. I have to choose an architect and speak with him and plan its chambers. I did promise Roberts there would be another chapel built, however."

"I hope you don't move the apartments. I am fond of these chambers. I would not want to leave the memories behind and stay elsewhere when we visit."

The sentiment charmed him. He did not think he would want to move the apartments either, now that he thought about it.

He rose and smoothed his hand down that curve. He pressed kisses along the same line. She closed her eyes and smiled, luxuriating in the sensation. She giggled when he kissed the nape of her neck, and started to turn into his embrace.

"No. Stay there." He kissed, then licked at the dimples at the small of her back and caressed her bottom more firmly. Her hips flexed gently in time with the pulse of her growing arousal. He slid his finger along the cleft until he touched her deeply between her thighs.

Her lips parted and she breathed sweet moans. She parted her legs, and he caressed more fully. Hard now, impatient, his mind darkened to everything except the howling urges, he swung up behind her.

She needed no help, no instruction. Her primitive essence knew what to do. Her bottom rose to him as she lifted on her knees. Gripping the sheets, hugging the mattress, she offered herself.

He resisted the impulse to take her at once, even though every fiber of his body called for it. Instead, he savored the additional torture of waiting while her erotic position tantalized and teased. He stroked her and her breath caught. He kept caressing her swollen flesh, with this hand, with his cock, until each breath she gave carried a begging cry.

Finally, he joined in a deliciously slow thrust that sent exquisite pleasure throbbing through him. He pressed her legs together to make it tighter yet and stroked in again, harder. He felt her reaching toward her orgasm and shed the ties that still bound him to his mind. He held her hips and, in a long, hard taking, drove them both over the brink of sanity.

Cold woke her before dawn. The fire had died and she lay uncovered and naked. She began to reach for the cloths when she saw she was not alone.

He had stayed. Normally, he left while she slept or even before, when he had come to her. Now he lay sprawled where he had dropped after that last lesson. Arms crossed above his head, face half-buried in a pillow, he almost filled her bed with his strong, muscular form.

She dallied in pulling up the covers. She moved so the dim light from the embers and one low lamp showed his body. She bent down to examine that scar.

He had been lucky. The back of his knee had been spared. Above and below it, however, the skin showed long streaks of the waxy, hard texture common to bad burns.

It could be worse. She did not find it unsightly, but many others would. Like most things, experience changed one's view.

She tugged at the covers and pulled them up. She made sure he was warm and snuggled in close beside him. She looked at his face, or what could be seen of it.

They would return to London soon. Her mission had been compromised by this marriage, but she did not dwell on that now. She wondered instead if the joy she experienced with him would continue. There was no other word for the emotions she experienced. Definitely at night, where their deepest intimacy took place, but even during the day, when she shared a meal with him.

That was not true. There was another word. One she dared not use because then she would have too much to lose, and to mourn, if it passed. And yet, in this darkest hour, she could not deny that her feelings had deepened so much that now, as she watched him sleep, she almost wept from how they moved her.

He stirred. His eyes barely opened. He turned. With one arm he gathered her up and brought her close to him, then fell asleep again.

Chapter Twenty-Four

The young woman's name was Bridget, and she was well along in her pregnancy. Word had come asking Davina to visit, because there had been some bleeding and Bridget feared for the baby.

"Your first?" she asked while she gently pressed her fingertips on Bridget's belly.

"It is. We are very happy to be blessed."

"Have you been pregnant before?"

"I said it was my first. Oh, you mean and lost it. No."

Davina kept chatting, all the while pressing. She could feel the baby. Finally, she also felt a definite kick.

"Oh!" Bridget cried out, then laughed. "He must not like you doing that."

"It was a good kick, wasn't it?" She sat back. "Who is the midwife?"

"Mrs. Malcolm. She goes to all the ones who need help. She's far enough that she may not make it here. My family is half a mile, though, and we have set up a big bell to ring if we need my mother."

"I want you to ring it even if you do not think you need her. I am confident all is well with the child and that the small amount of bleeding is not a worry. It would be best, however, if you have another woman with you."

Bridget struggled to her feet. "I feel better with you saying that. About it not being a worry. You must have some beer before you go, and I've a biscuit for you too."

Davina accepted the refreshments even though she was not hungry or especially thirsty. Bridget smiled broadly after putting both down on the table and watching Davina partake.

"Who would think I'd be having a duchess eat my baking? I had no idea duchesses were as nice as you are."

"The ones I know are very nice."

Bridget sat at the table. "I hear they are taking down that burned-out shell. Is it true? Was it your doing?"

"It was not my doing, but it is true."

"Terrible thing, that fire. I was a girl then. All the talk it was. And for that poor woman to die in it." She shook her head. "They say she was lovely. Beautiful. So sad."

The biscuit suddenly tasted dry in her mouth. Davina drank some ale. "I did not know it was a woman."

Bridget nodded. "A visitor. She and the duke—of course, he wasn't the duke then, but the marquess of something— had been there a fortnight, then suddenly that fire. You could see it for miles. Not the flames, but the whole sky over that way was bright with red and orange. It looked like hell had opened, my mother said. Those who came out of it said it felt like hell too." She reached for her tin and placed another biscuit in front of Davina. "It is so good to hear what remains is finally being removed. Like a scar on the land, it is."

Davina made heroic efforts with the second biscuit, but a thick sadness filled her from her ribs to her throat. When she could do so graciously, she took her leave and climbed into the phaeton beside Rufus. She said not a word all the way back. Her mind raced in circles, seeking a way out of the implications of what Bridget had told her.

She and the duke had been there a fortnight. A woman had died, but not any woman. Not a servant, as she had assumed. A lovely woman. A beautiful one.

No wonder he hated that house and that property. His lover had died there.

Davina was nowhere to be found. Eric had seen her return from today's mission of mercy, but after that, she disappeared. He finally looked in the garden, although the day's sharp wind hardly encouraged time there.

The overgrowth of shrubbery and intrusion of grasses meant most of it could not be viewed from the terrace. He plunged in, peering for her among the branches. Spying her blond crown, he changed directions.

He did not find Davina, but instead Roberts. Arms folded and brow furrowed, the steward eyed the wilderness swallowing the space like an invading army.

"Unsightly. A gardener could do wonders with it in a few seasons, though," he said.

It was in terrible condition, Eric had to admit. More negligence on his part. He had starved the house of funds, as if hoping it would waste away and disappear. "You should hire a gardener, then. Add it to the accounts."

Roberts looked around. "It is big. Two would be better. If you will be visiting regularly, you'll want a nice garden."

"What makes you think I will be visiting regularly?"

Roberts shrugged. "The duchess is a Scot by blood and heart. She's grown partial to the people in these parts too. I think it's her idea to come here frequently."

"Did she tell you that?"

"Not in so many words. She just stopped to chat when

she saw me. Told me to do something to make this garden usable. In future years there would be many visitors, she said. I suppose she meant parties and such."

She meant the visitors to her pharmacy and the inmates of her infirmary. "Where did she go after she spoke with you?"

"Toward the back." He jabbed his thumb over his shoulder.

Eric headed that way. He still did not find her, but he noticed a back portal stood ajar. He stepped through and the wilderness fell away.

No one had planted trees and shrubs on this side of the wall, so it was just grass intermingled with a few wildflowers still valiantly sending out blooms. A rough fence cordoned off a large section where the few horses at the house grazed. To the right, up a little hill, was the old graveyard amid a few trees.

He spied a sliver of blue and gold among the stones there and aimed for it. He found Davina, arms folded, eyeing the markers much as Roberts had been examining the wilderness.

He realized which grave arrested her attention.

She noticed him. Her gaze returned to the grave. He walked to her.

"Jeannette O'Malley," she read. "An unusual name."

"I don't think Jeannette was her true given name. I suspect she adopted it when she went on stage because it sounded French."

"An actress or a singer?"

"An actress."

"Not appropriate, then."

"Not in the least."

"I am very sorry she died and left you with so much

grief and guilt. I should have guessed there was a good reason you never came here and ignored this place."

She did not understand. Neither did he, not all of it. He never spoke of this, never thought about it if he could help it, but right now—He did not want her making new assumptions to replace her old ones. Yet to explain might destroy the joy he had known the last few days.

"Did you love her?" The question came on a small whisper of a voice.

"I was enthralled, even enslaved, but it was not a mature love. It was mostly carnal."

"Sexual."

He had to smile at her directness. "Yes. She was wild." How to explain to a respectable woman? "There were no rules. None. And I had lived with so many, for so long, that the freedom to be wild as well intoxicated me. Like a drunk, I lost sight of myself, my duties, my past and my future. I slipped out of my harness and broke through the paddock and galloped hard."

She smiled, which gave him heart. "No wonder you never lost control again if the time you did ended so badly." She looked out on the land surrounding them. "Why did you bring her here? So no one would know?"

Now they were down to it. Stupid of the king or himself to think this smart woman could ever be bought off with half a loaf. He could lie. Omit most of it. But she'd know eventually. Perhaps she already had figured it out.

"The affair was a secret, that is true. But we came here because I intended to marry her."

Davina had not expected to hear that. She was wrong when she thought she could take these revelations in stride. It had been a mistake, perhaps, to demand them.

He did not call it love, but he wanted to marry her. Not an arranged, appropriate marriage. Not one of convenience and obligation, such as he made with her. He had not taken this Jeannette's innocence and marched to the altar due to the gentleman's code of honor.

"Ah yes," she said. "The one thing Scotland is good for. No banns, no waiting, nothing much."

His hand moved just enough to touch hers, then hold it. "My father learned of the affair. I had told no one, but she had been indiscreet. He commanded me to break with her. I pretended to, but I didn't. I kept her in London for almost a year. I think he suspected that she— She was very changeable in her moods. Very extreme. When happy, she was delirious. When sad, melancholic and despondent. When angry, enraged."

She wondered how extreme she was when sexual. *No rules*, he had said. Small wonder a young man found her enthralling.

"I should have seen those moods and wondered about those extremes. Instead, I just made sure that when she was with me, she was happy."

"You should have told me that you married her. That one thing I had a right to know."

"You have a right to know all of it."

Perhaps, but she rather wished she didn't know anything. Of course there had been women—many women, most likely—but this one sounded very special. Special enough to marry, even though she was inappropriate in every way, even though his father forbade it. It had been years ago and she should not care, but she did.

"If I am not quick to share the story, it is because the whole of it reflects badly on me. One thing you definitely must know, however. We did not marry. It did not get that far. The fire interfered."

She looked at him, surprised by this turn in his story. In his eyes, as he stared down at that stone, she saw anger and grief and regret all mixed together.

"How tragic to have lost her just then," she said.

His hand holding hers gripped tighter. His jaw tightened like a vise. "Ah, Davina, you are too good. It is not what you think. She started that fire. That she tried to kill me might be excused as an act of passionate fury, but many others came dreadfully close to perishing as well. All because I refused to see what I had in her."

A weight lifted as soon as he said it. Spoke of it. Even with Roberts, who had been there and almost died too, he had never once done that. As so often happened with Davina, he found peace in her presence.

She did not ask any questions. She did not tell him that he was not to blame. Thank God for that. He couldn't have born the cheap sympathy of that reassurance.

He no longer wanted to stand in front of this grave. He led Davina out of the yard, down the hill and through the portal. They found the path Roberts's boots had made and followed it.

"You have not asked why she did it. How it happened," he said.

"Perhaps you will tell me one day, when you want to."

He wanted to tell her now. The start had been hard, but now the rest demanded to be heard.

"I told her my plan after we arrived here. Before we left, we would marry. She was happy. Delirious with joy. The night of the fire, however, she asked if my family would attend. I could not believe she did not understand. I am sure I had explained it all. I did again, however. They would not attend. They would not know. No one would until my father passed away. She said that insulted her, that to have such a marriage and keep it a secret was not fitting for her. She said I must write to my father and inform him before we left Scotland. I refused. He was already showing the signs of the illness that eventually killed him, and I would not burden him with this. We had a row. She was distraught, furious, despondent. Violent."

"You also did not want to tell your father for your own reasons, I think."

"I only realized that during the argument. Later, as I lay in bed, I admitted I should not marry a woman I could not claim publicly. It was not love but something baser that held me. My mind stepped to one side and saw how I was behaving. It was just then, as I slapped myself out of the madness, that I smelled the smoke. It came from my dressing room."

"There was no way it could have been an accident?"

"There were no candles. The hearth was cold. It turned out it was just one of several fires she had started." He looked above the plantings. He could just make out the wall of the ruin, and a man up there chipping at mortar and stone. "The one on the main stairway—the smoke overcame her there. I found her as I was leaving. I dragged her out, but she was gone."

The story exhausted him. He might have run ten miles.

He could not tell what Davina thought of the sorry tale. She appeared thoughtful, though neither shocked nor critical.

"I am told she was beautiful."

"I suppose. I never see her in my memories that way. I see her during that argument, and there was nothing beautiful then."

They had reached the house. "Thank you for telling me," she said. "It is better to know than to wonder."

* * *

She reached her chamber before the emotions she held in check burst from her. She paced out the agitation they created, tried to find rational reasons not to feel so empty and alone.

It was a horrible story. A dreadful one. She felt sorry for Brentworth. Sorry for that poor woman. Angry that medical knowledge of the human mind had not progressed much since ancient times. She must have been deranged to start those fires. Who but an insane person would do such a thing? She had been too lost to consider how she would get out herself. But then, perhaps she did not intend to get out.

No rules. She could guess what that meant. She was not ignorant of the more exotic sexual tastes some indulged in. What had occurred in their marriage bed was child's play in comparison. She tried to imagine what it was like to be a young man who pursues and catches a woman who has no rules. He would have been in his early twenties. She could believe he became enslaved to that passion. She pictured him throwing over all those duties and lessons and expectations that had bound him all his life and would tie him forever. She could believe the freedom had been its own kind of madness.

He did not call it love. Not now. He probably did then. She would take him at his word, though. Jeannette had not been the great love of his life. Fine. She would hold on to that. She had, however, been the great passion of his life. He knew he would never experience anything like it again. He would never allow himself to. Not with his mistresses. Not with his lovers. Not with the woman he married out of obligation and convenience.

That night at dinner they did not talk about it. She

doubted they ever would again. Both of them overdid the small talk and joking, as if each wanted to prove all was the same. Only it wasn't for her. That empty spot would not go away.

As the meal ended, he became more serious. "I think we should return to London. Tomorrow next, if you agree."

"Perhaps. I would like to sleep on it, and think whether there is anything more for me to do here."

"Our departure can be delayed a day or so if you prefer."

She only nodded. Her mission here, her great quest, had not even entered her mind today. She needed to remember why she had come, and what still could be accomplished.

She had the girl in that night to prepare her for bed. She hoped Brentworth would not visit. She wanted to be alone. She needed to accommodate all this, think about why that spot in her heart simply would not fill.

He did not visit. She did not sleep. Nor did her thoughts dwell on her legacy and her grandfather and all the other reasons she was here. Instead, Brentworth filled them. She even came to understand that odd sensation in her chest, that hollow weight, that void.

She had hoped—like a girl, she had thought that maybe— She laughed at herself, but it hurt to do so. She felt a little better, however.

She stopped dwelling on herself and turned to the man himself. He had risked much in telling her what he had today. It was not something she thought a man like him admitted to easily, or at all. She did not think his friends, the other dukes, knew of it. If they saw that scar and he said, *That? I was careless and got burned*, they might just accept it and not press for particulars. Men were like that.

Yet today, he had put it into words. Did it become more real when he did? Were the memories sharper? Saying the words, admitting the truth, was much harder than thinking about a transgression or guilt. There was a reason the Catholics insisted that confession be verbal.

Perhaps he did not sleep either. Maybe he lay awake too, also accommodating the revelations. He might be in his bed right now, reliving those weeks and that night.

She rose and slid on her dressing gown. She took a candle and eased into the corridor and walked to his chambers. She entered as silently as possible and went to his bed.

"Eric, are you awake too?" she whispered.

He sat up.

She set down the candle and blew it out. He threw the covers aside and she climbed in. He drew the covers up around them both.

She nestled beside him and closed her eyes. Already it felt better. "I thought that if we were not alone, each of us, it might be easier to sleep."

His arm slid around her and he pulled her closer. He kissed her temple. "Much easier."

Chapter Twenty-Five

Eric became impatient to return to town. This journey had produced far more than he expected, most of it good. His life was in London, however, and with November the bite of winter could be felt in Scotland's winds.

At least he no longer had to worry that some farmer would tell Davina about the fire, and about Jeannette. One had, and he did not regret it in hindsight. Speaking of it, finally, had freed him from much of the memory. He wondered if Davina would say it had all been a good thing, though. She seemed different in subtle ways. She was still full of bright lights, but one of them had dimmed.

"When you said there were no rules, what did you mean exactly?" She asked the question abruptly, interrupting his lesson on driving the phaeton. She had asked to learn and they set out in the morning to start. It was not the best kind of carriage for a woman to learn on, but she had insisted that she saw women in the parks holding the reins of such conveyances, and assumed she could manage it too.

He did not need to ask what she referred to. He supposed if she had said, *I had a sexual liaison with a handsome man, and we were wild and had no rules*, he might query her about it too. Though as a man, he might not have to because he could imagine the particulars. He doubted she could.

Which meant it was time to be vague. Or avoid the subject entirely.

"Move the carriage forward very slowly. Do not become distracted," he instructed.

"I won't. I can listen to you and do this as well, so feel free to answer my question. Unless it would embarrass you."

"Embarrass? Not at all. It might with another woman, one who had not explained to me despite her utter lack of experience that women could have orgasms."

"So, what did you mean?"

"You are pulling left too much."

She corrected that, then gave him a meaningful glace.

He sighed. No way out. "In these matters, some things are typical and done by everyone."

"Such as what we do."

"To be honest, not everything we do is typical."

"So you have lured me into more exotic love play. I think I know what may not be typical. Go on."

"Then there are even less typical things. The human mind has been very creative over the millennia and a long list of pleasures has been amassed." It almost sounded like a normal conversation. "Think of it as circles going out from a center. Typical is in the center. Things become increasingly less typical the farther away from the center."

"Not all the same, you mean. Some not typical is still not too exotic. Out at circle seven, it is shocking."

"Something like that."

She decided to try turning the carriage, even without his permission. She managed it fairly well so he could not interrupt the odd conversation with a scold. "Go a little faster, but stop well before you get to the paddock fence," he tried instead.

"Did you use whips on each other?"

She stunned him. "Whips? Where did you hear about that?"

"My father and I visited a woman who was always ill. Only she really wasn't. When my father said as much, she asked him to lie about it. It seemed her husband used a whip on her, for his own pleasure."

"Your father allowed you to hear such things?"

"It just came out, and I was there when it did."

"That was bad of her husband. If the pleasure is not mutual, it should not be done."

She reined in the horse and turned her head to look at him. "I would not like being whipped, but if you enjoyed it, I think I could whip you and derive some pleasure from it, so it would be mutual."

How had she pulled him into this astonishing conversation?

"Did you enjoy it?" she asked.

Now she assumed— He felt his face heating. Damnation, he never blushed. *Never.* She peered at him.

"It is not a pleasure I seek out," he said noncommittally.

"I see," she said. "You probably also had a third person with you on occasion. I will say now that while I am willing to try a bit of wildness with you, I will not countenance that."

"That goes without saying."

"It seems to me that on this topic nothing goes without saying because you were enthralled with having no rules. It is not the wildness of it that repels me, if that is what you think. After due consideration, I concluded it is adultery. A most peculiar form of adultery, but adultery just the same."

She had thought about this. Perhaps for the last two days she had been working her imagination for hours, trying to figure out what *no rules* meant. Which left him to wonder where in those circles fell the things that did *not* repel her after due consideration, and just what those activities had been.

"Have you decided when you will be ready to return to London?" he asked, as much to learn her answer as to change the subject.

"Two days hence, I think. I have something I have to do first. I had an idea last night, and now I need to see it through." ·

"Another visit to a farm?"

"I need not even leave the house, as it happens. I am going to turn this carriage around. I am very comfortable with the reins now."

"Just do it slowly. You are hardly an expert. I said *slowly*!" He gripped his seat while she continued her tight, fast swing. Then, with a wide-open pasture before her, she snapped the reins and they flew.

Davina tapped on the door. Mr. Roberts opened it with an exasperated expression. He saw her and immediately looked friendlier. "Your Grace. I thought it was the house-keeper. She has been peppering me with questions all day."

He stood aside and invited her into his office. Davina saw that the small space gave off to a bedchamber before Mr. Roberts closed that door.

He invited her to sit. She perched herself while she took in the wooden desk, the simple carpet, the nice prospect from the long windows and the shelves of books and ledgers.

"I have come for your expertise." She gestured to the ledgers. "Some of those appear very old. I expect none of them are ever thrown away."

"This office has been used for generations for the same

purpose, and some of those have been there since before I was born, I expect."

"So the fire did not take them. How fortunate. Tell me, do those contain the names of servants and retainers?"

"I doubt it. Those fees are recorded as one sum. Each servant is not listed." He opened the ledger on his desk, flipped back some pages, then turned the book toward her. "See, like this."

That dimmed her brilliant idea. "I had hoped you had records of servants from decades past."

He didn't ask why, but she could see his curiosity. "Other than occasional notes about some problem—such as a footman caught stealing silver or a cook starting a fire—we don't." He thrummed his fingers on his desk. "We do have names regarding pensions. The ones who serve here a long time are given one when they leave service. An annual sum, to keep them in their older years."

"That might be good enough. I would like the names of your oldest pensioners, and where they live."

"Only the living ones?"

"I think so, to start." It would be better to learn anything directly, but if she failed to discover something, perhaps she would see if any of those old servants had told stories to their families.

It did not take long for Mr. Roberts to make the short list. "Here it is. The oldest one is at the top of the list. He's been getting a pension as long as I have been working here, it seems to me."

She folded the list. "Thank you. I should tell you that I will be taking the phaeton out tomorrow, very early."

"I will tell Rufus to be prepared."

"I won't be needing him. I learned to drive it myself today. Brentworth taught me." She took her leave, but stopped at the door. "Speaking of the duke, there is no need to bother him with a report on my visiting you, Mr. Roberts."

"I understand, Your Grace. And I have received instructions to hire gardeners to fight that wilderness out there. I thought you'd like to know."

She took her list to her chamber, to do some calculations. The news about the garden pleased her. She supposed she should be content that the duke was taking an interest in this house at least, even if she would never be the great passion in his life. That had not been part of their arrangement, had it?

Davina woke with the dawn, dressed and went below for breakfast. None had been prepared yet, so she wandered to the kitchen and obtained some bread and cheese from the sleepy cook. Then she put on her pelisse and her bonnet and went in search of a groom.

She did not hide what she was doing from Brentworth. She merely neglected to tell him about it. To his mind, the problem regarding their conflicting claims on the property had been solved by saying those vows. He would find it unnecessary, perhaps even annoying to hear she planned to ride all over the countryside, seeking more proof when she no longer needed it.

But she did need it. He thought this was about her wanting to enrich herself. While no one would mind having a birthright of many acres of land, she also wanted to know if her family had lived here and belonged here. She wanted to know if those old portraits were her ancestors. She wanted to trace her father's lineage, no matter where it took her. She ached to know who her people were.

She climbed into the phaeton when the groom brought

it out. He handed over the reins. "You said you know how to manage this? It is not your typical carriage."

"His Grace taught me and said I had become quite good at it. I will not go fast."

He shook his head, then shrugged.

She got the horse going and jostled along. The carriage seemed very light without Brentworth beside her. She took it to a slow trot and followed the drive to the lane. When they rounded the corner of the house, a dark figure waited for her, hands on hips. She just barely managed not to trample him.

"That is a bad place to stand," she scolded. "I did not see you until I was upon you."

"It is an excellent position to grab the horse's bridle." His hand closed on it as he spoke. "Where is Rufus?"

"I did not need him. Nor do I need you. I am not going to tend to anyone sick."

His lids lowered. "Then where are you going?"

"For a ride. To try my new skill with reins and whip on the lane and road."

He strode around the horse and got in beside her. "I will go too, in case you find you are not expert enough to get home. Do not under any circumstances use the whip. The horse will bolt, and you have no experience in controlling him then."

He crossed his arms again. His expression fell into one of magnanimous tolerance. Her lord and master would indulge her but was not pleased.

What a bother he was. Even her father had not been this intrusive, and since his death, no one at all had told her what to do.

"Don't you intend to go for that ride?" he asked when they had not moved for several minutes.

"I am not sure I want to anymore." She let the reins go

slack. "Did Roberts tell you? He depends on you for his situation, so if he did, I can't blame him too much."

"Tell me what? Are you and he plotting together? Only about gardens, I trust. If he has shown any other interest, that would be unfortunate. He is one of the men I would prefer not to kill."

She laughed at that. He didn't.

She handed him the reins to hold and dug into her reticule. "This is a list of retainers of this house who are now pensioned. This man at the top is the oldest. I intend to speak with him."

She saw his response in his eyes. *There is no need. The question has been resolved. Made moot. Been dealt with.*

"Where does he live?" he said instead.

"Harrow Ridge."

He sighed. He climbed down and came around to her side. "Move over. That is at least seven miles from here. I will get us there faster than I dare let you do it. You can practice on the way back if there is time."

He moved the horse to a fast trot.

"You were joking, of course, about killing a man who showed an inappropriate interest in me."

"Not at all."

"That is hardly necessary. If anything actually happened, you could divorce me, then pick a new wife during the next season to replace me. Your reaction would not be rational."

"My dear Davina, you are irreplaceable, especially by one of those children lined up on the marriage mart. The mere thought of losing you turns my mind black. If it were due to another man, there is no telling what I would do."

The little speech stunned her, especially coming here and now. It was the first time he had ever said she mattered to him. He found her acceptable, yes. He enjoyed pleasure with her, it appeared. He had indicated that their conversations did not bore him. But as for truly mattering to the point where he feared losing her— Perhaps even his not wanting to risk her to illness not only derived from his sense of obligation and responsibility, but also because he did not want to lose her?

She had nothing to say that would not sound as if she begged for more declarations of her value. Much as she would like that, she just leaned over and kissed his cheek.

"I think you should stay away when I talk to him," Davina said while he handed the reins to a groom outside a coaching inn in Harrow Ridge.

"You are forgetting our reason for both making this journey north. We hear and see what is learned together." He helped her down.

"Then please let me ask the questions. Your presence alone puts them off, and your pointed questions help not at all."

"You are just vexed that you could not sneak off alone."

"I thought you would try to stop me. That you would say it didn't matter anymore."

He probably would have said that, or something similar. Damned if he would admit it, however. If she was determined to turn over every rock in Scotland looking for her proof, she would manage to do it no matter what he said.

It was already afternoon. They entered the inn and had a light meal in the public room. When they finished, he asked the proprietor where to find Mr. Rutherford's house.

"He lives down the back lane. A woman there lets out some of her chambers. But you won't find him there. He's right out back, working with the horses."

He returned to Davina and told her that Mr. Rutherford was at most a hundred feet away.

"He works with the horses here? He must be seventy years old. Eighty perhaps."

"Some men don't like gardening." He looked down at her feet, glad to see she had worn her half boots. "Watch where you step if we are going into the stable yard."

They circled the building and found the stable and the large yard and paddock next to it. Carriages of all sizes and kinds jammed the yard. Boys and men led horses to and fro.

"That may be him," Davina said. "He looks very old."

The man she pointed to had a skittish horse in tow, a bay stallion. The old man wore no coat or hat, and his white hair blew around his face. Although barely half as high as the horse's head, he held the bridle firmly, pulled the horse's head down and looked to kiss its eye. The horse snorted twice, but stopped stomping at the ground.

Davina marched over to him. "Sir, are you Mr. Rutherford?"

The fellow ignored her while he kept his face close to the horse's. One could almost see the horse calm in stages, until it appeared docile. Only then did the man turn to Davina.

"I am. Who might you be?"

"My name is Davina MacCallum."

Mr. Rutherford's gaze sharpened on hearing the name. He gave her a good, hard look.

"We have come from Teyhill. I was told you worked there many years."

He nodded. "For the dukes." He looked at Eric. "Your father, and his father."

Since Rutherford had surmised his identity, he took the opportunity to introduce himself.

"Well, now, what would the current Brentworth want

with me? Not going to complain that I am still working, are you? Nothing in the agreement said I couldn't be a groom elsewhere."

"No complaints. We seek information."

His face, wrinkled and weathered, did not reveal much, but his eyes, sparkling slits showing a sharp mind, gave them continued scrutiny and showed some impatience.

"I am wondering if, when you worked there, anything ever happened to give you cause to think that the last baron's son did not die," Davina asked, getting to the heart of it right away.

Rutherford turned to pet the horse's nose. "I never thought about it one way or another. But something happened that said someone else thought that." He turned back and peered at Davina. "Man came one summer. I heard he was in the area, doing odd jobs and such. Nothing to think about. Only one day he came to the house. I was at the stables, and this man just walks past, as if he knew what he was about. Wasn't a gentleman from the looks of him, but—there was something to him that said leave him alone. Had this determined look in his eyes and walked like he spoiled for a fight."

"Where did he go?"

"Into the garden, through the back portal. I didn't think much of it after that, except later, he comes back the same way, carrying a big box. He was a thief, and a bold one at that. He was much bigger than me, but I said he had to put it down. If he did, I wouldn't say nothing, and he could leave peacefully."

"He didn't put it down, did he?" Eric said.

Rutherford shook his head. "He turned to me and said *I've more right to it than anyone in there. A birthright.* He just kept walking. I went to the house and told the steward, but nothing was done that I know of. No search for him. No magistrates came. And that was that, for the most part."

"When was this?" Eric asked.

"Oh, long ago. Well before the war with Napoleon. I had, let me see, maybe thirty-five years. I wasn't even head groom yet."

"I don't suppose you know what was in the box?" Davina asked.

"Nothing too heavy, from the way he carried it. He didn't labor under it much, so it wasn't the family gold and silver. It wasn't too big. Not a trunk. Just a good-size wooden box."

Davina looked disappointed. "Thank you, Mr. Rutherford. For your time and your help." She came back to Eric. "I think I will return to the inn now and warm myself."

He let her go, then went over to admire the stallion. "You are one of them, aren't you?"

"One of what?"

"It is said there are some Scots who have a special way with horses. Whisperers. I thought that was folklore."

"I've a knack with them. Always have."

"If you ever want to return to Teyhill, you are welcome. There should be more horses there soon."

"I've settled here now. It suits me. Lots of different horses every day. It's more interesting. Also, I've a woman friend who would mourn my leaving."

"It is also said the whisperers have a way with women."

Rutherford grinned. "Is it, now?" He took the horse's reins. "I doubt the blood who came in on this horse would sell him, but if he would, you should take him. That young pup doesn't know how to handle him. Uses the crop too much." He began to walk the horse to the stable entrance.

"You said that after you told the steward of the theft, that was it for the most part. What was the lesser part?"

He paused his walk and thought a bit before replying. "No telling it was connected at all, of course. It was years later. Twenty or so. But your father came to visit the property—he was duke then—and he had me called in and asked about that theft. The man, the box. A little late to start caring about it, seemed to me, but I told him all of it that I remembered. Then, after he goes, maybe two weeks later, the steward tells me I am being sent out to pasture. A nice pension, though. Good money, secured by a trust. Well, I was not even past my prime and even by normal ways it was too early. It had been decided, however, and here I am."

"Do you think it was connected? That you were sent away because of what you knew?"

"Wouldn't make much sense, would it? Those who owned the house were the victims, not the thieves. No reason to send me away." He turned and took the horse into the stable.

"It was my grandfather," Davina said as they rode back to Teyhill. She had the reins now and, at his command, they traveled more slowly. "So was the man the minister saw, the one who looked like me. I thought it was my father, of course, but my father would never have been here as early as Mr. Rutherford says this man was."

Eric murmured agreement while she worked out what little they could surmise from Mr. Rutherford's memories. Most of his own thoughts were on that pension.

"And my grandfather would leave home at times. Once for a good, long while. It was assumed he would not be back. This is where he came. It seems on one of those visits, he entered the house and found what he needed."

Eric did some mental calculations. The theft took place as best he could guess in the eighties.

"Brentworth, I think he took the Bible. That was what was in the box. Some families keep their Bibles in one."

"It probably burned in the fire, Davina."

"It was that or something important that would help him prove who he was. I think whatever he took, he sent to the king."

"Possibly."

"Just possibly? You could say that about anything. You think I am right, don't you?"

"I agree it was your grandfather. However, he could have taken anything. Jewels, silver, anything at all. If he had convinced himself that he was the baron's son, he would believe he had a right to it, and that it wasn't theft."

She did not care for that view of things. "I don't know what you expect when you speak of proof. Do you want someone to come back from the grave and say *I know the baron's son did not die and was fostered in Northumberland*?"

Something like that would be useful, impossible though it might be.

Upon returning to Teyhill, Davina said she would start on her packing for the journey back to London.

"I do not think we will leave until late morning," he said.

"I assumed you would want to be off at dawn."

"There are a few things I need to attend to tonight. Enough that I won't be at dinner."

"Then I will take mine in my chambers and see you in the morning."

She went up the stairs. Eric instead headed past the library, on to Roberts's little apartment. The steward was not in his office, but came out of his sleeping chamber when he heard Eric enter.

"Do you need something from me, Your Grace?"

"Your time, and your records." He shed his coat and hung it on a peg. "I am going to walk back in time and you will be my guide. Make room on your desk for us. We will both have to do the search if we are to finish tonight."

"Search, Your Grace?"

He explained what he wanted to see. Roberts turned to the shelves.

Having someone rise from the dead would be the best proof, but a note sent from beyond the grave could work just as well.

Chapter Twenty-Six

Davina sat with the duchesses in the same drawing room where she had met Brentworth. No other guests attended tonight except he and she. With the informal dinner finished, the gentlemen were talking in the dining room, and the ladies had sequestered her in the drawing room.

They both almost ate her alive with the curiosity in their eyes. It had been that way all through this impromptu evening at Stratton's house, put together the night after their return to London. At the meal there had been much wheedling at Brentworth for information, and many leading comments that begged for the particulars.

"You are going to tell us now, aren't you? How you left here an enemy and came back his wife?" The Duchess of Stratton—*please address me as Clara now*—asked.

"Did he seduce you?" Langford's duchess, Amanda, blurted out. "Forgive me. That was too forward. But matters moved very quickly, and it seemed to me that—" She flushed and twirled her finger absently in one of her dangling dark curls. "That is what Gabriel thinks too."

What to say? She was not accustomed to confiding in other women, and these other women were not ordinary ones. Neither was she, officially, although right now she felt very commonplace.

"She doesn't want to tell us, Amanda. That is fine, Davina. You don't have to. Our husbands will get the story out of Brentworth and we, in turn, will learn it from them."

"That would be better," she said. "I will say that even when I left London, he and I had been less enemies and more two people in disagreement over an important matter. There is a difference."

"Absolutely," Clara said.

"Definitely," Amanda said. "Here is the puzzle, though. I hope you will not mind if I am direct, because you and I have a friendship. It is Brentworth, Davina. *Brentworth*. The unassailable, unapproachable, cut-from-rock Brentworth. However this came about, I hope that you think you can be happy with him."

"I think I will be very happy." She gave a bright smile when she said it, and she even believed it. In her heart, however, a little sadness lingered. She would be happy because she chose to be and because only a fool would not be happy if she was a duchess. While they remained in the first blush of marriage, she would even be very happy. She would know that he had already known his great passion with another woman, however. She would accept that he would probably seek out passion with others again, eventually.

At least with his insistence on discretion she might not learn about that when it happened. She could probably lie to herself for years.

Something passed between the two women in the looks they gave each other. "Well," Clara said, "there is much to do in the next days. You will need a wardrobe fitting your station, of course, and your own coach and pair."

"I would like my own phaeton."

"A phaeton no less. Can you handle one?"

"I began learning at Teyhill. Brentworth taught me."

"He sounds very accommodating to your preferences," Clara said, casting another look at Amanda. "Did he give you anything you wanted?"

"Not the land, of course. That is why we went there. I regret I did not find enough proof for him, although I found enough for me. However, he is rebuilding the manor house, and even rehabilitating the gardens, so I suppose he gave me that. I don't think it was his intention to do that otherwise."

"You astonish me," Clara said. "I find it difficult to see him doing anything he did not intend to do. He sounds almost romantic."

"We have become friends."

"Friends," Amanda said curiously. "Friends," she repeated to Clara.

"I do not think Brentworth ever had a woman friend," Clara said. "Most men do, but not him. He does not see either of us as friends. We are the wives of his friends, which is something else."

Davina shrugged. "I do not doubt I am his friend, so he has changed, it appears." It was the one thing she did not doubt, and she clung to it. If she loved this friend in other than friendly ways, at least there was some kind of affection returned.

"Did he give you this?" Amanda asked, touching her fingertip to a simple necklace hanging around Davina's neck.

Davina fingered the stone dangling on the gold chain. "Last night. He brought it to me. It was his mother's jewel. But he said it was mine, and *not part of the family hoard*, whatever that is."

"I will explain all of that, and other such things you

need to know. The lessons I received from Clara are still very fresh," Amanda said.

"You married in Scotland. Was there a contract?" Clara asked.

"No contract. Just the two of us and the witnesses. We signed the church book, of course."

"No contract," Clara murmured. "That will never do. One more thing to be handled soon. I will have my husband broach the matter with him. It was a mere oversight of the moment, I am sure."

"I have nothing, so it will not be complicated."

"It is always complicated. And utterly necessary. Leave it to me, however. Now, tell me, do you want some time to get your sea legs, or do you want us to start introducing you to people? I daresay you can call on whoever you like. No one refuses to receive Brentworth."

"Sea legs sound good to me, thank you."

"We will allow you a fortnight. We can address your wardrobe during that time, and you can demand the phaeton from Brentworth."

No one brought Brentworth to any back chambers when he entered St. James's the next drawing room day. The king left the diplomat he conversed with, crossed the chamber and greeted him as if they were brothers. With winks and smirks, he let it be known that this marriage to Davina pleased him very much indeed.

After Brentworth extricated himself from the king's attention, Haversham pulled him aside. "A splendid resolution, Your Grace. Felicitations on your nuptials."

"It was a most felicitous coincidence that I decided

she suits me and I her. It had nothing to do with the king's preference."

"We don't need to emphasize that to him, do we? He is happy. You are happy. All is well. As for your wife's claim, we have found nothing. However, I think if a bill is introduced to reinstate the lands to that family, with her as the inheritor, it will have no difficulty in passing both houses."

"I think it would be nice if the title is reinstated too."

Haversham's lips folded in. "That is more complicated. The baron was a rabble-rousing Jacobite. Had he not died in battle, he would have been among those executed. Our research into this entire matter uncovered evidence of *that*, unfortunately."

"It was long ago. No one remembers. No one will care."

"I am not so sure, Your Grace. After the recent Radical War, emotions can be strong on the question."

"Haversham, I have complete confidence that you can make it happen. Once the lands are returned, she will ask the Lord Lyon in Scotland to recognize her as baroness, which, because it is a feudal barony with the title derived from ownership of the land, they will do. What happens here will be a formality, and it would cause unnecessary hard feelings if it were resisted."

Haversham pondered the problem.

"Also, while the king remains under the illusion that I sold my manhood in marriage to save him from dishonor, tell him about our current attempts to return the slavery question to Parliament's attention. I do not expect him to speak in favor of any bills. I only ask that he not speak against them."

Haversham grimaced. "I'm not sure—"

Eric arched a brow at him.

"I will see what I can do, Your Grace."

He took his leave of the sycophants flattering the king

and now closing in to flatter the Duke of Brentworth. He rode back to Mayfair and stopped on Bond Street. He mounted the stairs to the dressmaker's shop Davina said the duchesses were taking her to this afternoon.

"Your Grace." The owner of the shop, Mrs. Dove, swept out and curtsied low. "It has been a long time."

"I trust you did not mention to my wife that there was ever another time." Clara and Amanda *would* have to choose a shop he had visited with several mistresses.

"Of course not, Your Grace. You have never been here before. The ladies are choosing designs and fabrics. If you come with me, you can inspect the orders submitted thus far."

He did not doubt Clara would see to this with good taste and aplomb. All the same, he followed Mrs. Dove for no more reason than he wanted to see Davina.

Davina jumped up when he entered and came over to him. The duchesses exchanged unfathomable looks with each other.

"How good of you to join us, Brentworth," Clara said. "I promise we are not bankrupting you, if that is your concern."

"They are rather overdoing it," Davina whispered. "They asked if you had given me an amount and when I said you had not, they went a little mad."

"I have no concern about the bills, Clara. I am just curious to see what you have chosen."

Davina took him to her place at the table and laid out fashion drawings and trims and pointed to colors. Her excitement touched him. He was glad he had interrupted.

He lifted one of the dinner dress plates. "Not this color. Primrose."

She looked up and blinked at him. Then she smiled. "Ah, I remember. Primrose it will be."

He glanced around the chamber, laden with fabric samples and stuffed with ladies' frothy things. He spied a Venetian shawl gently patterned with blue on cream.

"Have you chosen the carriage ensembles yet?"

"One. It is lovely." She pulled out a drawing. It appeared appropriate for London or the southern counties, but not for anything farther north.

"Davina will need a few more," he told Clara. "At least two with fur. Ermine for one, because I favor it. Also cloaks. One of those should be fur as well."

"Now *you* are overdoing it," Davina murmured. "I promise not to take chills."

"I'll not have you cold."

"Leave it to us, Brentworth. An excess of fur will be commissioned," Clara said. "Amanda, where is the drawing we set aside, the one with the fur mantle?"

The two of them shuffled paper. He took the opportunity to give Davina a kiss. "It will be our first evening at home alone in London. I have some gifts for you."

"Thank you, but this is already too generous."

"Nonsense," Clara interrupted, not even pausing in her perusal of the carriage ensembles.

"As she said, nonsense." He gave her another kiss, letting his lips linger on hers. "I am going to Whitehall. I will see you at dinner."

Chapter Twenty-Seven

The dining room at Brentworth's house in Mayfair would suit a state dinner. Davina almost giggled when she and Brentworth took their places at the table with all those other chairs empty. Three footmen served them, which seemed two too many to her.

"The cook is from Milan," Brentworth explained while she spooned some odd rice dish onto her plate. "He is full of fire and sends for ingredients from all over. Italy, Portugal, France. It was suggested to him by my father that the accounts had gotten out of hand. He threatened to leave. My father liked his food, so he stayed and I pay for things I can't pronounce."

"This is very good. Who would think rice could be so flavorful? And the joint tasted different from any other I have ever had. Am I supposed to supervise him, or will the housekeeper manage that?"

"No one supervises Marco Innocenti. You can try if you like, however. By all means, let him know what you want if you favor certain foods or preparations."

She peppered him with some other questions about his expectations of her. He told her about the bills he was shepherding and hoped to see pass. She thought it noble of him to fight the continued use of slaves in the Indies. Great Britain had outlawed the slave trade, and its navy even interfered with ships engaged in it. To still allow slaves in the colonies was a terrible hypocrisy.

As the dinner wound down and the last of the wine had been drunk, he took her hand. "I am glad that soon you will have that new wardrobe, although in my mind I will always remember how lovely you appeared in your simpler garments."

"I intend to keep them, so you may not have to rely on memories. There will be times I want to do something that might ruin those fine ensembles."

"I would ask what activities you refer to, but I think I will wait for another day to learn that. I told you that I have some gifts for you. Several. The first I will give you now. A bill will be brought to Parliament, reinstating Teyhill to you. The king will let it be known he supports it. You will have fulfilled your mission."

She should have been elated. She was happy, true, and she showed it, she hoped. She was getting what she thought her family deserved. But she had never found the proof that said it was in fact her family. She believed it was, but there would be those who always claimed she was a charlatan who only succeeded because she had turned Brentworth's head.

She admitted it might only be half a loaf, but it was the better half and she would take it. Perhaps one day she would stumble upon the evidence she had been trying to find. She would prefer this were not a gift, but a right.

"There are other gifts?" she asked. "This news would be enough for one day."

"There are several. Up in your chamber you will find

two of them. I would like you to be wearing them when I visit tonight."

"Do you expect me to sit here longer and talk, when I know surprises wait for me up there? That may be impossible. All I will do is try to get you to tell me what they are."

"I expect you to run up and see them, so I can spend a very long night with you." He raised and kissed her hand. "I have thought about little else all day and am half mad over it. Go now."

She went to give him a kiss before scurrying out and up the stairs. In her chamber, her ladies' maid had already prepared her bed and laid out a nightgown. A simple, practical one. After Brentworth had left today, after she assumed they were finished at Mrs. Dove's, Amanda had insisted that some other items be commissioned to replace these serviceable ones.

Charlotte, her maid, stuck her head into the bedchamber from where she had been working in the dressing room. "His Grace's valet brought something earlier. It is in here."

Davina went into the dressing room. It was a sumptuous chamber, as large as the one with the bed, with a big fireplace and two damask-covered divans and a special spot for a tub that waited in a cupboard built into a corner. Charlotte pointed to one of the divans. Two packages, one small and one large, both wrapped in silk, rested on the cushion.

"Are you retiring, Your Grace? Should I prepare water for you to wash?"

"Please do." She sat on the divan and pulled the ribbon on the little package. The cloth fell open to reveal a small wooden box. She pried that open to see the contents. Pearls. A string of them, perfectly matched. Beautiful. Priceless.

She called Charlotte over to see. She handed them to the maid, who ogled while she fingered the orbs. "Why, each one could keep a lady for a year," she said.

"Leave it on the dressing table." Davina opened the larger gift.

She recognized the shawl at once. It had caught her eye as soon as she entered that back chamber at Mrs. Dove's shop. When she asked about buying it before she left, however, Mrs. Dove had informed her it was spoken for.

She lifted one corner high, and the thin silk fell like luminous water. The blue sprigs on the cream background would look perfect with a dress the color of primroses. She rose and draped it over the back of the divan. Of all the purchases made today, this one pleased her the most because Brentworth had seen it and thought she might like it.

Charlotte began her duties. Davina submitted, although having a maid take care of her would take some getting used to. The notion of lying abed until another woman came to get you out of bed struck her as a little stupid, and she doubted she would ever conform to that practice.

Face and body washed, hair brushed, clean and ready in her simple nightdress, she sent Charlotte away. She draped the shawl around her shoulders. The silk's texture caressed her bare arms, but it looked silly with the muslin dress beneath it.

Feeling daring and naughty while she did it, she removed the dress and again draped the shawl. The silk created a wicked sensation on her whole body. She sat at the dressing table and began clasping the pearls around her neck.

Hands took it from her and finished. In her looking glass, she could see Brentworth's brocade banyan and a V of his skin above where it was buttoned.

She ran her fingertips over the pearls. "It is perfect.

Lovely. Thank you, and for this too." She smoothed her hand over the shawl.

His hands followed, sliding down from her shoulders and over her breasts. "You are perfect. Jewels and silks are mere decoration."

He caressed her like that, standing behind her, his strong hands visible in the looking glass while he touched her through that silk, and the fabric increased the sensuality. Watching that, feeling it, mesmerized her. Her head lulled back against him, but she did not close her eyes entirely. She kept watching.

He cast aside the edges of the silk and exposed her breasts. The pulse of pleasure made her sway against him and arch her back. Light touches, torturous ones, had her close to groaning. He circled and brushed her nipples, drawing gasps out of her, pushing her to the edge, where abandon beckoned. She felt his arousal, swollen and hard, heating the back of her neck.

A scandalous impulse joined her fever. A shocking one. The notion turned into an urge. Should she? Dare she? She heard his voice in her memory. *No rules.*

She was honest in her passion. Free. She did not resist what it did to her. How it transformed her. His desire turned savage when he saw her like this.

She sprawled in the little chair now, her legs parted, the silk of the shawl's ends falling between her thighs. Her head pressed him and her breasts rose high, their tips tight and dark. She shuddered whenever he caressed them. Lips parted, she watched through the slits where her lids had not closed entirely.

He cupped one breast and bent over and licked. A little cry escaped her, then another and more yet in a rising pitch of need. She raised her arm to circle his neck and hold him like that. He moved to the side of the chair for better purchase.

Only she did not want more. She took his head in her hands and held him to a deep kiss. Her tongue plunged and explored and demanded. She refused his attempt to join her, fending him off aggressively. While she kissed him, she unbuttoned his banyan.

He shrugged it off gladly. During the next kiss, she took his cock in both her hands. She stopped the kisses and pressed her lips to his shoulder, then his chest. He stood tall and watched what she was doing, balanced on rigid legs so pleasure did not bring him to his knees.

Her hands had him reeling. The path of her kisses made him grit his teeth. She could not know how suggestive this was, and what it was doing to him. He was on the verge of asking, begging, instructing when she showed she needed no encouragement. Her mouth closed on him, then took him in more fully. He threw back his head and closed his eyes, and his mind split while an ever-tightening pleasure thundered in him.

He lifted her up in his arms and dumped her on the divan. He dropped to his knees, spread her thighs and lifted her hips. He found enough sense not to ravish her, but to start slowly, but soon her cries begged for more, and he indulged what he wanted, using his mouth and tongue, claiming what was his, only his. Her surprised gasps drove him on. He made her moan with want, almost weep with it, before he felt the trembles that heralded her end. Her earthy scream almost took him with her.

Almost blind now, raging inside, he pulled her down onto his thighs, so her legs flanked his hips. Her head and shoulders pressed the seat cushion, and the silk still draped her like a Venus. He pushed into her and drove hard while the tremors of her orgasm still shook her, reviving them, taking her with him into a cataclysmic storm.

She slowly emerged from the bliss. She felt him still beneath her and in her. He braced himself on extended arms against the divan's cushion. Tiny shivers still tantalized her where they joined, like little echoes of what had just occurred. Eyes closed, passion spent, the face mere inches from hers looked so beautiful. Almost innocent in the absence of awareness and thought.

She watched as he regained himself, as the man emerged again and the jaw firmed and those crinkles at the sides of his eyes found their tiny furrows. He opened his eyes and looked right into hers. They wordlessly acknowledged the power of what had happened.

"Was that one of my gifts?" she asked.

"I was about to ask if that was to thank me for my gifts. If so, you will have to set aside a lot of room for all the silk shawls and pearls you will be getting."

"It was a wild impulse."

They disentangled, and he sat beside her on the floor. She noticed a book on her other side. It must have fallen off the divan. "What is this? Did you bring it?"

He looked over, then his head sank onto the edge of the cushion again. "I did. I want to show you something in it." He stretched, then stood. In his naked state, she was able to see the scars on the back of his leg very clearly.

He bent and took the book, then offered his hand for her to stand. Together they walked to her bed. He moved the light to a close-by table. She sprawled on the bed, pulling the shawl over her shoulders and back for some warmth. He sat beside her and opened the book. Inside was a folded paper, which he set aside.

"It is from Teyhill. Stewards keep logs, much like captains of ships do. They note anything of importance, problems that arise, episodes needing attention. It creates a little history of an estate and its lands. This one is from about forty years ago."

She turned the first few pages and saw what he meant. This was not like the ledger Mr. Roberts had shown her with the financial accounts. It was a personal record.

"I thought about what the whisperer told us and realized that if a theft happened, it might be noted in the log." He flipped through the corners of the pages, and turned to one far along in the book. "And it was."

She looked where he pointed. The steward had written about the theft.

> *Today, a stranger entered the house and removed several items in a wooden box. He claimed to be the last baron's son. Because I have reason to think he was telling the truth, I wrote to the duke to see if he wanted to lay down information with the magistrate before I did so on my own authority.*

"Then this, ten days later."

> *His Grace wrote that I am not to bother the magistrate, that the thief mentioned earlier was probably far gone by now.*

"I wonder what he meant when he wrote that he had reason to think he was telling the truth," she said. "Do you think this steward spoke to him?"

"There is no way to know. But for some reason, that steward accepted that the son had not died. Back then, there were probably those alive who knew about what happened to the son. It is not the kind of proof that would convince a magistrate, Davina, but it is one more piece of evidence that your grandfather was right, and that you have been too."

"I do not need to convince a magistrate. Only myself."

"And me too. Or, at least, you used to need to."

"Are you convinced?"

He closed the book and set it on the floor. "I am." He pursed his lips while he thought. "I need to tell you more. I think my father knew who that intruder was. Knew that it was the son of the last baron."

"I don't believe there is anything—"

"It was why he told the steward not to lay down information. And later, why he sent Rutherford away with that pension. The groom knew something had been removed. If your grandfather claimed he had some proof from the house—don't you see how it looks?"

She did, but she made light of it so as not to insult his father. "We do not know that. Nor should we assume it. And even if you are right, it does not signify today." She patted the book. "This, however, does. To me, at least. Was this one of the gifts? If so, I think it was the best one."

He reached for the paper he had set aside and placed it under her nose. "There is one more."

She unfolded the paper. Then again and again, until a large drawing made on several combined sheets spread on the bed. It was a drawing of Teyhill, only with a new wing where the burned one had been.

She examined the new chambers. In the end, near the gardens, she saw large ones labeled *Dispensary* and *Infirmary*.

"You will direct the architect on how to plan those chambers and that space. There can be beds on the second floor, or this one here, if you choose to take it that far," he said. "I only ask that you allow me to bring in physicians. That you not try to do this yourself."

"Of course there need to be physicians." Her eyes misted at the drawing. It would have taken her years, half her life, to achieve even half of this.

"If you—" He hesitated. "If you must continue, so you can be who you say you are, I pray that you will indulge me by trying to avoid danger."

She nodded. She would not need to continue all the time. There would be situations when she wanted to, however. She would try not to put herself in danger, as best she could.

"I think perhaps this is the best gift, Eric." She folded the paper again. "It is a wonderful plan."

He brushed back her hair with the backs of his fingertips. "I thought the last one was the best one."

"Oh, that was quite fine too." She raised her chin so she could show off the necklace. She flipped the end of the shawl. "They were all wonderful."

He leaned down and kissed the back of her neck. "None of them compare to the gift you gave me when you gave yourself, Davina."

"I'm glad you are pleased. Contented."

He embraced her, then rolled so she sat on his hips, looking down on him. She enjoyed the sight from this position, of his hard chest and astonishing face. Of his arms and the little line of hair going down his stomach to where she sat.

His gaze captured hers. "I am both pleased and contented, but also happy. Joyful." He fussed with the shawl, drawing its edges down over her body, then toying with the long ends. "I have sensed a sadness in you since I told you about the fire. About Jeannette. Did that old story disappoint you in some way? In me?"

The spot of emptiness she nursed widened and ached. It grew until it twisted against her heart. "Not in you. Not at all in you."

"In some other way, then." His hands smoothed down her shoulders and arms, until they took hers in firm holds. "Langford thinks it was a mistake to tell you about that. About her. He says you will believe the memory forever compromises what you and I share. That in my heart, she will be my first, best love."

Her throat burned. "Perhaps he should mind his own affairs and not offer advice so freely."

"I told him about it. And Stratton. That first night after dinner, while we drank port, I shared it. Langford always offers his opinion, and always minds others' affairs, so this won't be the last time." He looked right into her eyes. "Is he right?"

"A little," she managed to say. "It is not like those men pursuing me at the theater, though. I did not have expectations that have been denied."

He closed his eyes briefly, then joined their gazes again. "Sometimes the best things are least expected. You are so wrong about my memories. About my feelings for you. I told you early on that I was deranged by desire for you. My hunger for you was greater than I ever knew with anyone. When we embrace, I am freer than ever before. The contentment I know fills my soul. Do you not feel some of that too?"

Her eyes burned. The emptiness disappeared with his words, filled now with such joy, she could hardly hold it. His expression while he waited for her response touched her. So earnest he looked. So unsure what she would say.

She nodded. "Yes. Oh yes."

He pulled her forward, down into his arms. "I thank

God for that. To love you and not have you experience at least some of the same things—"

"All of it. I have lost my heart, Eric. Hopelessly so."

A kiss then, both raw and sweet in emotion, careful and ferocious at the same time. He set her up again. He lifted her hips, then lowered her while they joined. He separated the edges of the silk and took her breasts in his hands. "Take your pleasure, darling. Look at me and see my love while you do."

Chapter Twenty-Eight

"Will you tell me now where we are going?" Davina asked the question while the coach rolled through town. "South now. Are we going to St. James's?"

"Close to there. We are going on a hunt." Eric hoped the hunt succeeded. It had been planned meticulously, and all logic said it might, but one never knew. "Here we are."

"The Queen's House? We are hunting on a royal property?"

"Something like that." He handed her out. "It is not only a house. The King's Library is here."

She looked confused, but allowed him to escort her in. She stopped short once inside. "Why are all these people here?"

"This is our hunting party." Also, in the event of success, their witnesses. The group waiting for them included Stratton and Langford and their duchesses.

Langford brought over a man who resembled him, along with another very elderly gentleman. "Let me introduce my brother, Harold. And also Mr. Barnard, the Royal Librarian. Both are intimately familiar with the library and have agreed to aid us today."

Davina smiled graciously, but still looked confused. "What are we searching for?" she whispered to Eric.

He drew her a few steps away. "A Bible. Your family's Bible. We may not find it. I could be wrong. However, if that was what your grandfather took from the house, and if it was sent to the last king, and it was among his possessions when he died, there is a good chance it ended up here, in his library. Its significance to your cause would not have been known or recognized at the time. When a king dies, his household has other matters occupying it."

Lights of hope entered her eyes. "That is a lot of ifs, but I think you may be correct. It is wise you did not tell me this before you brought me here. I would have paced the house until we could come to see." She walked back to Mr. Barnard. "Can we go to the library now?"

Mr. Barnard led the way. Eric escorted Davina and their party trailed behind. Into the large octagonal room that held the library they filed. Davina's face fell. "There must be thousands of books here. We will never find just one."

"There are over sixty thousand," Mr. Barnard said. "However, they are all organized so they can be found without too much difficulty, so they can be used by scholars. The Bibles are all in one section, with pride of place, of course, going to that printed by Gutenberg. Come with me."

There were a lot of Bibles. Not only Gutenberg's, but also other early ones both in manuscript and early printing. "Once we get to more recent years, there is less differentiation to the shelving," Mr. Barnard said. "These cases here hold the ones from the last several hundred years. The last king bought many collections, and almost all had Bibles."

Davina looked up and down the cases. "It is a good thing we brought that hunting party."

Langford's brother took over. He divided up the party and assigned them shelves. He gave a little lecture on handling frail books. "We can assume it is in Latin, Gaelic or English. Any other languages you can reshelf immediately." They all went to work.

Even the best-kept library collected a lot of dust. Fifteen minutes later, clouds of it surrounded them. Tome by tome, Eric removed Bibles and checked for any in one of the languages noted. Those he examined more carefully.

They had been there almost an hour when he felt a pull on his coat sleeve. Clara stood at his side. She passed a book to him. "I think this may be it," she said quietly. "You and Davina can see if it is."

He appreciated her discretion. Should they find the Bible, and should it contain anything of use, there would be cause for celebration. If they did not, or if it held nothing of value to her, he did not want Davina's reaction to be too public.

He walked to her and showed her the book, then took her away from the others. He set it on a reading table. They both just stared at it.

"I am almost afraid to open it," she said.

"I understand. However, it is time." He turned back the front of the soft leather binding.

There, on the front pages, left blank of printing so as to accommodate such a use, were the family notations of the MacCallums of Teyhill.

He turned two pages full of writing, then stopped at the final one. It was only half-filled. Davina read the next to the last line in a whisper.

1746—James MacCallum, born 1740, was sent to Harold Mitchell of Northumberland for safekeeping after his father's death at Culloden.

Below it was one last note. *1748—Teyhill given to an English duke by the king. Household dispersed.*

Her breath caught. "Oh my. You have done it, Brentworth. You have found my proof."

He turned to where Clara watched them. He nodded. Davina's expression showed just how successful the hunt had been. Word spread, and the party closed in. Clara pushed Mr. Barnard forward. "You must verify this discovery here in this library, sir. No one can claim that *you* lied out of friendship for Brentworth."

Mr. Barnard examined the Bible, then smiled. They had cause for celebration after all.

"Thank you, Eric," Davina said before stretching up to kiss him. "Thank you, my love."

Epilogue

The garden flowers perfumed the air. Somewhere, birds sang, but they could not be heard. Rather, the children's squeals and cries filled the space. Servants ran this way and that, trying to keep them corralled in one section of the garden.

From the terrace, Langford watched a boy with dark, unruly curls and dark eyes. Davina doubted any other person except Amanda could bring such warmth to that duke's smile.

"Your heir is full of the devil," she said as the boy escaped a footman and ran for a tree. "He'll be up that trunk in two blinks from the look of him."

"He is a fine boy, isn't he?" Langford said, as if being a devil were a very good thing.

"He looks to be healthy and strong," Eric said. "And full of trouble."

"Not too much trouble. Nothing I can't manage." Langford turned his attention to the other children, and the adults in their midst. "Stratton and Clara are like children again themselves, guiding the play, although Amanda seems to be fomenting rebellion against their authority. His twins seem to get along well with your son, Brentworth."

Davina saw the gleam in Eric's own eyes while he watched their son play with the others. Benjamin was not a devil, but he knew more freedom than his father had. *Not too many rules*. It had been one of the first things Eric had said when the boy was born. She knew he had laid down the law for himself more than for her.

The baby in his arms began fussing. She let Eric try to sooth matters, but his own consternation only made it worse. He could not bear to hear this one cry.

She took the baby from him, gave a few bounces and cooed at the pudgy face. "You will get to play soon enough. You have to grow first."

Langford rested his hip against the terrace balustrade. "It is done, then? The title is settled?"

Eric nodded. "Word arrived yesterday. Isn't that so, Baroness? She prefers that address now, Langford. Don't you, darling?"

She laughed. "I can be forgiven, I think. Scotland recognizes me."

The decision of the Lord Lyon in Edinburgh had come by messenger sent by Brentworth to await the decision. Because the lands had been returned to her by Parliament, and because with baronies like Teyhill the baron was whoever held the lands, the conclusion had been a foregone one. The College of Arms would accept it, most likely.

"So we are all domesticated and appropriate now," Langford said. "The next time we meet at the club we should go out on the town and raise some hell, though. It doesn't do to be all about duty and responsibility, and we deserve a night of trouble. You in particular, Brentworth. It will be like old times. We can be the Decadent Dukes again."

"I'm not sure I remember how," he replied with a slow smile. His gaze slid to her, and she felt herself blushing.

Last night he had invited her into the fifth circle of acts not typical and astonished her anew.

"I'll remind you," Langford said with a laugh. He looked out at the children again. "Who would believe it? Married all of us, and each with his heir."

The baby in her arms began fussing again. A strong hand reached over and a masculine finger stroked the infant's cheek. "We have been fortunate. We should be forever grateful for our wives and heirs."

Yes, it had all worked out splendidly for them, and for those wives, Davina thought. Clara's journal and club flourished, and Teyhill now offered medical help to farmers and crofters for miles around. When she and Eric visited, she donned an apron and entered that wing to assist. Amanda had taken up the anti-slavery cause along with the dukes. The last effort had not succeeded, but new ones were coming and would continue to come until it was done.

Most importantly, the children were all healthy and full of love and joy. They filled the houses with chaos when they all played together like this.

There was much for everyone in this garden to be thankful for. Especially her.

She smiled down at her son, the next duke, then at the new daughter in her arms. The world was changing quickly in ways that would not be denied. Who knew, perhaps little Godania could even one day become a physician, if she chose?

Author's Note

In the early 18th century, there were over two hundred barons in Scotland, many dating from the late Middle Ages. The title in Scotland means something different from what it means in England, however. Scottish barons are part of the nobility, but are not peers. They are not part of the Scottish Parliament. In Scotland, baron is a minor title, and ranks below Scottish baronets in the hierarchy of titles.

The title historically derived from the land, which meant whoever held the land and manor (or *caput*) was the baron. A baron in Scotland is the Baron of X (land holding), not Baron X as in England. If someone lost the land he ceased being a baron. The title did not follow blood lines unless the estate continued down as well. This tie between the land holding and the title continued until 2004 when it was ended by law.

These feudal baronies could be bought and sold, since the land might be bought or sold. If a baron died without heir, and in Scotland a daughter could be an heir, the lands reverted to the Crown because the charter of erection for the barony came directly from the Crown.

A baron was and is not the same thing as a laird. As the Lord Lyon has made explicit, laird is not a title, but a description. It was a term used for the owner of an estate, usually by those who lived or worked on the estate rather than by the estate owner himself. So barons were also lairds, but not all lairds were barons. While laird is a Scots word for lord, a laird is not a lord in the official meaning of the word. A baron is.

This holiday season, steal away with the
reigning queens of Regency romance . . .
plus one or two dukes, one heiress, and
one headstrong beauty—to a surprise snowstorm,
the comfort of a blazing fire,
and the heat of a lover's kisses . . .

Don't miss

Seduction on a Snowy Night

by
Madeline Hunter
Sabrina Jeffries
and Mary Jo Putney

Available everywhere books are sold
in Fall, 2019!

Connect with  Us

Visit us online at
KensingtonBooks.com
to read more from your favorite authors, see books
by series, view reading group guides, and more.

Join us on social media

for sneak peeks, chances to win books and prize packs,
and to share your thoughts with other readers.

facebook.com/kensingtonpublishing
twitter.com/kensingtonbooks

Tell us what you think!

To share your thoughts, submit a review,
or sign up for our eNewsletters, please visit:
KensingtonBooks.com/TellUs.

More from Bestselling Author
JANET DAILEY

Calder Storm	0-8217-7543-X	$7.99US/$10.99CAN
Close to You	1-4201-1714-9	$5.99US/$6.99CAN
Crazy in Love	1-4201-0303-2	$4.99US/$5.99CAN
Dance With Me	1-4201-2213-4	$5.99US/$6.99CAN
Everything	1-4201-2214-2	$5.99US/$6.99CAN
Forever	1-4201-2215-0	$5.99US/$6.99CAN
Green Calder Grass	0-8217-7222-8	$7.99US/$10.99CAN
Heiress	1-4201-0002-5	$6.99US/$7.99CAN
Lone Calder Star	0-8217-7542-1	$7.99US/$10.99CAN
Lover Man	1-4201-0666-X	$4.99US/$5.99CAN
Masquerade	1-4201-0005-X	$6.99US/$8.99CAN
Mistletoe and Molly	1-4201-0041-6	$6.99US/$9.99CAN
Rivals	1-4201-0003-3	$6.99US/$7.99CAN
Santa in a Stetson	1-4201-0664-3	$6.99US/$9.99CAN
Santa in Montana	1-4201-1474-3	$7.99US/$9.99CAN
Searching for Santa	1-4201-0306-7	$6.99US/$9.99CAN
Something More	0-8217-7544-8	$7.99US/$9.99CAN
Stealing Kisses	1-4201-0304-0	$4.99US/$5.99CAN
Tangled Vines	1-4201-0004-1	$6.99US/$8.99CAN
Texas Kiss	1-4201-0665-1	$4.99US/$5.99CAN
That Loving Feeling	1-4201-1713-0	$5.99US/$6.99CAN
To Santa With Love	1-4201-2073-5	$6.99US/$7.99CAN
When You Kiss Me	1-4201-0667-8	$4.99US/$5.99CAN
Yes, I Do	1-4201-0305-9	$4.99US/$5.99CAN

Available Wherever Books Are Sold!

Check out our website at **www.kensingtonbooks.com**.